Eagles
Flying High

The Eagle Wings Series

Eagles Flying High

Linda Rae Rao

Fleming H. Revell
A Division of Baker Book House Co
Grand Rapids, Michigan 49516

Published by Fleming H. Revell
a division of Baker Book House Company
P.O. Box 6287, Grand Rapids, MI 49516-6287

Printed in the United States of America

Library of Congress Cataloging-in-Publication Data

Rao, Linda Rae, 1943–
    Eagles flying high / Linda Rae Rao.
        p.   cm. — (Eagle wings)
    ISBN 0-8007-5548-0
    I. Title. II. Series: Rao, Linda Rae, 1943– Eagle wings.
PS3568.A5957E25   1995
813'.54—dc20   94–28705

To Buzzy,
the most supportive husband ever,
and my sister Sheri,
whose encouragement and advice
have been immeasurably appreciated

Acknowledgments

I wish to thank those people who have been most instrumental in bringing this book about. The Lord has truly blessed my life with loving, supportive family and friends, for which I am eternally grateful. Without their faith and encouragement, becoming a published author would have remained merely a dream.

My beloved husband, Buzzy, who didn't laugh when I told him I was writing a book, took my efforts to be a writer more seriously than I did at first, and gave me the moral support and encouragement to continue, even when it seemed an impossible dream.

My dear sister, Sheri Griscom, for years was the only person I allowed to read my stories. She is the one who first encouraged me to type up this little story for her to read, and then introduced me to the wonderful world of word processing when it became more than a "little story." Her interest in reading and making constructive suggestions has been invaluable.

My wonderful parents, Ray and Anita Scott, have served as loving examples of people of integrity and strong character. It is from them that I learned the truth in the lesson of the eagle as told in the prologue.

Our precious children, Jeff and Jennifer, and my brother, Dan Scott, in addition to their unfailing faith and encouragement, served as models of a sibling relationship marked by superficial conflict but grounded in a deep protective affection.

As important as the moral support and encouragement of a family is, I'm convinced that without a good literary agent, a writer has little chance of success in the publishing world today. I still consider it a miracle from God that brought Helen Hosier to be my literary agent. It had to be a miracle for a well known author/lecturer in her own right to take the time to read my first rough manuscript and agree to become my agent. I will never be able to express the depth of my appreciation for her unfailing faith and tireless efforts on my behalf.

As part of the miracle of having Helen Hosier for my agent, I must acknowledge my dear friend, Ruth Earhart, who knew of Helen through their mutual friends John and Goldia Mills. On the very day I finished the first draft of this book Ruth called and, learning of my project, directed me to Helen. I'm so thankful she did.

And last but not least, the editors at Fleming H. Revell who have worked so hard to prepare this work for publication. It's been a marvelous learning experience that I appreciate very much.

My deepest and sincerest thanks to you all.

Prologue

Jagged fingers of lightning darted across the dark thunderhead above the valley. The thunder that followed clapped and crackled, its throaty boom echoing against the surrounding hills.

Feeling the earth tremble beneath his moccasins, the young boy looked up at his father standing beside him and was reassured by his calmness. A strong hand clamped the boy's shoulder, and he looked up to see Quiet Bear, his father's blood brother. Standing between the two men, the boy felt his apprehension dissolve as he watched the storm play out its grumbling passage before them.

The hunting had been good that day, and the boy had watched with pride as his father and Quiet Bear had skillfully stalked and taken the gray doe. It was the first time he had been allowed to accompany them hunting, and he'd watched it all with great care. He'd even joined in when the two men thanked the swift creature for providing food to keep their families strong and healthy, and then added thanks to God for his bountiful provision.

They'd been on their way back to the village when they had noticed the freshening wind running ahead of the summer afternoon storm. Stopping along the trail for a moment to rest from carrying their heavy burden of fresh venison, they peered over their valley, nestled among the southern peaks of the Appalachian Mountain chain.

Standing between the two strong hunters, feeling protected and safe, the boy was enjoying the dramatic display before them when his father drew his attention to a tall skeleton of a dead chestnut tree along the ridge to their right. There, perched among the topmost limbs, sat a large bald eagle, his snow-white feathered hood contrasting sharply with the blackening sky. The boy watched as the eagle suddenly lifted from its perch. Certain the magnificent creature was preparing to fly for cover, he watched in amazement as the regal bird spread his wings to head straight for the thunderhead, as if to challenge the overwhelming power of the swiftly moving storm.

"What's he doing?" the boy asked, looking up at his father.

"What did Quiet Bear tell you about the eagle?" his father asked in return.

"That the eagle is the bravest of all creatures," the boy replied, looking up at their Cherokee friend standing beside him.

"Yes," Quiet Bear agreed. "He also has wisdom with his courage. Watch how he rises on the winds of the storm and is carried higher and higher until he is flying above the storm. He teaches us that we must not cower before the difficulties we face. We must meet them head-on, and many times we will be lifted up by the very whirlwind that threatens us."

The boy watched as the great bird performed exactly as Quiet Bear predicted, flying into the storm. Then, as if without effort, he soared higher and higher until he disappeared in the upper fringes of the dark clouds.

The boy looked up at his father, who smiled and added, "No matter how big or strong a problem might be, if you are in the right, our Lord will give your heart the courage to face it and the wings to fly up and over it."

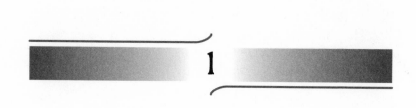

1

"I just don't like the idea of takin' Jess along. We'll be passin' through some rough country, and no tellin' who we might meet up with." Rob McClaren paced back and forth in front of the fireplace of the farmhouse. He rubbed the back of his neck with the rough brown hands of a man who had worked hard for most of his fifty years. A stocky build, snapping gray-green eyes, and a thick shock of curly, sand-colored hair evidenced his Scottish background even without the thick Scottish burr in his voice. His wife, Cara, a wisp of a woman, sat in her rocker, busily darning a small bundle of socks.

"I don't like it any better than you, dear, but we haven't much choice, now do we? Robbie can't go, not with that broken leg, poor dear. With so many of the hands away with the militia, there's no one else to spare with the planting season on us.

"The contract says you have to have Ettinsmoor and Lady Heather Star down in Charleston on June 15.

"Besides, you know how skittish the filly can be. Jess is about the only one who can handle her."

Rob nodded resignedly and looked out the window across the rolling green hills of the large plantation. In the distance stood the main house with its grand columns and manicured gardens. He half expected to see his old friend and employer, Lord John Keene, standing on the wide portico surveying the vast plantation; it was still difficult to realize his old commander was gone. The present situation only magnified the sadness of losing such a valued friend. He pounded his fist against the mantel.

"How could he do it, lass? How could Lord John's own son turn his back on his father's wishes and betray the land that's been so good to him? Instead of usin' his influence and money to help fight for our rights as free men, he turns and declares himself a Tory and goes on sellin' his grand thoroughbreds as if the world was calm and peaceful."

"You know why, Papa."

They turned at the sound of their daughter's voice. Dressed in a Brunswick riding habit of hunter green, Jess cut a trim figure. Not yet twenty years old, she had her father's gray-green eyes, and although not beautiful, she had attractive, even features framed by thick, chestnut-colored hair that hung loosely about her shoulders. Removing her riding gloves and jacket, she continued in an angry tone.

"Because Bradford Keene is a pompous, arrogant man," she said, "more concerned with the number of people who will come to his fancy dinners than the number of men lost at Savannah."

"Jess . . . " Her father started to reprimand her, but stopped. How could he chastise her? He shared the very feelings she had voiced.

Her mood softened a bit and she strode to her father's side. She slipped an arm about his waist and gave him a hug.

"I'm sorry, Papa. I know you'd like us to be as loyal to Bradford as we were to his father, but it's not easy. We all loved Lord John and held him in high regard; but Bradford Keene is nothing like his father."

"Aye, lass," he agreed grimly. "That's what makes it so hard to ask you what I must." He'd been dreading this moment all afternoon, ever since Bradford had told him about the sale of the horses. He still had not found the words to help him break the news to her.

Looking up at him, she tried to quell the sense of dread that began to grow as she watched his obvious difficulty in choosing carefully the words he needed. She had never cared for beating around the bush. It had always seemed to her that bitter medicine tasted worse the longer one dreaded taking it. She asked bluntly, "You mean he's . . . he's done it? He's sold Lady?"

Her father nodded sadly. "Aye, and Ettinsmoor. I've got to take them to Charleston to be shipped to the West Indies, June 18."

"That's less than a month away. But Robbie won't be able to ride for at least six weeks."

"That's right, dear," her mother said gently. "That means you'll have to go along and help your father by driving Lady's van."

Jess sat down staring silently at the floor, fighting back angry tears. The memory of a wobbly-legged, chestnut-colored foal taking halting steps toward her outstretched hand flashed across her mind.

"Try not to take it so hard, darlin'. I know what Lady means to you, but she belongs to Bradford and he can do what he wants to with her."

The disappointment in her father's eyes belied his matter-of-fact statement.

"He may own her legally, but I've raised her. I've taken care of her since she was just a tiny foal, when Bradford didn't think she was even worth saving and ordered her destroyed."

There had been something special about the newborn filly that cold December morning three years ago. The birth had been difficult and premature; the valuable brood mare had not survived. Considering the time of year, and the fact that it was born four weeks early, the foal was thought a hopeless case as well. Jessica remembered vividly the look of contempt in Bradford Keene's eyes for the weak, helpless animal. He had turned on the heels of his highly polished boots, slapped his glove against his thigh, and coldly ordered the foal destroyed.

Whether it was her displeasure with the way Bradford had been undermining his father's control over the plantation, the stubborn streak her brother Robbie had always teased her about, or simply the way the tiny foal had so gamely struggled to her feet, blinking large black-brown eyes at her, Jess had begged her father to spare the foal and let her take care of it. He had granted her a week; if there was no improvement, he would then have to carry through with Bradford's order.

She had spent seven very cold nights in the stall with the little filly, who seemed to have a tenacious streak as strong as Jessica's. During those first days and nights, a bond of trust and affection developed between the two.

Jessica had laughed when her brother Robbie teased her, saying the foal thought she was its mother.

Her loving care was not wasted; to everyone's surprise, the foal developed into a beautiful thoroughbred, displaying some of the best attributes of her distinguished lineage. Lord John Keene, Bradford's father and builder of Cheltenham Farms, had still been in control then, and he allowed Jessica to name the little filly. Jess dubbed her Lady Heather Star.

Though Bradford had grudgingly admitted that the decision to spare the foal had been correct, the filly was a constant reminder that his authority had been usurped by a wisp of a young girl. Well, now he would have the final say in the matter, as well as receiving a substantial financial benefit and strengthening his position with some very powerful Englishmen. The stallion, Ettinsmoor, and the three-year-old, Lady Heather Star, had been bought by the powerful Duke Wilton to be taken to his plantation in the West Indies where they would bring prestige and a strong new bloodline to his thoroughbred race horses.

The news about the sale had dealt Jess a wicked blow, and she was having difficulty recovering her composure. "What about shipping from Charleston?" she asked her father. "Will Cornwallis and Clinton allow such a thing now that they hold the city?"

"Bradford's been sending special messengers back and forth, and Clinton is very eager to keep the Tories happy. It seems the General is cooperating in any way he can. Today Bradford gave me the papers of identification that will permit us to pass without difficulty. The British merchant ship, *Westwind*, is scheduled to set sail the eighteenth."

16

Jessica could just imagine Bradford cunningly using the desperate political situation for his own benefit, taking advantage of the protection and power of the British army as they endeavored to strengthen Loyalist support in the colony. He was a man of immense ego and ambition. He was also a very petty man. He had several other fine mares he could have sold. Selling Lady would not only erase the reminder of her insubordination, it was also retaliation for Jessica's rejection of his unwelcome attention over the past year.

After a long silence, McClaren finally cleared his throat. "Well, I guess there'll never be a better time for some good news. I was going to wait for supper to tell it, but I canna wait a minute longer."

He went to his coat, which hung on a hook by the door, and brought out a long white envelope.

"What is it, Rob?" his wife asked curiously.

"It's our new home."

"What?" she asked, standing to reach for the paper he had just taken from the envelope. "Jessica, darlin', do look at this."

Still distracted, Jessica glanced at the piece of paper her mother held before her. The letter informed them that their down payment had been accepted on a small farm in the Matokee Valley just across the dividing line between North Carolina and Virginia. It was a beautiful valley with good rich grassland, perfect for starting their own horse farm. They had fallen in love with the area two years earlier when they had traveled to Virginia to purchase two new breeding mares.

"Rob, it's wonderful," Mrs. McClaren exclaimed as she grasped Jessica's hand. "When do we go?"

"First of September, if everything goes well." He turned to his daughter. "Jess my girl, I know this trip won't be easy ... but maybe ... maybe knowin' we'll soon have our own horses will help."

"Yes, Papa, it's wonderful." She smiled. She was pleased with the news, for it would be a relief to escape the unpleasant influence of Bradford Keene. Still, her enthusiasm was dimmed by the shadow of the upcoming journey.

The next two days were spent busily making preparations for the trip. Robbie, who was three years older than Jess, cursed the green stallion that had thrown him, badly breaking his left leg. Attempts to prove that he could manage by hopping and using a crutch had only resulted in a painful demonstration of how impossible it would be to climb up onto the wagon, let alone control the foot brake and manage a high-spirited thoroughbred.

When he finally resigned himself to the inevitable, Robbie suggested that Jess should dress like a boy in breeches, knee stockings, vest, and coat, explaining that a young farmhand would attract less attention than an attractive young girl. To complete her disguise, Robbie contributed an old flat-brimmed hat to conceal Jess's long hair.

On the morning they were to leave, Jessica stopped by Robbie's room to bid him good-bye. Knowing his leg had been giving him quite a bit of pain, she was concerned about his grim countenance as she told him they were about to leave. The look in his eyes hinted at something else, however; something that puzzled Jess.

Though they had always been close as they were growing up, Jessica sometimes felt Robbie's mission in life was to make her life miserable with his teasing. She had, for the most part, been able to hold her own, and Robbie had generally been able to tell when he had pushed her to the limit. Quick to spar, they were also quick to sense when the other was troubled about something. Jessica knew that Robbie felt bad about not being able to carry out the job that should have been his, but she thought she sensed something else, something that disturbed her, because his grave expression was so uncharacteristic.

In an attempt to discover what lay behind his troubled demeanor she grinned and teased, "Don't give me that look, trying to pretend you would rather spend the next two weeks jolting over those wagon tracks on a hard wooden seat and sleeping on the hard ground rather than stay here in your soft feather bed."

He smiled and nodded with a wink. "You found me out," he said. His smile faded, and he started to say something with a serious expression that reflected their father's image.

Physically, Robbie resembled his father a great deal, but their personalities had always been vastly different. Robbie's happy-go-lucky spirit had concerned the elder McClaren, who worried that his son would never take anything seriously enough to be able to accomplish much. Robbie had always loved to read, becoming so engrossed in the books borrowed from Lord John's library that he would forget to eat. Somewhat of an enigma, the young scholar never seemed to mind the hard physical labor required in helping his father with the never-ending chores involved in managing a stable. He and Jessica had both inherited their father's unique ability to care for and train horses. However, those who knew him well were also aware that while Robbie was mending a corral fence or pitching hay to the stock, his thoughts were more often than not roaming the mythical lands of Homer's *Iliad* and

Odyssey or the brooding realms of Shakespeare's royal courts. To most, he appeared a carefree dreamer with a fun-loving spirit who managed to make the hardest work seem easy.

For just a moment now Jessica caught a glimpse of an uncharacteristic exasperation. She couldn't remember ever seeing him so perplexed. Even in severe pain when he broke his leg, he had quipped about not having to carry in the wood for a long while.

"What is it, Robbie?" she finally asked seriously.

"I'm truly sorry you have to go in my place, Jessie. Before long, we'll have our own horses." He seemed ready to say something else, but didn't.

Unconvinced that this was the only reason for his grave attitude, she was nevertheless touched by his sympathetic expression. She nodded, not daring to trust her voice. She kissed him on the forehead and turned to go.

"Jess." The urgency in his voice startled her.

"What?" she asked quickly, wheeling to face him again.

If he hadn't been the one to suggest her disguise, he would have teased her about her appearance. He wasn't in a teasing mood, however. He had been wrestling with a dilemma ever since his accident; he knew something about the journey that no one else knew. He had finally concluded that Jess and Father would be in less danger if he kept silent than if they knew his secret.

Seeing Jess prepared to leave, he again was tempted to tell her, but after a long moment his only remark was, "Be careful."

She waited, for she was sure there was something further he meant to say. His countenance brightened, however, and he said, "Don't poison Papa with your cooking."

She picked up a small hand-stitched pillow from the chair by the door and threw it at him in mock anger, then turned and tossed a casual wave over her shoulder. She was still puzzled by his behavior and couldn't help wondering what it was he had wanted to tell her.

Outside, before climbing up onto the wagon, Jessica hugged and kissed her mother, and teased a bit to help them both blink back their tears of parting. The journey would take just over a month, and both were acutely aware that during these uncertain times any travel could be perilous.

"Robbie told me to be careful not to poison Papa with my cooking. I promise I won't."

"Oh, don't pay your brother any mind, darlin'. You're as good a cook as they come. When you get back we'll make you a new dress." Mrs. McClaren looked at Jessica dressed in her brother's clothes and shook her head in dismay. "Oh, my lovely little lass in those old clothes. Ah, well, I guess you're not goin' to the parade, are you?"

They hugged again and laughed. As Jess climbed up on one of the wagons, Rob McClaren took his wife in his arms and kissed her. Watching them, Jess felt a sudden pang in her heart. She was reminded of the young man who would never be able to hold her as his wife, as they had planned. As her father climbed up onto the wagon in front of her, her hands tightened on the reins; she reflected on the terrible toll of the war that had taken the life of her fiancé, Evan Collingsworth. The thought made her snap the whip over the mule team's rumps harder than necessary. They sidestepped a little in surprise, but stepped out to begin their long journey.

She was instantly sorry for taking her bitterness out on the animals. Robbie had warned her not to let the sorrow etch itself too deeply into her spirit. For the most part, she had been able to recover from the grief she had endured those long months after Evan was killed. Once in a while, however, something would remind her of him, and it would all come washing back over her—the grief, the anger, the empty place he'd left in her life.

The Collingsworth plantation bordered Cheltenham Farms on the southeast. The Collingsworths' small but elegant plantation had gained a worthy reputation from producing an outstanding grade of tobacco. Therefore, while not as large as Cheltenham Farms, the Collingsworth plantation was just as prestigious and profitable.

Evan, the younger of two sons, had been the same age as Robbie, and the two boys had become good friends. Evan's brother was nearly ten years older, and the two were not close.

Even as a twelve-year-old, Evan had dominated Jessica's life, for she was constantly following on the older boy's heels. With his deep blue eyes and blonde hair, he had reminded Jessica of an illustration of the handsome knight Lancelot in one of Robbie's books. His daring antics were often performed for her benefit, as Evan was well aware of the admiration and awe with which she beheld him.

As they grew older, there was never any question that one day they would marry and Jessica would move to Collingsworth Plantation, where Evan had helped his older brother manage the growing operation since their father's death from a heart attack.

That terrible day when he had come to tell her he was going off to Savannah to join the militia there, she had been furious with him. She suspected it meant no more to him than another daring escapade to break the monotony of the day-to-day business on the plantation, and her protests had only been laughed aside. Evan had smiled his wonderful, heartbreaking smile and assured her that as soon as he had tasted the excitement and glory of battle, he would come back to her the conquering warrior, worthy of her beauty and grace. He would, he promised, come back to sweep her off her feet and carry her off to the church to become his wife, and they would live happily forever and evermore.

With a broken heart, she had watched him ride away, for with a tragic certainty she knew she would never again see his smiling face, hear his contagious laughter, or be held in his strong embrace. She had been frightened for him, but angry, too, that he should risk their future together on a whim.

When the terrible news had come, she was numb with grief, doubting if she would ever be able to feel anything again. As the numbness passed, however, she indeed felt something: an acute, searing pain that overwhelmed her heart. The pain had diminished over time, but never completely dispelled, lingering as a dull, aching loneliness just beneath the surface. She was learning, with some difficulty, to live with this gaping hole in her heart, its jagged edges healing ever so slowly—a process that would certainly be hindered by the loss of her cherished Lady.

The journey to the seaport of Charleston began slowly. They traveled along the narrow, rough, post road, barely more than two ruts following a southeastward trail that had once been used by the Indians. Lord John had designed two wooden box-shaped vans to transport his expensive horses to buyers or those needing the services of his fine stallions.

The floor of the narrow van was lined with a thick bed of hay, and the opening in the back was blocked by a hinged gate that dropped down, transforming into the loading ramp. The sides were thickly padded to provide a safe and comfortable support for the animals to lean against as they fought the rocking movement of the wagon. Each van was pulled by a matched team of sure-footed mules capable of traversing the rough-hewn trails that passed for roads.

The plantation was situated in the piedmont of the South Carolina colony. The countryside was an expanse of rolling hills with an occasional high hill called a mo-nadnock, a solid rock formation that had resisted the rav-ages of erosion. The piedmont extended from the lower section of the Appalachian highlands to the fall line where the land dropped down to the wide coastal plain and stretched to meet the cold Atlantic Ocean. Barring disas-ter, the journey would take them about two and a half weeks, one way.

Jess tried to see the time as two and a half weeks more that she would have Lady, instead of thinking about the ship that would take Lady to the West Indies.

If Lord John Keene had still been alive, she knew, things would be different. He would never have approved of his son's actions. The elder Keene had been a titled gentle-man; Jessica's father had served in the British army with him in India. Retiring from the army, Lord John had moved to the colonies, where his younger brother had set-tled several years earlier. Lord John had offered Rob McClaren Sr. the job of stable master in charge of his excel-lent line of thoroughbred horses. McClaren had accepted the offer, bringing his young wife and infant son, Robbie

Jr., to the colonies, where Jessica had been born three years later.

The plantation had been named Cheltenham Farms in memory of Lord John's birthplace in England. Over the years, the plantation had prospered and grown into an agricultural and horse breeding operation that spread over nine hundred acres.

Jessica's father was paid well for his expertise and provided with a very comfortable house set apart from the servants' quarters.

Everything had gone very well until matters between the colonies and England began to deteriorate from difficult to impossible. Now a full-fledged war for independence had been raging up north, and the British had been trying to encourage the Tory sentiment that existed among many in South Carolina. The occupation of the colony's major seaport of Charleston was part of a concerted effort to retain control over the whole of the South.

Lord John had spoken out sharply against the British conquest of Savannah two years earlier; but, later that same year, he had fallen ill. Upon his death, his son Bradford had taken over and made public his Tory sympathies. Bradford's sale of the two thoroughbreds was, in fact, a direct slap at the colonial boycott of trade with England.

At every turn, Bradford had made a point of belittling the "revolutionary rabble of the Continental army" and had attended parties given by the British General Clinton in Charleston. His fortune continued to increase, as did his landholdings (with the purchase of an adjoining farm when the owner and his son apparently decided to return to Ireland).

Bradford's Loyalist attitude, along with his tyrannical administration of the plantation, had convinced Rob

McClaren that it was time to move on and establish a place of his own. Out of loyalty to Lord John, he had promised to stay until Bradford could find a replacement.

A year and a half after Lord John's death, Bradford had not been searching very diligently for a replacement, for Jessica's father had a reputation as the best stable master and trainer in all the southern colonies. She wondered what Bradford's reaction would be when her father told him about the purchase of their own farm. It would be a moment she would not want to miss.

The first five days of the trip were uneventful as they rolled steadily through green hills and wide grassy meadows. The spring rains had been light, and the road was passable; aside from one cracked wheel rim, they had enjoyed a fairly easy time. Even the cracked wheel had not delayed them long, as they were carrying two spare wheels atop each van for just such an event.

Each tiny village through which they passed seemed to be a parade of curious people stopping to stare. Due to the dreadful road conditions, there were few wheeled vehicles in the colonies, and they were always a source of curiosity. Though they were more common closer to the larger centers of population where the roads were somewhat better, only those of means owned coaches and wagons on the frontier.

Rob McClaren noticed that the people were not only curious, they seemed apprehensive, uncertain of how the events unfolding along the eastern seaboard would affect them. Meeting several of his acquaintances from previous trips, he heard the rumors about British troops poised at Charleston, ready to swoop down upon the entire colony in a military siege to crush all opposition to the crown.

They were not quite halfway to their destination and, concerned about Jessica, he couldn't help wondering what the situation really would be as they drew nearer Charleston.

On the sixth day, about midmorning, the two wagons were moving along as they had each morning before. Jessica was humming dreamily as she watched the clouds skimming above trees bursting with the brilliant green of new growth. They were beginning to see the last of the dogwood and redbud blossoms before the coming heat of summer. Along the sides of the road stretched fields splashed with bright patches of wildflowers. A gentle breeze floated past them, cooling the sun-washed scene.

A sudden shout interrupted Jessica's dreamy state and the wagon in front pulled to a stop. Reining in her team, she craned her neck to see around the wagon in front.

Two soldiers approached her father. A strong surge of resentment and anger swelled inside her at the sight of their powdered wigs and bright red uniforms.

In a moment, her father came back and told her everything was all right. The soldiers were just looking for some crazy Cherokee who had gone on the warpath and scalped two of their sentries.

Jess's anger and sorrow over Evan's death at the battle of Savannah had dulled somewhat with the passing of time, but it had settled within her a grim bitterness toward anything remotely British. She therefore found it difficult to pity the dead sentries, especially after hearing about the British paying some of the Indian tribes a bounty on colonial scalps. Jess couldn't help thinking it was merely poetic justice.

The soldier in charge checked the papers Bradford had given them, and quickly looked inside the horse vans; Jessica refused to even look at the soldier walking by. In a matter of minutes, they had been waved on their way.

They passed two more British patrols before stopping to make camp for the night.

The western sky was beginning to change from blue to evening lavender when they pulled off the road. Stopping in a small clearing surrounded by white oak, they set up camp on the grassy bank of a narrow stream. Aside from the ever-present mosquitos, it was the perfect place to stop for their teams and their two prize animals.

"Poor Lady," Jess said soothingly, stroking and patting the beautiful chestnut-brown neck as she prepared to back the filly down from the van. "Let's have a wee bit of a walk, and stretch those legs."

She led the two horses to the stream and let them drink long cool drafts of water while her father unhitched the two mule teams and brought them around. After strapping a feed bag of oats onto each of the animals, McClaren joined his daughter by the campfire she had started. He stretched out on the grass to light his pipe while Jessica started the coffee and prepared some boiled cornmeal mush for their supper.

Daylight was evaporating into the cool of evening by the time they finished eating. It had been an uneventful—but long and tiring—day. McClaren reminded Jessica that to stay on schedule, they would need another early start in the morning. He suggested she get their bedrolls from the wagons while he checked the animals' picket lines.

Jessica had just pulled the bedrolls out of Lady's van, and was closing the van up when suddenly a hand landed heavily on her shoulder, and a rather deep voice said, "The eagle's flyin' high, Robbie."

2

Whirling around in surprise, Jess looked up into the darkest brown eyes she had ever seen. The smile quickly turned to a quizzical frown as the stranger suddenly realized he was not speaking to the person he had expected. He backed away and turned to go, but suddenly stopped. Clutching his side, he swooned and collapsed beside the wagon.

"Papa!" Jessica cried. "Papa, come quick."

"What is it, lass?" Her father came running to find her kneeling beside a young stranger.

"He's hurt, Papa . . . I think he's been shot."

"Let's get him over to the fire and have a closer look," McClaren said.

Half dragging and half carrying the stranger over to the campfire, they laid him carefully beside it. In the firelight, they could see a large red stain surrounding a torn place on the left side of his buckskin shirt just above his belt.

"Not a bullet wound. It's a knife or maybe a bayonet wound. Lost a lot of blood," McClaren said after raising the leather shirt to examine the wound. "I wonder if this could be the Cherokee the soldiers were lookin' for."

"Not exactly the wild Indian I had pictured," Jess said. Glancing briefly at the young man's face, she opened the black satchel of medical supplies they carried for the horses. "I wonder why he would have attacked their sentries? I thought the Cherokees were fighting on the British side."

"True, but the redcoats said he must be a renegade; and look at this—if that's not a Cherokee belt and tomahawk, I'll be a kipper fer breakfast." Her father held up the tomahawk he had removed from the stranger's belt.

As Jess began cleansing the ugly wound she said, "Papa, I think he was expecting to see Robbie."

Her father chuckled. "What gave you a crazy notion like that?"

"Well, he grabbed my shoulder and said something about eagles flying and called me Robbie." Wincing with concern at the still bleeding wound, she gingerly applied the poultice paste she had prepared, then pressed a thick bandage directly over the cleansed wound. McClaren propped the young man up while she wrapped a long strip of bandage to hold the pad in place.

"Eagles, heh? Maybe he is daft," McClaren mused. "More likely, just delirious from blood loss."

"Papa, did you hear me? He called me Robbie. Then when he saw me, he turned to leave. How could he know Robbie?" She began putting away the supplies in the black bag; McClaren removed his jacket, folded it, and placed it under the young man's head for a pillow.

"You must have heard him wrong, gal. I think we better tie his hands, just to be on the safe side."

She didn't press the matter further, but she couldn't accept her father's reply. She was certain of what she had heard.

"What are you going to do with him, Papa? You're not going to turn him over to the soldiers, are you?" She couldn't imagine her patient scalping anyone.

"We'll wait to see what he has to say for himself before we decide what we'll do with him." McClaren leaned back, lit his pipe, and studied their strange visitor. Dressed in a suit of buckskin with knee-length moccasins and a weather-beaten felt hat, he looked like many of the frontiersmen. His dark hair was cut short, not long or braided like most Native Americans he had seen.

At her father's instruction, Jess sat on the other side of the fire and kept Robbie's hat pulled down over her face so the stranger would not be able to see her well. She peered curiously at the wounded man from beneath the hat brim.

It wasn't long before he regained consciousness. At first he was silent, apparently trying to get his bearings. She could see him watching her father intently. Then he squinted to see her shadowy form beyond the circle of firelight.

McClaren knelt by the young man with a cup of water and spoke matter-of-factly. "We're not goin' to hurt you now, lad; and those ropes are meant to make sure you don't do us any harm. What's your name? How were you hurt?"

The young man took the drink McClaren offered and silently studied his situation.

"You'd better tell us, son. I don't want to have to call them redcoats of King George who stopped us today."

After a moment more of silence, the stranger began, "Thanks for patching me up, Mister . . ."

"McClaren. Rob McClaren. Now, you know my name and considerin' we did patch you up, don't you think you could tell us who you are and what happened to you?"

"Name's Andrew Macklin," he started. "I, uh . . . was robbed by three scavengers down the road."

McClaren raised an eyebrow and said skeptically, "Macklin is a fine name for a Scot, but in these buckskins you could pass for a Cherokee."

The young man raised himself up on one elbow and, looking at his bandaged side, said absently, "My father was from Scotland."

Although not convinced by the stranger's story, McClaren could tell by the sound of his voice that he was exhausted and very weak. "Rest now. We'll talk more in the mornin'. If we can get a straight story from you, then we'll decide where we'll go from there." Turning to Jess, he said, "Better get to bed, son. I want to get started early in the morning."

Nodding silently, Jess pulled her blanket up over her and glanced at the stranger. For an instant their eyes met. She felt him studying her as curiously as she had regarded him before he awoke. She pulled her hat down further and closed her eyes, but the vision of Macklin's dark, perceptive eyes remained before her. Although as skeptical as her father about the man's story, she was struck by her impression that this mysterious stranger was no threat to them.

Rob McClaren dozed lightly through the night. Occasionally he rose to add more wood to the fire. He felt fairly safe with the young stranger tied, but with Jessica along, he would not take any chances.

How proud he was of his daughter. Although he knew her heart was breaking, she had not complained nor protested as they continued each day of their journey. The thought of such pain for his child caused the anger to boil in him anew as he thought about the man responsible for this trip.

Bradford Keene was not an easy man to work for, especially now that they differed so completely in their view of independence for the colonies. However, it had been the last straw when Bradford began to pay uninvited attention to Jessica shortly after Evan's death. The man was nearly old enough to have his own child Jess's age. Before McClaren had been able to give Bradford a piece of his mind, Jess told Keene graciously, but in no uncertain terms that she was not interested. A heated confrontation had been avoided; however, Rob McClaren knew that there was no time to waste. They must establish their own place and move far away from Bradford Keene. Lord John had left his faithful stable master a nice bonus, and saving every penny possible, McClaren finally had enough to make a down payment on their new farm. If all went well on this journey, it would perhaps be the last order he would have to take from Bradford Keene.

The past year since Lord John's death had been difficult to endure. After his military experience and working for his old commander for so many years, McClaren was used to taking orders. He'd had to obey orders he did not agree with before, but working for Bradford had become an increasing burden. He was constantly at odds with his employer. It grew clearer each day that the time had come to set out on their own. Jess was on constant guard against Bradford; and even his affable son, Robbie, grew more resentful and impatient with the Tory sentiment being forced upon them.

McClaren and Lord John had talked at length about independence for the colonies. Each had been loyal members of the King's military for years, and the transformation to colonial patriot had come about slowly. Robbie knew only the colonial life and felt no special obligation to the crown. This thought made McClaren begin to consider the possibility that Jess had not heard wrong when she thought Macklin had called her brother's name. Could it be the young lad he had worried would never take anything seriously was involved in something very serious indeed? It was not difficult to remain awake with so many ideas stirring in his brain.

3

The next morning Jess woke to a gentle shake and sat up. In the gray light just before sunrise, she saw her father kneeling beside her with a cup. "Here's some coffee. I didn't want you workin' around over there, now that it's gettin' light."

"Has he said anything else yet?" she asked, stretching sleepily.

Her father shook his head no. "I hate to do it, 'cause there's something about him that I like, but I'm afraid we'll have to turn him over to the soldiers. We must be on our way and he could use a doctor."

"Not the soldiers," she protested. "He'll get no doctoring from them. If you have to, turn him over to the constable in Barleyville. You said we'd be there by midmorning. Besides, what if he does know Robbie?"

"Robbie? I think it's highly unlikely, Jessie, gal. Don't you think your brother would have mentioned an Indian friend named Macklin?" His eyebrows rose in a gesture of skepticism before he responded to the pleading in her eyes. "I suppose the constable would do. All right, drink your coffee and go pack up our gear; just keep your head down and don't get too near him. I'll hitch up the teams and then you can bring Lady and Ettinsmoor over."

By the time the first rays of the morning sun spilled over the eastern hills, they were preparing to leave. The stranger was sitting up, leaning against a tree. McClaren had given him a cup of coffee, which he managed to hold with little trouble even though his hands were still bound securely in front of him. He waited in silence for the horses to be loaded and to be taken to the wagon himself.

Jess was just tying the gate closed after getting Lady into the van when suddenly the still morning air was pierced by a shrill panic-stricken whinny.

Dashing around the van, Jess was just in time to see the huge stallion strike her father down with a wild blow from his thrashing forelegs. Screaming, she ran at the wild-eyed horse, waving her hat to scare him back. Rushing in closer than she meant to, she closed her eyes at the sight of those deadly hooves flashing toward her face. In the split second that she expected to feel the crushing blow, she was suddenly pulled aside. A rush of air touched her face as the flailing hooves passed within inches.

In only a moment Ettinsmoor was quieting down, and Jess saw the stranger holding him by the mane and the halter at the throat latch. "Whoa, boy, whoa," he said, speaking in soothing tones to the nervously dancing stallion.

With Ettinsmoor under control, Jessica turned and knelt beside her unconscious father. Blood flowed freely from a frightful gash on the right side of his head.

Laying her head against his chest, she detected a steady but very weak heartbeat. Kneeling across from her, the stranger quickly examined the head wound and directed, "Get some water and a bandage."

36

Without another moment's hesitation she ran for the canteen and the medicine satchel. In only a few minutes, they had ministered to the injury, bringing the bleeding under control.

"There's a doctor at Barleyville," the young man said, glancing up at her. "He'll be able to help him, Jess."

Nodding, silently grateful for his calming assurance as well as the steady efficiency with which he tended the wound, she quickly repacked the medicine satchel.

The stranger picked McClaren up and gently laid him on a blanket that Jessica quickly spread on the hay in Ettinsmoor's van. The stallion was tethered to the back end of the van, where he would have to walk the distance to Barleyville just like an ordinary horse.

Picking up the hat she had dropped when she was pulled out of harm's way, Jess hurried back to Lady's van and climbed onto the wagon seat.

The next three hours of slow traveling seemed torturous. Having calmed down from her initial fright for her father, she still couldn't seem to think very clearly. A myriad of questions swam in her thoughts. Most of the questions bombarding her senses concerned the stranger driving the van carrying her father.

Who was he? How had he gotten free to get Ettinsmoor away and save her and her father? Had she been mistaken or had he called her by her brother's name the night before? Even if she were mistaken about that, she had clearly heard him call her by her own name when they were tending to her father. She was fairly certain her father had not called her by name in front of him. How could he know? Could he really be the one the soldiers were looking for? His hair and eyes were dark, but his features were not especially typical of most Indians. If not for the Indian moccasins and feathered tomahawk removed from the belt of his buckskin clothing, he resembled the dark-haired clansmen, the fierce guardians of the highland moors described in the fireside tales spun by her father.

She was no nearer to an explanation of the mysterious stranger when their seemingly unending journey brought them at last to Barleyville. The sight of the small village tucked neatly at the edge of the forest was a great relief to Jessica.

Without hesitation or stopping for directions, the wagon ahead of her turned onto the first lane that crossed the road into town. In a few minutes they pulled up in front of a two-story, whitewashed frame house where Jess saw the young man swing down from the wagon seat. Grabbing his side, he held onto the side of the wagon for a moment before going up to the house.

She tied off the reins and jumped down to check on her father. As she let down the back gate, she glanced over at the porch to see that a tall, thin man in shirtsleeves had answered the door. He greeted the young stranger happily with a vigorous handshake and a slap on the back.

As soon as Jess saw the man she assumed to be the doctor coming down the steps, she climbed into the van, hoping to find her father awake at last.

Her anxiety increased as she found him still unconscious, and she turned a fear-filled glance toward the two men as they appeared at the back of the wagon.

"Miss McClaren, this is Dr. Barton," the stranger said.

"Miss McClaren," the doctor said with a nod of greeting. "Let's get your father inside. Help me here, Mac."

After the men had gotten Rob McClaren inside and under the doctor's care, the young man turned to Jess and

38

said, "Instead of sitting around waiting, let's go see to your horses. There's a paddock and barn out back."

She reluctantly agreed when reassured that they wouldn't be long; and if the doctor needed her, all he had to do was call out the back window.

Once outside again, as they walked down the path to the gate at the front of the yard, Jess asked, "You and the doctor are friends?"

He nodded.

She felt the color rising to her cheeks as she asked the next question, knowing the answer already, "And Mac is short for Macklin? Andrew Macklin?"

Again he nodded.

"Then you were telling us the truth last night?"

Expecting another affirmative answer, she was embarrassed over their suspicious treatment of him, especially tying him up when he had been wounded.

"Well, not completely," he confessed.

His answer caused her to stop abruptly, but he continued on down the walk ahead of her without further explanation.

Macklin led one mule team while Jess led the other, moving the vans around to the back of the house. They exchanged few words as they worked to get the horses settled in the paddock. The mules had been turned out and Ettinsmoor was led in to join them before anything further was said. Jess brought Lady in and was checking her over as Macklin checked Ettinsmoor's hooves for stones and began rubbing down the stallion's legs with liniment.

Jess was unable to hold her questions any longer. "What did you mean when you said you hadn't been completely truthful with us last night? You weren't robbed?"

He shook his head.

Perturbed by his reluctance to communicate, she persisted. "You're not the 'wild Indian' the soldiers are looking for, anyway," she declared with certainty.

He spoke as though he hadn't heard her. "It was a fox that spooked this one," he said reaching to pat Ettinsmoor's neck, and avoiding her questioning glance.

"A fox?"

Nodding, he said, "Must have been sleeping in the hay and ran out when your father let the gate down."

Although momentarily sidetracked, she refused to be swayed from her line of thought. "Well, even if you are the 'wild Indian' they're looking for, I don't know how we'll ever be able to thank you. He could have killed Papa and me both."

Macklin said nothing.

Thinking he might be angry because of their plans to turn him over to the constable, she tried to control her growing exasperation and apologized. "I'm sorry we tied you up last night, but . . . by the way, how did you get loose to help us?"

Leaning over, he lifted the fringed cuff of his moccasin boot to reveal the bone handle of a knife.

"You mean you could have gotten away any time?"

"We'd better get back to the house," he said. "Doc Barton should know about your father by now."

Noticing how tired he appeared, she realized he must still be quite weak from his injury; and being anxious to hear about her father, she reluctantly let the issue drop for the moment. Although she followed him silently up to the house, she fully intended to learn the answers to her questions before all was said and done.

A lively little white-haired lady greeted them at the door, and after a hug for Macklin she introduced herself to Jess as Mrs. Barton. Assuring Jessica that her father was resting comfortably, she led them to the doctor's office.

"Well, it's a rather serious concussion, but it might've been worse," the doctor explained soberly. "It's still a bit soon to know for sure, but there doesn't seem to be any brain damage. He will have to stay quiet and in bed for two weeks."

"May I see him?" she asked.

"He's still unconscious, could be for some time yet. Why don't you just rest a bit yourself? Mama here will show you where you can freshen up."

"Thank you. You've been very kind," Jess said absently.

"Come on, dearie, I'll show you where you can freshen up and then we'll have a nice cup of tea. Sassafras, I think. 'Twill bring the bloom back to your cheeks." Mrs. Barton took her arm to lead her up the stairs.

Jess stopped and turned. "By the way, Dr. Barton, Mr. Macklin's been hurt himself and has lost quite a bit of blood."

The doctor turned to Andrew Macklin with a raised eyebrow. "Come in here," he commanded.

Jessica couldn't help smiling a bit wryly at Macklin's frown.

4

Jess felt much better after washing away the dust of the road. The bracing cup of sassafras tea she sipped with Mrs. Barton restored her even further. As they relaxed with their tea, Jessica took the opportunity to satisfy some of her curiosity about Andrew Macklin. Mrs. Barton was happy to oblige. She told Jess that Mac's father was indeed Scottish and his mother was Delaware Indian. Hearing this, Jess was glad to dismiss the suspicion that he could be the Cherokee Indian the British were searching for.

Although the elder lady suggested she lay down for a while, Jess was too unsettled to rest and decided to check on the horses.

Passing the doctor's study on her way out, she could hear raised voices. It surprised her after the enthusiastic way Macklin had been received by the doctor and all the nice things Mrs. Barton had told her about him during their tea.

She tried not to listen, but as she went by, she heard Macklin firmly say, "No! and that's final. I'll get there some other way."

Outside at the paddock she was greeted by a low whinny as Lady shook her mane, impatiently waiting for Jessica to come to the fence. Stroking the velvet nose, she murmured a soft greeting to the filly. The attention was received with soft little nickers in reply.

"What are we to do, Lady?" Jessica sighed. "If I don't get you and Ettinsmoor to Charleston by the fifteenth, the contract will be broken and Bradford will never let Papa go until he's made up for the loss." Remembering Bradford's pettiness, she struggled to imagine a way to keep the contract for which her father was responsible.

She twined her fingers absently in Lady's mane. "What would Robbie do if he were here instead of me?" she murmured. "Of course, I know what he would do, but how can I go off and leave Papa when he's hurt so badly?" She stood silently petting the filly. Finally, she drew her fingers out of the thick mane. "Maybe if we take a ride things will look a little clearer."

She took a bridle from the van and put it on Lady. Then, climbing atop the fence railing, she slipped lightly on the chestnut's bare back. Jess walked Lady through the back gate of the paddock, letting the thoroughbred's well-muscled legs warm up gradually. Soon, Lady was straining at the bit, eager for the run.

The thoroughbred's gait was as smooth as glass as she raced across wide meadows and jumped tiny brooks. The late spring air rushed past them, playing with Jess's hair and Lady's mane. The exhilaration of the flying pace had never become old hat to Jess; she knew this was as close to soaring like the birds that she would ever come. Horse and rider were like one in a fluid motion fairly flying over the lush meadow grass.

She rode out over the heath until she worried she might lose her way. Circling back, she slowed the pace gradually, finally dismounting at the hedgerow that grew along the far end of the field behind the paddock. Walking slowly, in deep thought, she led Lady back to cool her down.

The filly nudged her playfully as if to hurry her along, and Jess turned to teasingly scold her. It was a little game they had played when Lady was just a yearling and always ended with Jess holding out some apple chunks as a treat. Such behavior was not encouraged with most of the horses in training. Lady, however, seemed to possess an unusually keen sense about the more fragile nature of human creatures. Even in her youthful exuberance, the filly had never taken advantage of her strength and size, taking great care to avoid causing any injury to her mistress.

Jessica had no apple chunks today and slowly stroked the silky neck, dark brown with perspiration. Looking into those big trusting eyes caused a lump to swell in her throat.

"Surely Bradford couldn't hold Papa responsible for not making it to Charleston under these circumstances."

Lady watched her closely as if understanding every word, nodding her head up and down. Jess laughed; the action appeared to be Lady's answer to her statement. She stopped laughing, though, remembering an incident last fall when the foreman of the field hands became seriously ill and so was unable to oversee the cutting of the hay. His nephew had taken the crew into the fields. Not being the forceful man the foreman was, the nephew failed to complete the cutting before a late season downpour. Bradford held the foreman responsible for the costly ruined hay.

44

The size of the debt was such that the foreman would never be able to redeem himself.

Thinking it would have all been so different had Lord John still been alive, she found it hard to believe the two men could be related, let alone as father and son. Bradford Keene was a hard man. His hardness was not the tough, determined kind of steel possessed by his father and most of the colonials. Bradford Keene's hardness was the cold, ruthless kind. Even in the local social circles he was a feared man—not respected, but feared.

Over the last year and a half, she had avoided any contact at all with the heir of Cheltenham Farms, especially after the news had come about Evan, when Bradford had come to express his condolences and hinted broadly that he would be very willing to help mend her broken heart. If she hadn't been so appalled by the suggestion, it would have been laughable. Her rejection of his attention had been costly, however, for it was just a short time later that he had first threatened to sell Lady. Jess could still remember the cruel smile as he told her of his plan. Now, the memory of his humorless smile and the coldness in his voice left her shivering, even though the sun was shining brightly.

"Have a nice ride?"

She jumped with a gasp, startled from her thoughts by a pleasant, deep voice that seemed to contrast dramatically with the cold voice in her memory. Macklin sat on the fence railing, wearing a clean shirt of faded blue homespun that seemed to make his complexion look more deeply tanned and his dark hair and eyes even darker.

She turned away from those dark, perceptive eyes when he asked, "Are you all right?"

She drew a deep breath and tried to sound casual as she explained, "It's beautiful country and Lady's been dying for a good run." Then, glancing back up at him, she asked, "Has Papa awakened yet?"

He climbed down from the fence rail and said, "No, he's still sleeping. But Doc Barton feels pretty sure he is going to be all right."

He picked up a grooming brush and began helping her as she started tending to the horse.

"Are you feeling better now?" she finally asked. "How's your side?"

"Doc said you did a good job on it; probably saved me from bleeding to death. Thanks."

Watching him across Lady's back, she ventured, "Does that mean you've forgiven Papa and me for tying you up last night?"

"Nothing to forgive," he said with a slight grin to put her at ease. "There are some pretty rough characters roaming around these days. It doesn't hurt to be cautious."

As he was apparently in a much more talkative mood now and bearing no ill will toward her, she seized the chance to satisfy her unanswered questions from earlier that morning. "You never did explain why you didn't escape when you had the chance."

"The fire was nice and warm, and I needed a few hours of sleep. Besides, I took your father at his word that you didn't wish me any harm." A slight smile punctuated his words.

She narrowed her eyes suspiciously. "Or . . . could it be you wanted to know about Robbie? That's it, isn't it? That's why you didn't try to escape during the night." She was determined to know the truth about this stranger, no matter how charming his smile. "Mr. Macklin, how do you know my brother?"

He did not look at her. "You've taken good care of this filly. She's a real beauty. By the way, lunch is almost ready."

She held her temper in check with effort. "You always change the subject at the mention of my brother. Why is that, Mr. Macklin?"

Having finished currying Lady, he put the brushes away and turned to look toward the house. "There's Mrs. Barton, callin' us for lunch." He grinned back at her innocently. "She's a gentle little lady, but she can sure get upset if people don't get to the table on time. Come on."

She placed her hands on her hips in exasperation, and watched him stride back to the house. There were many unanswered questions about Mr. Andrew Macklin, but of one thing she was certain: He was the most perplexing person she had ever met.

When they were all seated around the table and Mac had said the blessing, they began to visit like old friends. They discussed the promise of a bountiful year for the farmers and plantation owners.

Dr. Barton brought Mac up to date on some of their mutual friends; when he mentioned that a well-known planter, Ronald Gallagher, had given up and sold out, a strange look flickered in Macklin's eye that made Jess all the more curious about this young man. Why would the mention of the Gallaghers, who had sold their neighboring plantation to Bradford Keene before returning to Ireland, mean anything to Andrew Macklin?

There was little time to contemplate the curious facts about the young stranger as Jessica was included in the lively discussion during the rest of the meal.

The meal itself warranted special attention. The sliced cold beef, hot vegetables, and homemade bread, with a thick apple pie for dessert, was heavenly. After nearly a week of their Spartan diet along the trail, Jessica savored every tasty morsel.

The Bartons and their home were so congenial Jess's spirits were lifted, and she was sorry to think she would have to be leaving soon.

As the meal drew to an end, her thoughts turned to the decision she had made earlier. Taking a deep breath, she asked, "Dr. Barton, do you know of any young men in the village who would consider taking a job driving our other wagon?" She hoped she sounded more certain of herself than she actually felt.

"So you've decided to go on, have you?" the doctor asked.

She bit her lip slightly. "I don't know what else I can do. If we don't have Ettinsmoor and Lady in Charleston by the fifteenth, Papa may never be able to . . . well, we just must deliver those horses on time." She stopped short of going into the details, reluctant to air family problems before strangers, even very nice strangers.

"I'm afraid there's no one really reliable." The doctor sighed, leaning back in his chair.

"No one at all?" she asked.

The doctor cleared his throat. "As a matter of fact, there might be someone quite suitable who is on his way to Charleston on business of his own."

Mac directed a grim glance at the doctor. "That would be perfect," Jess said hopefully. "How can I get in touch with him?"

The doctor took off his glasses and began cleaning them. "Turn to your right there and ask him."

Jess turned to Mac, but he spoke immediately. "I'm sorry, Miss McClaren," he said politely. "The doctor's right, I am going to Charleston, but I have to get there as quickly as I can."

"Oh, I see," she said. Determined not to let her disappointment show, she turned to the doctor and asked, "Are you sure there's no one at all?"

"Well, it's the war, you see," he explained. "We lost two of our village boys at Savannah two years ago, and almost all the rest have gone north to join the Continental army or have joined the bands of rangers intent on harassing the British troops in these parts." He cast a sidelong glance at Mac. "Of course, there are the Larkin boys."

Macklin nearly choked on a mouthful of milk. "Larkin boys? Seth and Caleb?"

"Well," the doctor drawled, "one of them would probably be willing to go with Miss McClaren and help her."

"Help her?" Mac declared, raising his voice slightly. "That'd be like sending a hungry timber wolf out to escort a lamb back to the fold. How can you even think of the Larkins, knowin' what they're like?"

"Well, they *are* available," Dr. Barton declared with certainty, looking to his wife. Her wide-eyed expression echoed Macklin's incredulity.

"About the only other one who could handle a team would be Jake Sandy," the doctor continued.

"But he's only twelve years old," Mac countered.

It was clear to Jessica that the young man was mystified by his friend's rather careless attitude. "My advice, Miss McClaren," he said, still staring at the doctor, "would be to just wait till your father is well enough to travel on to Charleston."

Before Jess could reply, the maid entered to announce that her father was awake.

Excusing herself, Jess anxiously hurried down the hall to see her father. Inside the room, she stood quietly beside the bed and clutched his big rough hand.

"Hello, Papa," she said softly, trying to hold back tears of relief.

"Jess," he replied in a hoarse whisper. "Jess, are you all right, lass?"

"I'm fine, Papa. No, don't try to get up. The doctor says you must stay still."

He weakly submitted to her restraining hand on his shoulder and lay back. The terrible throbbing in his head seemed to rob him of any strength. With some difficulty, he tried to sort through the jumble of questions plaguing his battered senses. "Where are we?" he asked. "What's happened to Ettinsmoor and Lady?"

"They're fine, too," she assured him. She explained where they were and how they had gotten there. When she finished, she said, "You just rest now. You mustn't worry about a thing."

He drifted off to sleep again, and she sat beside his bed for a long time as the shafts of midafternoon sunshine cast an inviting golden glow throughout the cozy room. She braced herself, resisting her desire to stay in this place of peace and safety; she knew she must begin taking steps to complete the task at hand.

Mrs. Barton was just closing the front door after showing a patient out as Jess approached her.

"Excuse me, Mrs. Barton, could you please tell me how I might find the Larkins?"

50

The little lady stammered just a bit, then motioned for her to come a step closer. "My dear," she whispered conspiratorially, "the doctor just mentioned the Larkins to try to convince Mac to help you. He really didn't mean . . . oh my, no, not the Larkins, no, no, dear."

"Is there someone else, then?" she asked in a determined tone.

"I'm afraid there really is no one else, dear. The rest of what he said is true, but perhaps Mac . . ."

"Mr. Macklin made it clear that he isn't interested. I think I'd better speak to the Larkins."

"Isn't interested?" the little lady chuckled to herself. "Oh, I'm sure he's interested, mighty interested; but there are other matters he's concerned about. Mind you, given a little time and a push at the right moment, I think he'll come around." An impish gleam danced in Mrs. Barton's bright blue eyes.

"I'm afraid I haven't time to wait for him to make up his mind," Jessica said, a little more impatiently than she intended. She certainly didn't want to offend this charming little lady, but she refused to be deterred or delayed— no matter what Andrew Macklin did. "If you don't mind," she said, "please direct me to the Larkins."

"Well, that might do it," the little lady murmured. "Just a minute, dear. Mac knows the way. I'll ask him to take you."

Jessica started to protest, but the woman scurried off down the hall to her husband's study without listening. She came out a few minutes later; Mac followed, wearing a stony expression.

"Mrs. Barton says you're determined to talk to the Larkins."

She lifted her chin slightly, and nodded without looking him directly in the eye.

"You're just asking for trouble, you know." He glanced at Mrs. Barton, sighed with resignation, and said, "All right, come on."

They took the doctor's buggy and rode without speaking. A mile past the edge of the village, they turned down a twisting lane that ended in front of a ramshackle cabin surrounded by old discarded bottles, scattered refuse, barrels, and rusting farm implements. Four hounds bounded up to them and commenced a chorus of mellow baying.

A voice spoke from the shadow on the front stoop. "Halloo there. Why, look. If it ain't that half-breed fella, Macklin."

"Who's that he got with him, Caleb?"

"Don't know, but sure gonna find out. Lookit that purty hair."

In a moment, two tall, lanky figures emerged from the porch. One of them impatiently kicked a hound out of his way. Their appearance nearly made Jess forget why she had come. The men were dressed in patched and grimy homespun clothing; their battered old hats were pulled down over mats of straggly hair. The only evidence of care taken by the repugnant pair was the shining gleam of the sharply honed steel blade of the hunting knife Seth held. The handle of an identical weapon was tucked in a scabbard on Caleb's belt.

Jess glanced uneasily at Mac, then back at the two approaching figures. The thought of either man touching her horses made her shudder and place an uncertain hand on Mac's wrist.

"I'm sorry, Mr. Macklin," she whispered quickly. "You were right. I don't think either of them would be suitable."

As they drew closer, their leering gazes caused the hair on the back of her neck to prickle. Realizing she was clutching Mac's wrist tighter, she quickly pulled her hand away in embarrassment. She shot him a glance and turned back with the distinct feeling that he had been watching her to witness her reaction to the unpleasant pair standing before them.

"Macklin." Caleb called to Mac, never taking his eyes off Jess. "Aintcha gonna interduce yer lady friend here?"

"Not necessary, Larkin," Mac answered coolly. "We aren't staying. Just passing by and made a wrong turn. Sorry to disturb you."

"Well, that ain't very friendly. Is it Seth? Don't seem quite right that a purty little gal like that oughta hafta go ridin' aroun' with no redskin, does it?"

Jess marveled at Mac's unflappability. He calmly pulled back on the reins to start backing the buggy, but Seth caught the horse's halter with one hand, the other still clutching the large hunting knife.

"Come on down an' set a spell, Missy." Seth grinned, showing brown teeth. "We're real friendly folk here."

"Let go of the lines, Seth," Mac warned calmly.

Seth let out a whoop. "Listen to that, Caleb."

"Mighty big talk fer one feller agin two." Caleb grinned menacingly as he stepped closer.

"You boys go on back to your porch," Mac suggested, "and we'll be on our way."

Jess watched uneasily as Caleb ignored Mac's suggestion and continued his swaggering approach. She wished they'd never come.

She heard Mac sigh wearily, then watched with growing apprehension as he rose to step down from the buggy. It seemed incomprehensible that he really intended to stop and confront the brothers.

Just as he started to step down, Caleb rushed forward. Mac caught him with a sudden kick to the chin that sent him reeling backwards.

Mac jumped to the ground. Jess shouted a warning; Seth was right behind him, but Mac seemed to know already. Using the attacker's own momentum, he grabbed the knife-wielding hand and quickly flipped Larkin over his head. The surprised man crashed heavily into his brother, who was just getting to his feet. The two fell to the ground in a groggy heap, Seth's knife falling harmlessly in the dust.

Jess could scarcely believe what she had seen. The two menacing characters, no longer threatening anyone, were pulling themselves up to a sitting position, glancing around to see what had happened. Holding his side, Mac stepped back up into the buggy, turned it around and, without a word, calmly clucked to the horse. They were off again.

5

The late afternoon sun was hot, and the dust of the road came swirling up to meet them in a suffocating cloud. They rode in silence along the winding lane, and eventually turned back onto the road leading into the village.

During their short acquaintance, Jess had begun to realize that Andrew Macklin was a man of few words. Nonetheless, she was wishing he would go ahead and tell her, "I told you so," and get it over with. As much as she hated to admit he was right, she shuddered at the thought of spending the next week traveling with either of the Larkins.

As they came to a bridge crossing the river, Mac surprised Jess by pulling the buggy over in the shade of a huge oak tree. He stepped down and, after helping Jess down, led the horse to the river's edge for a cool drink.

Jess sighed deeply. "I'm very sorry about the trouble back there. I . . . I guess you were right."

He nodded, studying her face.

She turned and walked along the river's edge. The early summer air was sweet with honeysuckle; the cool freshness of the damp earth rose up from the river's bank. Grimly realizing her problem was still unsolved, she took a deep breath of the fragrant air, and said, "Of course, maybe I was too hasty. If there were only one of them . . . looks can be deceiving. They say not to judge a book by its cover."

"In this case," Mac said, walking up to stand beside her, "the cover is only a hint of what's inside. They were drunk today, and easy enough to handle, but they don't use those knives for whittling wood."

"Well, of course, I'd keep Papa's pistol with me all the time," she said.

"Eight days is a long time to keep guard without going to sleep. Look, you might as well face it: There isn't any other way except to wait until your father is well enough to continue."

"There has to be a way," she insisted, clenching her fists. "Even if it means hiring a twelve-year-old boy."

He removed his hat and ran his hand roughly through his dark hair. "I don't get it. As much as you seem to care for that filly, it seems like you'd be happy for any excuse to keep from taking her to Charleston. Is Bradford Keene's business so important to you that you'd risk your life with some stranger?"

She looked up at him, her eyes flashing with anger. Afraid to trust her voice, she bit her lip and turned to walk away.

"Why can't you just wait until your father is well? There will be other ships," he called after her.

She wondered how he dared to say such a thing. Bradford Keene's business success was the last thing that interested her. Strangely, she realized that the thing that disturbed her most as she had stood there next to Andrew

56

Macklin was the fact that he had so misinterpreted her motives. Why should she even care what this man thought? She had no time to be concerned about him or his opinions.

Seeing her despair, Mac began to apologize. "Miss McClaren . . ."

Rebuffing his attempt at an apology, she quickened her steps and hurried back to the buggy.

Mac started after her, catching her arm and pulling her back around to face him.

"Let me go," she demanded. "Just leave me alone, please." She tried to pull away, but he held her fast. Emotion she had been suppressing since she and her father had left Cheltenham Farms welled inside her. The added burden of her father's injury so far from home, and being frustrated in her attempts to carry out the task herself, had been bad enough; Mac's assumption that her determination to complete the trip was motivated by a desire to impress Bradford Keene was the final straw. Meeting his questioning gaze, her anger dissolved into tears of frustration, and he drew her into his arms. She cried against his shoulder for a few moments, refusing to admit how very grateful she was for his strong, comforting embrace.

Her sobs subsiding, she began to explain the story of Lady Heather Star and the situation they now faced. "Almost four years ago they said she'd never make it, but I couldn't give up on her. She trusts me. She'll never understand. I've thought of every way in the world to avoid taking her to Charleston and putting her on a ship to the West Indies. I even considered stealing her and running away. But of course, that was foolish."

She had calmed down at last and, although she was reluctant to break Mac's embrace, embarrassment got the better of her and she gently pushed away from him.

"Forgive me, Mr. Macklin. I . . . I'm not usually given to hysterics." As she wiped the tears from her face, her eyes focused on a dark stain that dampened Mac's shirt. "For goodness sake," she said, "you're bleeding. All that fighting has opened up your wound again. I'm so sorry. We'd better get back to the doctor."

He answered without looking at the stain on his shirt. "It'll be all right."

Taking hold of his arm, she turned him toward the buggy.

"Why don't you buy Lady yourself?" he asked.

"Don't think I haven't considered it, but she's a very valuable animal. She's descended from the Royal Barb; she's worth more money than I'll ever see. Besides, I'm the last person Bradford would sell her to now."

He was curious about this remark, but didn't question it. Instead, he asked, "What about your father?"

"He's just put every penny of savings into a farm of his own. That's why I have to deliver the horses on time. If that contract is broken, Bradford Keene will plague Papa to his dying day. Bradford is a ruthless Tory; it would break Papa to suffer the humiliation of Bradford's revenge."

They reached the buggy. Mac led the horse back to the road, then gave Jess a hand up. He walked around and stepped into the buggy.

A long moment passed, and he did not start the horse. She finally looked at him. "We'd better get back to the doctor," she said, "so he can rebandage your side."

He did not respond. His wound seemed of little consequence compared to the dilemma he faced. Although it had been part of the original plan, did he dare to allow Robbie's little sister to become involved? Glancing over at her, he met her look of concern and knew that she fully intended to complete this journey with or without his help.

As he remained silent, he appeared a bit drawn and weary. Jessica worried that he might be injured more seriously than at first thought. "Mr. Macklin, are you all right?"

"I'll help you get to Charleston," he said, still looking straight ahead.

"What?" she asked, startled by his comment.

"First, I want you to know, you could be shot or hung as a spy if you're caught traveling with me." He turned to study her reaction to his statement.

Oddly enough, the tears shed earlier seemed to cleanse her senses. She felt renewed, alert. Although bewildered by his statement, she was not especially shocked by it; she waited for him to explain.

He urged the horse forward at a walk. "I am that 'wild Indian' the redcoats are looking for."

"The one that . . . scalped two of their men?" she asked in astonishment. She peered into his face, into those deep brown eyes. It couldn't be true.

"We did have a fight," Mac explained. "I was the only one to walk away, but taking trophies has never been a habit of mine or any of the Cherokee I've known."

"Mrs. Barton said you were Delaware, not Cherokee."

"The British can't tell one Indian from another and there aren't that many Delaware left anymore, especially this far south. I've spent a lot of time with the Cherokee, though; my Grandmother and Grandfather Macklin are missionaries at the Iron Mountain settlement in the Chalequah Valley not far from here. They came from Scotland to work in Pennsylvania with the Lenapi; Delaware is what we're usually called now.

"That's how my father and mother got together. Mother was very small when an epidemic of measles wiped out most of her village. Grandmother and Grandfather Macklin took her and my grandmother, She-wan-ikee, in. My mother and father grew up together. They . . ." He stopped, suddenly surprised at how much he had told her. He cleared his throat. "Enough of that, though. I'm acting as a courier and agent for the army right now and that's why I'm on the way to Charleston. That's also why, if we're caught together, we will both be shot or hung."

His revelation explained much, but not all. "What does Robbie have to do with all of this?" she asked.

"Aye, you're a true Scot: bulldog determination and single-minded to a fair fault." The perfect Scottish accent he assumed surprised her. She had to laugh, although she did not consider his description flattering.

"Well? What about him?" she insisted with a wry smile.

He smiled a wonderful smile, chuckled, and shook his head in surrender. "Robbie is in this, too. He has been since shortly after the fall of Savannah. He's been supplying information and doing odd jobs for us all along. I was supposed to meet him at the white oak glade and travel to Charleston as a hired hand."

"I knew you'd called his name," she declared with satisfaction. "But how did you know he'd be coming?"

"He contacted me after he overheard Keene making arrangements to ship the horses. It seemed like a good way to get in and out of Charleston through the British lines. Where is he, anyway?"

"He was breaking in a new stallion and was thrown, a few days before Papa was given the orders to go to

Charleston. His leg was badly broken . . . no wonder he made such a fuss when we were getting ready to leave. I think he nearly told me about you, but changed his mind. I suppose he didn't want to give you away."

She fell silent, letting this news about her brother sink in.

Their conversation was cut short by their arrival at the doctor's house. While Mac tethered the horse, Jess ran in to alert Dr. Barton about his wound needing attention again. As she was coming out of the doctor's office, she ran into Mrs. Barton.

"Whoa, goodness child, what's wrong?"

"Oh, excuse me," she said. "I was just telling the doctor that Mr. Macklin's wound needs attention. There was a fight and . . ."

They were interrupted by Mac's entrance. The women watched as the doctor ushered him into the treatment room once more. Mac sighed a little with impatience at the fuss over him, but submitted to the doctor's help silently.

As the door closed behind the two men, Mrs. Barton's bright blue eyes danced with expectation as she asked, "And what? What happened?"

Jess tried to appear nonchalant about the whole thing, but couldn't help lapsing into a gleeful conspiratorial attitude to match Mrs. Barton's.

"Oh, the Larkins were unsuitable, to say the least. On the way back, we had a talk and, well, he agreed to help me take the horses to Charleston. I only hope he's up to the trip," she added thoughtfully as she glanced at the closed door of the treatment room.

"Don't worry, dear. He's young and strong. He'll be fine." Mrs. Barton clapped her hands in delight. "What did I tell you? I knew he'd not let you go off by yourself. Why don't you run on and tell your papa the good news, and I'll pour us a nice cup of tea; the kettle is just about ready."

Jess nodded and hurried down the hall to her father's room.

"Come in, lass." The tone of his voice alarmed her. He was weak as expected, but his words were marked by a note of hopelessness she had never heard before.

Watching him closely and choosing her words carefully, she told him the news. He objected strenuously at first, forbidding her to even think about finishing their journey with a stranger. Jess explained that Mac really was an acquaintance of Robbie, and related all the complimentary things Mrs. Barton had told her. Being very careful to avoid any mention of the army or spies, Jessica assured him that everything would be fine.

He had always trusted her judgment and, while he felt helpless for the time being, McClaren managed to shake the despair he had felt earlier; hope flickered again.

Leaving him to rest, Jessica went out to join Mrs. Barton on the front porch for tea. During their morning visit, the little lady had made her feelings about the current conflict between the colonists and England known in no uncertain terms. She had grown up in England and felt there was no harm in clinging to English customs—such as morning and afternoon tea, which she served with delight. However, as for the rest, she had pledged her allegiance to the colonies and was pleased to let everyone know it.

Watching Mrs. Barton pour the aromatic tea into delicate china cups, Jess observed, "You seem to know Mr. Macklin very well. He said his grandparents are missionaries at a Cherokee settlement not far from here."

"Oh, yes." Mrs. Barton smiled fondly. "The Macklins are wonderful people. Getting up there in years, though. I wonder how much longer they will be able to continue their work. You know, Mac grew up here, in Barleyville. His father, Andrew Macklin Sr., had a silversmith shop. I told you his mother was Delaware, didn't I?"

"Was?"

"Yes. Precious thing Lelia was, too. Died when Mac was fourteen, along with Mac's youngest brother. Little James was only six. Terrible scarlet fever epidemic. The only reason Mac and his other brother, Roger, were spared is that they were with their father on a trip to Lexington to see his uncle. By the time they got back it was all over. Mac's father was devastated. He tried to pull himself together for the sake of the boys, but the pain was too great. He fell ill several months later and had neither the strength nor the will to recover.

"Mac and his younger brother, Roger, were sent to his grandparents at the Iron Mountain settlement. His grandmother, She-wan-ikee, was there already. She had stayed on with the Macklins when Andrew had taken his wife and baby Mac to Lexington to work out his apprenticeship with his uncle. They moved here after the apprentice term. By that time, Roger was two and Mac five. Our son, Franklin, and Mac became best friends. Franklin was like a lost pup when Mac had to go to Iron Mountain every summer; especially so when he went there to live permanently. Franklin's a doctor now, too. He's serving with the Delaware continentals under the command of Baron de Kalb."

Remembering when the boys were growing up brought a wistful sigh in thinking how quickly those days had passed. The thought of the fine young men they had grown to be brought a smile. Her face beaming with pride, she declared, "With fine young men like our boy Franklin and Mac, these colonies could manage quite nicely on their own without His Mad Majesty, King George."

Jess was fascinated by Mrs. Barton's story and eager for her to continue, but her storytelling was interrupted when a young boy came dashing up with a bandage wrapped around his hand.

"Is Doc and . . ." The boy stopped and eyed Jess suspiciously. He held up his bandaged hand. "Pounded it with the hammer. Nigh unto broke, I bet."

"They're inside, Jake," Mrs. Barton said.

They watched him hurry into the house, slamming the door behind him. "Oh, that boy. Excuse me, dear. If I know Jake, he's run the whole four miles from his pa's farm; he'll be needing a nice glass of lemonade and some of these cookies."

Jess sat alone and reflected upon the things she had just been told about Andrew Macklin Jr. Soon, however, the beauty of the June day intruded on her thoughts. The spreading oak trees that lined the lane up to the post road looked like glistening green fountains in the late afternoon sunlight. The meadows seemed alive with the clear trill of larks and the monotonous hum of bees sampling the fresh spring clover. She was suddenly struck by the thought that even the bleakest of winters was always followed by the beauty, vitality, and new life of spring.

Dare she hope that a season of happiness and a vital new life awaited her family—and the colonies—if they could manage to survive this bleak period of trial? Just as she longed to escape the tyranny of Bradford Keene, the colonies were struggling to be free of the British sovereign. She was only one of many who mourned the loss of someone dear due to the conflict between colonist and

British soldier. How much longer would it drag on? How many more lives would it take? she wondered.

Now, her father's injury had burdened her with the responsibility of completing a task that, at the end, would break her heart. She dared not imagine what dangers might lie in wait along the way.

Leaning back in her chair, she closed her eyes and breathed in deeply of the warm fragrant air. She mustn't try to think of it all at once. It would overwhelm her.

Praying silently for the strength and the wisdom to do what must be done, she became aware of a mockingbird in a nearby bush singing his wide repertoire of songs. In listening to the feathered aria while the warm afternoon breeze played gently in her hair, she slowly realized an inner calm had replaced the tight dread that had filled her before. She breathed a thankful prayer for the peace she now felt.

Mrs. Barton returned, breaking in on her thoughts. A worried frown darkened the lady's face. "Better come inside, dear," she said. She seemed a bit distracted.

"Is it Papa?" Jess asked, jumping to her feet.

"No, no. He's fine. Something else. Come on in. Mac and the doctor will tell you all about it."

She entered the doctor's study and saw the two men bent over a crude map spread out on the desk.

"Come in, Miss McClaren. Seems a problem has arisen," the doctor said.

She looked to Mac, who was donning his shirt after having his bandage replaced. He answered her questioning look with a nod toward the map. "They've set up a roadblock down the road about three miles. Jake tells us they're checking papers and searching everyone coming through."

She looked from Mac to the doctor. "Is that it?" she asked. When the two men exchanged bewildered glances, she continued. "Our papers are in good order. They've brought us through three blockades without a problem. Bradford Keene is quite influential with the British command in Charleston, so anything to do with his business is handled with special attention."

"You still want to go through with it?" Mac asked.

"I haven't any other choice."

"You fully realize the danger, Miss McClaren?" the doctor asked solemnly. "If Mac is discovered, you'll be considered his accomplice; that means death. If they discover that you're a young woman it won't necessarily make things any easier for you."

"I know what the British can do," she said bitterly.

"A lot of good men were lost at Savannah, Jess . . . Miss McClaren," Mac said. "Don't let your hatred goad you into something you might regret later."

"What about Savannah?" Dr. Barton asked. Jess was curious about Mac's comment too.

"Robbie told me your fiancé was killed there," he explained. "I want to be sure you understand . . ."

"I'm thinking about the future, not the past, Mr. Macklin," she answered.

"It'll be dark in about an hour," the doctor said seriously. "If you leave now, you'll get to the roadblock shortly after nightfall. You'll pretend you've been traveling all day and are looking for a place to camp for the night.

"Miss McClaren, if I may, I'll add Mac's name to your papers as Jonathan McClaren, your father's nephew and your cousin. I've already written a letter explaining the accident and the fact that your father is remaining here. They may check pretty closely and, if it is someone your father's met on other trips, we must keep close to the truth."

He turned to Mac. "You'd better change out of your buckskins. I'll get you something from Franklin's trunk."

Jess went to get their papers while the doctor assembled a set of clothes for Mac.

She was talking to Dr. Barton after giving him the papers when Mac joined them, dressed in a cream-colored shirt of homespun, with dark blue breeches and jacket. He carried a dark tricorn hat. He had changed his moccasins for a pair of light jackboots that came up just to the knee.

Except for the fact that Jess's clothes were a size or two too large, and she wore low buckled shoes with knee stockings, they were dressed very similarly. They looked very much like an overseer and a young farmhand; they were unlikely to draw any special attention.

"Mama's packing some food for you," the doctor said. "Better get started right away. I'll take care of these papers while you get your wagons loaded." The doctor seemed quite satisfied with the situation and hurried off to add Mac's assumed name to their papers.

With surprising speed, Jessica and Mac hitched the vans and loaded the horses. She returned to her father's bedside, clutched his hand, and told him that she'd written a letter to her mother telling about the accident. Dr. Barton would see that it got delivered to her.

"Send in Macklin," her father said. "I want to talk with him."

She obeyed his wish and watched from the door as Mac bent close to hear what her father had to say. She couldn't hear, but Mac appeared to agree to whatever was said.

The two men shook hands. She returned to her father's side, kissed him good-bye, and left with Mac.

Outside, Dr. Barton grasped Mac's hand firmly. "God be with you both." Turning to Jess, he took her hand and said, "Don't worry about your father. He'll be just fine by the time you return. Take care, young lady, and trust Mac to get you through to Charleston. He'll do it if anyone can."

Jess climbed onto the wagon seat of Lady's van and lightly flicked the buggy whip over the mules. She fell in behind the other wagon driven by Mac as they headed up the lane toward the post road. The shadows lengthened across the road in the waning light of day, and she took a deep breath to quell the anxiety welling within her again. As the last rays of sunlight shot through the tree branches in splashes of yellow and orange, she prayed she had made the right decision. She felt that this day, now drawing to a close, had been a turning point in her life; but where, she wondered, was it leading her?

Mac was also wondering if he had made the right decision. Right or wrong, however, he knew he never would have been able to watch her drive away to make this journey without his help.

It was dark by the time they reached the roadblock. Her pulse quickened when she saw the light of a campfire beside the road with several soldiers standing around it. Jess could hear them talking to Mac, but she couldn't hear what was being said. She saw one of the soldiers reading the papers with the aid of a small lantern. Presently, two young soldiers approached Jess; one checked the cargo in Mac's wagon, and the other inspected the van she was driving.

She heard Lady stamping nervously as the young man dropped the gate and held up a lantern to see inside. At the sound of the gate being locked back in place, Jess released the vise-like grip with which she had been holding the reins.

In just a few minutes, the inspection was over and they were rolling along again, apparently without having aroused the slightest suspicion. The road was very dark; the spreading branches of the trees closed in above them. She braved a peek behind her, and sighed with relief as she saw the light of the fire fading into the darkness.

They traveled for another two miles or so, wanting to get well down the road from the blockade before making camp for the night.

Jess had begun to wonder if Mac planned to travel all night, when the wagon in front finally pulled off the road into a small clearing. After climbing down, she stretched stiffly and rubbed her backside. A circle of light appeared by the front of the other wagon; she could see Mac coming toward her, carrying one of their small lanterns.

"You were right," he said. "Keene carries a lot of weight with the British. One look at his name on the papers and they hardly noticed anything else." He paused. "Tired?"

"A little," she answered. "This has been quite a day. It seems like ages since this morning." She wrinkled her brow. "How's your side?"

"I'm fine. I'll see about gathering up some wood for a fire while you unload the horses," he suggested. He reached up on the wagon for the other lantern and lit it for her.

After caring for the horses and mules, they ate the ham slices and cold potatoes Mrs. Barton had packed, and washed it all down with strong hot coffee.

Sitting wearily by the fire, they watched the flames flicker hungrily about the wood, creating a bright circle of light against the dark of the summer night. They had spoken very little since their trip began, and the silence hung rather heavily until Jess asked, "How long have you been doing your work for the army?"

"Practically since General Washington first said we were an army. I was in Lexington when it all began. My great-uncle has a silversmith shop there. That's where I was serving my apprenticeship. Uncle Wesley had grown too old to carry on the business and my cousin needed help. Jeremy knew Mr. Revere and Dr. Warren, so we made several trips back and forth to Boston."

She listened in fascination as he told her of that volatile period in the Massachusetts colony. Mac, his cousin Jeremy, and Franklin Barton—who had been going to medical school in Boston—had attended meetings of the Sons of Liberty, and Mac had been greatly influenced by Mr. Revere. When the first shots were fired at Lexington on April 19, 1775, Mac quickly vowed his allegiance to the struggle for freedom. He had even seen Revere ride by the previous night to warn them that British troops were approaching to confiscate a store of munitions hidden there, and to arrest Sam Adams and Dr. Warren.

Mac continued at the silversmith shop until the end of June. As soon as word reached him that Washington had been elected commander of the Continental army by the Continental Congress in Philadelphia, Mac went to join. Jeremy, unable to leave his ailing grandfather, remained in Lexington and acted as a local contact for the earliest agents. Franklin had remained in school, but joined the Delaware continentals two years later after completing his medical training.

Mac's linguistic abilities recommended him for a role as an agent and courier. He had learned to speak the Delaware tongue from his mother, and French and Cherokee from his Grandmother Macklin. He had also been tutored on the history of Scotland by his Grandfather Macklin. Such knowledge had enabled him to move with relative ease among the native tribes and among the British and Scottish population throughout the entire length and breadth of the colonies.

He stopped suddenly and apologized for talking so much.

Jess shook her head. "Oh, please don't apologize. We have had so little reliable news since it all began. It's been hard to sort the truth from the rumors."

He placed another small log on the fire. "You look exhausted," he said. "You'd better get some rest. We still have a long way to go."

She nodded wearily, handed him one of the blankets, and then wrapped the other one around herself and lay down using a canvas knapsack as a pillow. She lay a moment, watching Mac across the firelight. Leaning back against a log, chewing on a twig, he appeared to be deep in thought. Before long, she slipped into a deep slumber, too exhausted to worry about what would come tomorrow.

Mac remained awake, gnawing a green twig and staring into the darkness beyond the firelight. Relating the story of his involvement in the war to Jess had created a new feeling in him, a feeling of fear—not for himself, but for her. He scolded himself for letting himself be talked into traveling with her. He was wrong to place her in jeopardy, to let her risk being caught in the company of a wanted man. He was overwhelmed with the desire to turn around and take Jess back to the safety of Cheltenham

71

Farms, far away from the dangers they would soon be encountering.

He looked at her sleeping form in the flickering glow of firelight; she looked very fragile and vulnerable. The desire to protect her from harm began to overshadow his devotion to duty. He began seriously considering turning back at daylight. The war had dragged on for five long years already. Was this mission really so important to the final outcome that it warranted risking an innocent girl's life?

There were other lives involved. However, it may already be too late to change that situation. The best he could hope for would be to gain the necessary evidence surrounding the Gallaghers' rather suspicious departure to implicate Bradford Keene's involvement.

The Gallaghers and Keene had been at odds over the issue of loyalty to the Crown. Just when it appeared that Ronald Gallagher was beginning to sway the opinion of some of the plantation owners away from the Tory point of view, Ronald and his son Michael suddenly sold out to Bradford Keene. If Mac could find proof that Keene had been party to some underhanded scheme, the precarious balance of influence between Tories and Patriots in the entire colony could be affected. It could be an important factor in the war. His mission was based largely on speculation. However, there was no question about what would happen if he was caught.

Looking at Jessica now, he was sure he must take her back. He would never forgive himself if he was caught and she was hurt in any way.

A frown appeared on Jess's face, and he was again reminded of her determination to go to Charleston with or without his help. He smiled as he remembered the tilt of her head and the serious, steady look in those soft gray-green eyes; he knew she would never agree to turn back, and would try to get the two horses to the port city one way or another.

He sighed in resignation and pulled the blanket up. Whether he liked it or not, she had become a significant part of his mission. He would simply have to do what he could to keep her out of trouble.

6

The next four days of the journey were uneventful and they prayed the weather would continue to hold for them. They watched as large banks of thunderclouds began piling up behind the rounded peaks of the Appalachians to the northwest. So far they had been spared the heavy rains that were characteristic of the late spring and early summer.

Mac was quickly regaining his strength, but his wound still bothered him. If he turned or reached a certain way, the jab of pain made him reach for his side and his face wrinkled in a grimace.

Their trail gradually descended across the ten-mile stretch called the "fall line," the area where the piedmont of the uplands dropped down to meet the coastal plain. The stream that they had been following for two days had changed character the last few miles. Instead of the wide lazily flowing river, it had narrowed down between steeper, rocky banks. The gentle gurgling of the slow stream had become a rushing roar of powerful currents churned by massive boulders strewn along the riverbed.

When they pulled up to take their noon break, Mac removed saddle gear from the tack box of Ettinsmoor's van.

"What's the matter?" Jess asked.

"Wait here while I ride downriver to find a new ford. Those rains up in the mountains have the river in an uproar; that means the regular ford will be pretty high. If we can find a better place, I'd rather go a few miles out of the way than have trouble crossing up ahead."

He had been saddling Ettinsmoor as he spoke, and she watched a bit apprehensively as he swung easily up on the large thoroughbred's back. Ettinsmoor was unpredictable and temperamental; he had bested many experienced riders. Today, however, the horse politely stepped out and submitted to Mac's direction.

Mac returned a half hour later. "There's a place about a half mile downriver that we'll have to try. The ford up ahead is jammed with a couple of big logs. The river's spread out a bit, but it's fairly shallow down there."

Jess noticed the concern in his eyes. "Do you think we can make it?" she asked, squinting up at him as the sun bore down from straight overhead.

"We've come a long way without a speck of trouble; I guess it would have been too easy if we hadn't come up against something sooner or later. We'd better get to it. The river's rising still."

Standing on the riverbank at the ford, Jess and Mac exchanged quick glances. They had forded several small streams already, but nothing like this. It was only about knee-deep most of the way across, but the current was treacherous. They had almost bogged one wagon down once before, but a few tree branches and rocks dropped in front of the wheels had worked like a charm. This crossing could more than make up for the easy traveling they had enjoyed so far.

Mac tethered Ettinsmoor behind his van, climbed up on the seat, and urged his reluctant team forward. The wagon lumbered out to midstream and stopped. Mac jumped down from the seat, splashed into the stream, and worked his way along to the head of the team in order to coax them forward.

Jess watched anxiously as they struggled, bunching muscle and might to get the wagon moving once again. Finally, the large wheels began turning and the cumbersome box-on-wheels lurched forward, making it to the far shore slowly, but without further trouble.

Mac signaled Jess to wait where she was, then mounted Ettinsmoor and came back across.

"There's a hole there, Jess," he said when he returned, "but there's no way around it. There's soft sand on the downstream side and a submerged log on the other." He dismounted and tied Ettinsmoor's reins to the back of the wagon beside Lady. He began leading the team forward, walking next to the lead mule; Jessica handled the reins.

"Don't let them stop, Jess. When I tell you, hurry them on with the whip."

She nodded at his directions and took a deep breath as they started across.

Mac was just raising his hand to signal for the whip when suddenly a large log came rushing toward him. She cried out a warning, but the log caught him behind the left knee, knocking him off balance. He grabbed for the harness on the team but was swept away by the swirling current.

Jess looked on with horror and indecision as the river began to carry him away from the wagon. He flailed and splashed against the current, fighting to regain his footing on the uneven river bottom.

She thought about jumping in after him, but she had never learned to swim. She sat frozen to her perch on the wagon, and gripped the reins tightly.

Finally, after what seemed an eternity, Mac found his footing, and stood several yards downstream from the wagon, wobbling and spluttering.

Jess's eyes were wide with concern, and she called above the roar of the water, "Are you all right?"

He waved a weary hand, shook the water from his hair, and whooped. "Whooo that's cold."

She grinned with relief.

"It really isn't funny," Mac protested as he made his way back to the van, against the current.

"I know," she said. "I'm sorry." She tried to stop smiling, but he smiled too, and she felt suddenly happier and more alive than she had for a very long time.

The light moment was suddenly clouded by the realization that the wagon was standing still except for a slight rocking from the river current.

Mac's smile vanished, and he waded back to the mule team. He gripped the bridle of the lead mule and nodded seriously to Jess.

She flicked the mules with the light whip and they strained forward. The wagon groaned and slowly began inching forward, then stopped. The mules had not stopped their pulling; the wheel rims had wedged deep in the rock and mud. After a few more futile attempts to pull it free, Mac waded back to the wagon.

"We'd better take Lady and Ettinsmoor on over," he said.

Jessica looked around the side of the wagon; Lady stamped nervously, uncertain of her footing and the rushing water swirling about her.

As Jess climbed down from the box, Mac helped her gain her footing on the uneven bottom.

The strength of the current took her by surprise. It was one thing to see it, but another to be pressed by the power of it. Jess held on to the wagon as they made their way back to the horses. Both animals were jittery, and it took Jess a minute to calm Lady down as she untied her. Jess was able to coax her across, walking on the downstream side of the animal, holding on to the tuft of mane at the withers to keep her own footing.

About twenty feet from shore, Lady misstepped and nearly went down, knocking into Jess. The icy water swept Jessica's feet from beneath her and she went down with a splash. A sharp pain seared her knee as she struck a rock. The current began dragging her away, but her hand had become entangled with Lady's halter rope and she dangled like a fish on a line, unable to get back to her feet. She could not keep her head above the water; she had slipped into a deep hole. She thought frantically that she was going to drown.

Suddenly a strong hand closed about her wrist and pulled her up out of the suffocating coldness. She came up spluttering, gasping for air, and clutching Mac's arm. He helped her over to where Lady was standing, nervously watching them.

"Are you okay?" he asked, still holding her to make sure she was steady on her feet.

"You're right, it is cold," she declared through chattering teeth.

They were only a few yards from the opposite bank and, a few moments later, they finally stepped onto dry ground. Jess sat down on a large stone to catch her breath. She looked out to the middle of the river; the mules stood forlornly in the swift water.

"We'll have to use the other team," Mac said. He flashed her a worried look. He unhitched the other team and led the two mules to the water's edge. Jess stood and followed him.

"Where are you going?" Mac asked.

"You'll need help rigging the traces to the wagon tongue," she answered.

He opened his mouth to argue, but hesitated. She was right. And he had learned that determined look in her eyes meant arguing was futile. "Okay," he said. "But hang on to this one's harness."

The river was still rising. They would have to hurry. The mules balked at the water's edge; it took a hard slap on the rump to get them moving. It was slow work, fighting the current and working the lines together to attach them to the wagon tongue, but at last both teams were ready to pull together.

Mac handed the reins to Jess. Standing on the lee side of the wagon, she slapped the leather ribbons down across the mules' backsides to start them off; Mac put his shoulder to the wheel to urge it up and over the rocks. The slack was drawn tight and the four mules pulled as one, straining against the unyielding trap of mud and stone. The wheel started forward, imperceptibly at first, and at last jolted free. Mac helped Jess up onto the wagon seat and walked alongside the teams while Jess directed them to the other side.

The effort of the river crossing had spent the strength of animal and human alike; it was already late afternoon. They decided to make early camp once they got back to the trail.

As they made their way back to the road, Jess looked to the northwest; blustery thunderheads billowed above the mountain range. They were little more than two days away from Charleston. If the rain would only hold off just a little longer, they would be able to make the remaining miles with little trouble. Mac told her there were no more rivers to cross and only an occasional gully or two to manage. If it rained, however, the red soil would become a bog, slowing them down at every turn and low place.

They chose a campsite in a small thicket beside the river, overlooking a lower valley due south of them. The river tumbled away into the distance toward the valley of rolling green hills.

Since they had stopped so early, Mac decided to try his hand at fishing to give them a treat for dinner. They took off their jackets and hung them on some bushes to dry. Jess took off her cotton stockings and laid them next to her shoes and Mac's boots on a flat rock to dry in the sun. She pulled up her pant leg to look at her knee; a large, dark blue bruise swelled on her kneecap. Her muscles felt like she had been tied in a big knot and bounced around before coming unraveled. Stretching out on the soft grass along the riverbank, she let the warm afternoon sun soak into her cold, aching muscles.

Propping herself up on one elbow, she looked around drowsily. The horses and mules grazed contentedly along the bank. Mac knelt on a large slab of rock that jutted out over dark, cold pools. He was barefoot, his sleeves rolled up and his shirt hung loose over his breeches to dry faster.

His dark wet hair fell across his forehead as he bent over the water.

She watched in fascination as he raised a slender wooden rod he had cut and sharpened from a hardwood branch. His hand moved so fast, she hardly saw it; he yanked on the string tied to the end of the stick and drew it out of the stream. A brook trout wriggled on the spear point.

"Hungry?" he called, holding the catch up for her approval.

"Yes, but what are you going to eat?" she answered.

He smiled easily, warmly. She returned his smile, and lay back down in the grass. Closing her eyes, she dozed off with a contented smile on her face.

She was awakened by Mac's voice calling from his rocky platform. He proudly lifted an even larger fish, all shining silver with green and pink stripes along its sides.

After they had eaten their fill of the tasty fish and cleaned their tin plates, they reclined beside the fire, talking quietly over a hot cup of tea.

Mac looked at Lady and Ettinsmoor standing quietly in a drowsy pose. "Robbie said you were really good with horses. I'd say he understated it some. I've never seen anyone handle animals so well."

The color rushed to her cheeks and she smiled. She had never been one to enjoy flattery, but Mac's words had an intoxicating effect.

"I guess I was probably on horseback before I even started crawling," she explained. "My mother had to care for my invalid grandmother until I was about seven and it was necessary to keep the house very quiet, so I tagged along after Robbie and Papa most of the time. After my grandmother passed away, I loved riding and being out-

81

doors, so it was nearly impossible to keep me in the house learning all the proper things little girls must learn. Mama nearly gave up. If she hadn't loved horses so much herself, I doubt if she would have been able to cope with me. Finally, she said that as long as I kept up with my lessons and spent at least half the morning in the kitchen with her, the rest of my time could be spent down at the stables and training corrals. I suspect she thought I would outgrow it. Maybe I will, someday."

He smiled.

She continued. "Papa always said, 'Horses aren't pets, they're work partners. They have all the brawn so we have to use our brains to keep them in line or someone is bound to get hurt.' "

"Good advice." He paused. "What about Lady? She seems like a pet."

"Lady is special." Her voice caught a little and she looked away.

Mac tensed suddenly. The animals had raised their heads; their ears pricked forward. He spoke her name in a low voice, then cleared his throat and began speaking casually with the thick Gaelic accent he could assume so expertly. "Aye, hope Ettinsmoor takes the voyage a'right; 'e's mor'n a wee bit skitterish these days."

She stared at him for a moment, puzzled by his words until suddenly she heard the jangle of metal, wood, and leather. Turning, she saw four redcoat soldiers approaching. A grizzled old sergeant came forward and eyed the pair.

"Care for some tea?" Mac offered. "Ran out of coffee yesterday, but this is hot."

"First we'll see your papers, son," the old sergeant growled.

Mac rose, took the papers from a knapsack, and handed them to the sergeant. The man read the papers and looked over the top of the page, first at Mac, then at Jess.

"McClaren, eh?" he said.

They nodded, and he signaled his men. Instantly, they raised their muskets, holding the couple at gunpoint.

"What's wrong, man? Can't you read?" Mac asked.

"I can read just fine. I also know Rob McClaren and his boy, and I never heard him talk about any nephew, Jonathan. So you better put your hands up. Search him, Cooke."

Jess watched as the soldier came toward Mac, knowing that if he was searched, they would probably discover his wound. Before she realized what she was doing, she jumped up. "So, you say you know Rob McClaren do you?" she said defiantly. "Well, then, who are you?"

"Sergeant Arnham's the name. You're a might feisty there, laddie. You'd better hold your tongue."

"Not the Sergeant Arnham who fought with Papa along the road to Calcutta?"

The sergeant straightened in the saddle. He studied Jess and nodded. "The same," he said slowly. "Now who are you supposed to be? Rob McClaren has but one son, and you're not him."

"You're right, Sergeant." She took off her floppy, wide-brimmed hat, letting her hair tumble about her shoulders. "I'm Jessica, his daughter, and this is my cousin, Jonathan."

The sergeant seemed speechless for a minute, then sputtered, "What the . . . Jessica McClaren? What's going on here? Your papers say . . ."

"I know. It was Robbie's idea. He thought it would be safer to travel if everyone thought I was a boy since we were traveling by ourselves till we reached George's Crossing. That's when Jonathan joined us."

"But where's Robbie?" the sergeant asked.

"At home with a badly broken leg. That's why I had to come along to handle Lady Heather Star. The doctor's letter there will explain about Papa. There was an accident with Ettinsmoor, and now poor Papa is hurt, confined to bed at the doctor's home in Barleyville."

The sergeant looked at her with a squinted eye. "If you be who you say, then you'll know the name of the horse your papa used to ride during our campaign in India."

Jess bit her lip thoughtfully and said slowly, "Papa hasn't talked about that horse for years. I was only a child, but . . . but I'll never forget how he used to go on about old Salty. His real name was Sultan, but Papa said his disposition was like a salty sea captain who didn't know when to quit."

The sergeant slapped his knee, laughing heartily. "Aha! No one would know that but a McClaren. Come to think of it, you are the picture of your mother. How is she?"

"Fine." She smiled and glanced sideways at Mac and the soldier about to search him.

Sergeant Arnham noticed her glance and said, "That won't be necessary, Cooke. These people are friends of mine. You'll have to excuse me, darlin'," he said to Jess. "But I don't recall your papa ever talkin' about a nephew. In fact, I didn't know he even had a brother." He seemed to be waiting for an explanation.

"Oh, well, you see, Uncle Hugh came to the colonies many years ago after he and Papa had a fight. You know Papa's temper. Well, Uncle Hugh was just as bad. The two of them couldn't seem to get along. Finally, Papa brought Mama and Robbie over here, found Uncle Hugh, Aunt

Sarah, and cousin Jonathan and reconciled their differences." She did have an Uncle Hugh who didn't get along with her father, but he was her mother's brother-in-law, married to Jess's Aunt Sarah. She swallowed hard. She had always detested lying; it left a bitter taste in her mouth.

"Ah, that's good to hear." Arnham turned to Mac and stretched forth his hand with a sheepish smile. "I beg your pardon in not trusting you, lad, but we can't be too careful now. We're looking for a desperate, mean character that's supposedly headed our way. They say he's a wild one. Scalped four of our lads in their sleep. You two be sure and keep an eye open. We'd stay and keep guard for you, but we've got to push on to Collier Forks tonight.

"Is there anything I can do for you, Jessica? I feel just awful about your papa. He saved my life once, you know."

"Yes, I know, but you did the same for him and he's never forgotten your friendship."

"That's kind of you, lass," the sergeant said. He smiled wistfully. "When I get to Collier Forks, I'll see about getting you an escort on to Charleston. That way you won't have any more trouble about your papers."

They exchanged good-byes and the party left. Jess and Mac sat down slowly side by side and listened to the sound of boots marching away from them off into the dark. Each let out a long sigh of relief. They traded glances, and began chuckling at the irony of the situation.

"I almost believed it myself," Mac said. "You spin a very convincing yarn. You'd make a fair spy."

"Oh, no," she said, taking a deep breath. "I wouldn't last long in this business. I'm still shaking." She held out her trembling hand.

Gently taking her hand, his eyes still sparkling with pleasure, he said, "You did very well."

She felt a sudden flush of embarrassment as she looked up at him. For a long moment they seemed transfixed, studying each other's face.

Mac cleared his throat and let go of her hand. "Let's hope the sergeant forgets about the escort. It would just draw more attention and maybe even some unwelcome company. Bands of continental rangers have been working in this area; they might get the idea we're carrying British supplies, and start shooting first and ask questions later."

"Your fame seems to be growing. Four soldiers in their sleep?" Jess replied wryly.

"There were only two," he said. "But it seemed like four." He touched his wounded side. "And they certainly were not sleeping."

Jess's smile faded suddenly and she gazed into the fire.

"What's wrong?" Mac asked.

"Sergeant Arnham." She looked at Mac, then turned quickly back to the fire. "The redcoats are men with families and friends, Mac. They're not exactly the monsters I had conjured up in my mind. I feel bad about lying to him. He and Papa were such good friends."

"If you hadn't, we would both be on our way to British headquarters and very likely sentenced to be shot." A hard edge crept into his voice. "All armies are made up of men with families and friends. And all wars are ugly business. But there *are* things worth fighting and dying for.

"There's something more at stake here than freedom for the colonies. It's something bigger than just us. I'm not sure I can even explain what I mean. It has a much deeper purpose than just a squabble over some taxes. We have the opportunity to establish something the world has never seen, a country where the will of the people, under the grace and guidance of God, is the law of the land. Where the people decide who its leaders will be and those leaders must be responsible for governing the country to benefit the whole, not just the ruling class. It could be a place where the people's freedom would be protected by the government, not threatened by it." He realized she was watching him closely, listening intently to each word. He had talked more these past few days with her than he had in his entire life. Glancing away, he was more than just a little unsettled by the fact that he had opened up to her so easily.

"You make me believe it's possible, Mac," she declared softly, her eyes aglow with admiration. "It is a wonderful idea. Is it possible? It would be something worth fighting for, wouldn't it? It would help to know that lives aren't being spent uselessly. Now I see where Robbie has been getting a lot of his ideas," she smiled.

"Robbie's a clever fellow. He can think things out for himself," he said, pouring another cup of tea.

"I know," she answered. She refused his offer of more tea. "But you're the kind of man he admires and respects; with good reason, I suspect."

"He reminds me a lot of my brother, Roger."

"Is he still at Iron Mountain?" she asked, watching his face.

"He was until two years ago. You're not the only one to lose someone at Savannah, Jess. Remember, I told you before, a lot of good men were lost there."

Seeing the deep hurt reflected in his eyes, she suddenly felt very selfish for wearing her self-pity and bitterness like some badge of honor. Imagining the pain he must have felt in losing the last member of his immediate family caused a lump to catch in her throat.

The only sounds for a long time were the crackling of the fire and the insistent chirping chorus of crickets serenading their nighttime audience. Off in the distant hills sounded the deep-throated rumble of thunder.

Mac's voice finally broke the silence, "What was he like?"

"Who?" she asked.

"Your fiancé."

She didn't respond immediately. "You don't have to tell me," he said quickly. "It's none of my business."

"I don't mind," she answered, looking down into her empty cup. "His name was Evan Collingsworth. I grew up tagging after him and Robbie. He was charming, witty, always laughing—hardly ever a serious thought in his head. I think he even joined the army just as a lark. He said he wanted to taste the excitement and glory of battle before settling down on the plantation." She wrinkled her forehead in a frown. "It seems so long now since I last saw him, I can hardly remember." She caught her breath, slightly overcome by the realization that she hadn't thought about Evan now for several days. The realization flooded her with guilt.

Mac's voice was quiet and deep as he said, "My grandmother, She-wan-ikee, used to say, 'Brother Time is a weaver of magic thread, spun from the gold of yesterday's sunset. He uses his magic thread to weave soft pouches for storing memories in, to be laid away—not to lose, but to make room for more memories to be made.' "

"That's lovely," she sighed, looking up at him.

His dark eyes glinted reassuringly in the firelight. "The time always comes to let go of the past, Jess."

As he looked at her, she felt as though a fresh breath of new life was filling her and suddenly she wished desperately that she could let go of the past, but Evan had been a part of her life for so long. They had promised to always care for each other, to be faithful to each other. She had loved Evan deeply, but she could not deny how her pulse quickened when she looked into Mac's dark eyes. She pushed the feeling back, not ready to face it, and quickly looked away.

A sudden thought darted across her mind, disconcerting her more. It bothered her that he could mask his feelings so well, while he seemed adept at reading hers. She resolved to try to be a little less transparent.

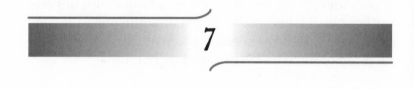

7

The next morning broke clear and fresh. The rain had stayed in the high country again, but the river was so swollen and swift, it was clear that if they had not crossed when they did, they wouldn't have made it at all.

As they packed to go, Jess felt a deep reluctance to leave this place. Their afternoon yesterday had been almost set aside in another world: a gentle, pleasant place with no room for war.

Later that day, as they passed a checkpoint just outside Collier Forks, they were greeted apologetically. Amid a flurry of activity, the corporal who checked their papers said, "Sorry, McClaren. Sergeant Arnham wanted us to hold a couple of men to act as your escort, but I'm afraid we can't spare anyone. We're headed west to set up some new positions."

"That's all right, Corporal." Mac said with his Scottish accent. "I'm sure nothing will happen in the next two days till we get to Charleston. But I will mention your courtesy to General Clinton when I see him."

"Afraid you just missed him, sir. General Clinton sailed for New York yesterday. He left General Cornwallis here to occupy the whole colony."

"Well, another time, maybe," Mac said, tipping his hat.

The two wagons were ushered on their way. They were only one day from the port city, and the relaxed feeling they had enjoyed together the day before was gone, pushed aside by the harsh reality of the war. Mac had been reminded of his mission and was all serious business once more. As they ate the last of their noon meal, Jess watched his stern countenance; she would never have guessed he could talk and laugh as easily as he had yesterday if she had not seen it for herself.

They had been passing through pine woods, past several plantations boasting wide fields of carefully tended crops of cotton, tobacco, and rice. The azaleas and camellias had already been replaced by the bougainvillea and wild roses everywhere. Honeysuckle and yellow jasmine fragrances filled the air. The early summer grew hotter with each passing day.

The pines had given way to cypress trees festooned heavily with wispy, gray Spanish moss, and they knew their travels were coming to an end. The hint of salt in the air from the marshes and tidal rivers mingled with the sweetness of wisteria and clover. Flocks of snowy white egrets, herons, and large wood ibises entertained them with a graceful ballet in flight over the saltwater marshes.

Coming to the battlements built to defend the city by the colonial General Lincoln, they were stopped by more sentries; then allowed to pass courteously.

Finally rolling into the outlying areas of the city, each click of the mules' hooves against the cobblestone street seemed to be counting off the seconds until Jessica would have to part with Lady forever. Her throat constricted with a large knot and she forced her hands to direct the team to follow Ettinsmoor's van.

Charleston was a much larger city than Jess had imagined. The cobblestone-paved streets were lined with lovely brick homes and imposing businesses.

At first glance, the activity along the streets appeared normal. Vendors pushed their colorful carts slowly along the curb of the narrow sidewalks, hawking their wares to those passing by. Shopkeepers emerged from their businesses to nod greetings to potential customers. Fine carriages moved sedately along the cobblestone streets carrying ladies and gentlemen in splendid fashion.

Highly visible, too, were the bright red coats of the British soldiers. They stood on every corner it seemed, or strolled two abreast patrolling the streets with their muskets held casually, but at the ready.

Even in her anxiety, Jessica noticed the grim countenance of soldier and citizen alike. Here and there a tight knot of people stood, engaged in serious discussion. The moment a redcoat appeared, the group would sullenly disperse.

As the horse vans came closer to the docks, it became more and more evident that the city was enveloped in a tense atmosphere of distrust and resentment.

They finally arrived at their destination. Mac swung down from the wagon and came back to tell her he would take care of everything for her. She nodded gratefully, too upset to trust her trembling voice. Her heart felt as heavy as if it were lined with lead and she tried to keep from thinking about her lovely little filly being confined in the hold of some ship for a month or more.

Mac was gone for some time. When he finally came out of the shipping office, he said, "There's some question about the papers. You'll have to come in and talk to the man."

They had been traveling hard the past two days, stopping only for a few hours each night to rest the mules, then pressing urgently onward. Mac had become very quiet again, reluctant to talk as he had only a few days before. The tension had been growing tangibly. At the moment, she was very tired and miserably sad. Now this apparent last minute problem made her snap irritably. "What could possibly be a problem?"

"Come on in and he'll explain it." Looking about cautiously, Mac helped her down and ushered her into the shipping headquarters. It was a musty, dank-smelling place crowded with wooden cartons, kegs, and odd parcels with strange looking marks.

An elderly gentleman in a white shirt and grubby gray knickers sat perched on a tall stool behind the clerk's counter. His unkempt hair was a dingy gray, but when he turned to look at her there was an odd sort of twinkle in his eye.

"You Mr. McClaren Jr.?"

"Uh, well no, not exactly," she said. "I'm Jessica McClaren. My father is Robert McClaren Sr."

He peered at her over his wire-rimmed glasses. "Haven't seen many young ladies dressed like that."

She glanced down at her brother's breeches that hung baggily from a wide leather belt to dusty stockings tucked under the knee bands. She self-consciously dusted off the sleeves of the brown woolen jacket that covered an over-sized shirt of white homespun and tried to think of an appropriate retort.

"Where is Mr. McClaren?" the little man asked, changing the subject. The man's tone remained very official. She looked to Mac for a clue, but he maintained a stony silence.

"Didn't Ma . . . my cousin tell you?"

"He gave me some story, but I'd like to hear what you have to say."

She looked at Mac again; he nodded for her to go ahead. After telling the clerk about the accident and where her father was, she asked if he had read the letter from Dr. Barton.

"Just want to make sure your story checks out. Can't be too careful these days. Okay, just a minute." He began stamping the papers and finally asked Jess to sign them. She managed to control her trembling hand with some difficulty, signed each paper in two places, and stepped back, wishing the whole dreadful thing was over.

"The *Westwind* hasn't made port yet. You'll have to take them down to the holding pens." The man stood and gathered up the papers.

"Not here yet?" she asked uneasily. "Who will be caring for them until it arrives?"

"You need not fret, girl. This here Duke Wilton has two stable boys all set up down there to take good care of them. Besides, they're my worry now. You have no say about them now that these are signed. Come on, I'll show you where to unload them."

They walked out the door and into the courtyard; it was empty. Jess stood rooted to the spot, looking all around the square, but neither wagon was to be seen.

"Well, miss, where are these thoroughbreds?"

"They . . . they were here just a minute ago." She looked up at Mac frantically.

"Would anyone have taken them to the holding pens?" Mac asked the clerk.

"No. Nothing moves down there without these here papers. Well, little lady," the clerk grumbled as he scratched his head, "looks like someone has made off with my fancy horses."

"Oh, Mac. Do you think he's right?" Her heart pounded and she felt dizzy.

"Don't worry," he said. "We'll find them."

The shipping clerk called to a red-coated soldier patrolling the dock area and told him what had just happened.

"We'll keep a lookout, Miss," the soldier said, "but these are bad times. They could be on their way north or west by now. Ever since Tarleton lost most of his horses in the transport last February, he's been snatching up every horse he sees."

"You idiot, Tarleton left a week ago," the shipping clerk growled. "You've got to find them horses. They're my responsibility, you see. She signed them over to me. We've got to find them or I'll lose my job."

"Take it easy, old man. I'll check around. In the meantime, don't be loiterin' about. Get back to your work, and you two be on your way. The general don't want no gatherin' mobs."

Jess stood silently watching the men, but she hardly heard what they said. She was torn. She was in agony, wondering what had happened to the two horses, but also rejoiced inwardly. She imagined that Lady had been saved from that awful sea voyage, and perhaps was headed for a newfound freedom.

It also occurred to her that her father could not be held responsible for the loss of the animals; the shipping clerk had just said as much. Secretly, she prayed that Lady had fallen into gentle hands and would be well cared for.

"Jess." She snapped back to the scene before her; Mac had called her name. "We can't stay here any longer."

"No reason for you to wait around here, Miss. It's my headache now." The old man sounded grieved and irritated; Jessica was glad they had finished their dealings with him.

She walked along in a daze as Mac led her by the arm into the heart of the city. She hardly noticed the people passing by, nor the British soldiers keeping a watchful eye on the passing citizens, an occasional rude remark passing between them.

Mac turned, led her down an alley, and stopped in front of a dark, stained door. He knocked out a distinctive rhythm and they waited a few moments before it opened.

He ushered Jess into a dimly lit room, led her to a chair, and asked her to wait there for him. He had disappeared into the dimness before she could answer. In the uncertain light, she discerned large shapes of furniture shoved together and covered with dusty shrouds. Ominous shadows filled the room, and she waited nervously for Mac's return. After what seemed like an eternity, she was relieved to hear her name and see his tall, broad-shouldered silhouette appear. She hurried toward him. He started to say something when a loud banging at the door made her jump. Shouts sounded outside. She clutched his hand and his arm went protectively around her shoulders.

"This way," he said. He led her through the building and back out into the brilliance of the afternoon sun. They emerged onto the front walk and looked both ways, as if preparing to cross the street. They suddenly heard a shout and saw two men in civilian clothes and two soldiers with flintlocks coming around the corner of the building. Mac grabbed her hand and started running. They ran until she felt as though her lungs were about to burst. "I have to stop," she cried.

Mac ducked around a corner, dragged her halfway down the alley, and pulled her into a shadowed doorway.

"Why are we running? Who are those men?" she gasped breathlessly.

He pulled her close and put his finger on her lips to signal silence. She heard the sound of running, the heavy footsteps of the four. They stopped. Then, with one gruff voice directing the others, they separated; two of the soldiers trotted past them and the sound of the footsteps blended into the noise of the city.

"Someone you'd rather not talk to, I gather," she said, still out of breath.

"Afraid so." He still held her close. "Can you run just a little farther now?"

She nodded, although her side was still aching and she had not yet completely caught her breath. If Mac said she must run, somehow she would run.

Slipping carefully out of their place of concealment, they kept to shadowed lanes and alleyways until they came to the edge of the city and a small whitewashed stable.

Inside, the warm sweet smell of dusty hay and leather greeted them. Mac led her to the ladder and, though her feet felt like lead, she climbed up to the loft, where she collapsed in a breathless heap on a thick bed of hay. Mac collapsed next to her. For a long time, they lay still, restoring their strength and listening.

A million thoughts raced through Jess's mind and finally, when she had caught her breath, she turned a serious face to Mac.

"Who are we running from?"

"Those two and I have crossed paths before. They're Clinton's men. We'll wait here till nightfall. Then we'll meet a contact on the edge of town. There'll be horses for us and provisions. We'll have to break out through the lines tonight."

He raised up on one elbow. "I'm sorry you're in this, Jess. I had planned to leave you here with my friends until they could arrange transportation for you back to Cheltenham Farms. Now that you've been seen with me, the redcoats would never believe you weren't helping me.

"I'm afraid it might be a little rough getting out of here, but if we can meet with Garrett's raiders tomorrow night at Hollow Creek, we'll be okay."

Considering the situation, she marveled at the strange sense of security she felt as she lay there looking up at him. There in the warmth of a sunlit loft, they silently searched the depths of each other's eyes. For a moment, she thought he was going to kiss her, but he lay back against the hay once more, looking at the roof above them.

Jessica finally broke the silence. "Do we really have to leave tonight? Can't we wait and see about Lady and Ettinsmoor?"

He closed his eyes. "I'm afraid we can't take the chance of being seen," he said. "I don't want to take the chance of running into those two again. There's also some information that I must report without delay."

"I wish I knew what happened to them." She propped herself on one elbow and turned toward him. "If you ask me, that shipping clerk was acting very suspiciously. Do you think he just got us both inside so some of his men could steal the horses?"

"You should rest for our journey," he said drowsily, his eyes still closed.

She watched him for a long moment, studying his face. It was a very nice face. Hard. But she had seen laughter in that face, and gentleness too.

He opened his eyes, catching her staring at him.

She looked quickly away, and blushed with embarrassment. When she looked again, his eyes were closed.

"I just wish I could be sure Lady's all right," she said.

She lay back in the hay and surrendered herself to sleep.

Mac lay with his eyes closed, smiling at the memory of the admiring look in Jessica's eyes a moment ago. The smile faded, however, as he remembered the fear and anger that had gripped him when he realized their identity had been discovered. Jess was in imminent danger of being caught in the company of an American agent. His fear for her safety only magnified his anger with himself for ever allowing her to make this trip in the first place. They were safe for the time being, but he wouldn't rest easy until he had gotten her safely away from Charleston.

8

Unable to sleep, Mac spent the late afternoon keeping watch through the loft door. He noticed Jess slept fitfully at first, but soon seemed to settle into a deeper rest.

Drawing the documents he'd been given out of his jacket pocket, he studied them for a long time. A distant rumble of thunder drew his attention to the dark clouds of an approaching storm. The rain had finally caught up with them. The sounds of the city died away with the closing of day and the approaching rain. As the light faded, Mac found himself watching Jess. She was sleeping so peacefully, he decided to wait until it was dark to awaken her. Although the situation was difficult, he had to admit he was glad they would not be going their separate ways just yet.

With the failing light, the rain began to patter against the roof and a chill damp crept into the loft. He noticed Jessica pull her jacket close as if to ward off the chill. Removing his own jacket, he carefully placed it over her. Returning to his post by the loft door, he leaned back, studying her soft features in that pale light. It occurred to him that it had been some time now since he had thought of her simply as "Robbie's little sister."

Jessica awakened from a deep sleep. She felt a gentle touch on her hand, and heard her name called softly. She opened her eyes to darkness and sat up quickly.

"Mac?" she called.

"Right here." His low voice sounded close. His form knelt next to her in the shadows.

"It's time to go," he said.

She started to put on the jacket that had been covering her against the coolness of the evening, and she realized she was still wearing her own jacket.

"Thank you for the use of your jacket," she whispered. "It has gotten a bit chilly, hasn't it?"

"It's started raining. It may be a little uncomfortable, but it will give us good cover. Ready?"

They descended the ladder. Mac carefully opened the stable door and peered out. Satisfied that the way was clear, he took her hand and led her into the drizzling darkness. They hurried silently down a tree-lined lane to a large brick home and ducked behind the stone fence that surrounded the backyard. Following the stone wall away from the house, they navigated a small incline to a grove of pecan trees. They stopped, and Mac whistled the sleepy night call of a mockingbird. An answering whistle came from the shadows along the wall.

"Come on," he whispered. He led her carefully through the still, wet darkness. Heavy drops of water slid off the leaves and pelted them as they ducked under the low-hanging limbs. Two dark shapes suddenly loomed before them.

"Lieutenant Macklin." A voice spoke in the darkness. "I was beginning to wonder if you were coming. Everything is ready, just like you wanted. Here's your flintlock and powder horn. Everything else is in the packs on the horses."

"Good. Thank you, Corporal."

"Just one thing, Lieutenant. These mounts are so skittish; are you sure it's safe to try it with them?"

"They'll be fine. They're fast, and speed is what we need now. Besides, they're old friends."

He turned to Jess and guided her toward their horses. She heard a strangely familiar whinny as she approached. Her heart leapt for a moment; she reached for the smaller horse.

"Lady?" she whispered incredulously. "Lady!" She hugged the filly's neck and was greeted with happy little nickers of recognition.

Jess turned to Mac, who stood next to her. Salty tears of joy mingled with the rain on her face. Her eyes widened in an unspoken question.

"No time to explain," he said quickly. After boosting her onto Lady's back, he quickly mounted Ettinsmoor. "So long, Corporal," he called. "Give my regards to Marion."

They started off slowly, keeping to the woods. Several times they came close enough to the sentry line on the right flank of the British force to see the dim flicker of their lanterns. By dismounting and leading their horses silently, they were able to steal through the ring of British troops occupying the city.

Once past the line, they rode steadily northwestward for about an hour before finally stopping. Finding a break in the underbrush, they led the horses down a steep embankment where years of eroding water had carved a deep ravine. A small brook gurgled noisily along the bottom of the embankment. About halfway down the sloping side, they came to a large granite overhang that would afford dry shelter for them until dawn.

The overhang was large enough to shelter the horses as well. They were soaked to the skin, and Jess was shivering as she dismounted. After traveling long into the night, her eyes had become accustomed to the dark, but her vision could not penetrate the pitch black shadow under the ledge. Hearing the sound of snapping twigs, she guessed Mac was gathering wood for a fire.

"There's not much dry wood," came his voice, reassuring her through the darkness. "But maybe we'll have enough of a fire to warm our hands."

She heard the click of a flint striker and finally saw a tiny spark, which grew to a glow as the dry tinder caught. It was just a small flame, but it danced brightly in the surrounding darkness.

She knelt beside the tiny fire and held out her trembling fingers, stiffened from the cold. In the dimness of the flickering light she looked at Mac and asked, "Are you going to tell me how you managed to get Lady and Ettinsmoor out of Charleston? And why did you let me fret about her?"

"I didn't want to raise false hope because I wasn't sure my friends could manage it. We needed two fast mounts to get us back to our men, and these two happened to be handy. The Continental army will reimburse Keene's estate of course . . . someday."

"I'm sure there is more to all this than you're telling me; but for now I'm just happy to have her back. However you did it, and for whatever reason—thank you."

A smile brightened his face for a brief moment before he cleared his throat. "All in the line of duty," he said.

She smiled. "Of course, just in the line of duty."

The little bit of wood that Mac had found did not last very long. Soon, only the glowing embers were left to ward off the chill in the damp night air.

"We should reach Hollow Creek around noon," he said. "They'll have a warm meal for us. Until then, this will have to do." He handed a piece of pemmican to her. "It's not very tasty, but it will help keep up your strength."

"Thank you," she said through chattering teeth.

He took the two bedrolls from the packs on the horses and layered them together on the ground at the base of the rock wall. Sitting down on part of it, he pulled the rest up across his back. He grasped the blanket and extended one arm like a large bird's wing. "Come over here and sit down. We can't have you catching pneumonia."

She hesitated only a moment before settling next to him. His arm closed the blanket around her, and soon the chill began to subside.

"I promise I won't tell Marion about this," she said, trying to sound very nonchalant. "She might get the wrong idea."

"Marion?" he asked.

"The one you sent regards to by way of the corporal."

He was silent for a moment. Then he began to chuckle. "Well, you don't have to worry about that. Marion couldn't be jealous of you."

"Oh?" she stiffened. "Of course, there's nothing for her to be jealous about, is there. I mean, I'm sure Marion and I are probably very different, aren't we?"

"Oh, that you are," he smiled. "You're not at all like Marion."

She grew quiet trying to imagine what this Marion must be like.

"You know, come to think of it, though," Mac said, "if Marion knew about you . . ."

"Yes?" she asked when he hesitated.

"Well, he'd probably be jealous of the fact that I've been your escort on this trip instead of him."

"He? Him?" she asked.

Mac chuckled again. "Francis Marion is one of the captains of the rangers in this area. His boys supplied these provisions. He's getting quite a reputation; the British are beginning to call him the 'Swamp Fox.' "

She felt a wave of relief and chuckled too. Their laughter died away, and they sat in the dark watching the curtain of rain falling outside of their shelter.

"This reminds me of the summer I was eight, the first time I camped out at Iron Mountain by myself," Mac said. "It started raining such a downpour the river began flooding. I found a small cave to take shelter in, but I lost my food and bedroll climbing up to it. It was midsummer, but that was the coldest cave and the longest night I ever spent in my life."

Jessica tried to picture him as a little boy, all alone in a wilderness cave. "It must have been frightening." Her teeth had stopped chattering, and she was no longer shivering. She imagined a young boy, curled up by himself in a cold cave, waiting for the light of day to make his way home.

"It was the first time I'd been out there alone, but I'd been camping out every summer from the time I was five. My father and his blood brother, Quiet Bear, taught me how to survive in the forest." A melancholy tone crept into his voice. "I've felt more at home there than almost anywhere else."

"One of my favorite things," Jess mused sleepily, "is the forest just after it's rained. The way the shafts of sunlight come streaming down through the leaves. It's like a smile from heaven. Everything is so alive and fresh."

They sat in contented silence until Mac finally asked, "Still cold?"

She did not respond. He looked down at her head snuggled against his shoulder; she was asleep. Dawn approached, and a day full of unknown risks and dangers lay before them. For now, however, the world was quiet, allowing them a short time of rest and a closeness he found especially pleasing. He hadn't been really close to anyone for a long time now and he realized just how much of a loner he had become. Growing up, he'd been surrounded by loving family and good friends. He hadn't realized how much he missed that. The nature of his duties in the war effort meant he had to be able to travel light, at a moment's notice. There hadn't been time to develop any close friendships after the war began. Maybe he hadn't wanted to—until now.

He must be more careful, he decided. He reminded himself pointedly that he had known this young lady little more than a week.

His arm was beginning to cramp a little, but he was reluctant to move at all, afraid she might awaken and move away. As he finally shifted ever so slightly to a more comfortable position, she raised her head sleepily, but he gently pressed it back against his shoulder. A small sigh escaped her lips as she nestled comfortably against him again, not having fully awakened. Leaning his head back against the rock wall, he listened to the patter of the rain outside their shelter before closing his eyes to sleep. He was in no hurry for morning.

The gray misty light just before dawn greeted them as they began the rest of their journey to Hollow Creek, some twenty miles to the west. They picked their way slowly along the ravine until they could follow it no farther because of the tangled growth of underbrush.

With some difficulty, they were able to scramble up the side of the gully. The horses' feet slipped in the mud and rock, but they soon reached level ground.

Jess and Mac checked the horses' hooves for imbedded rocks and gently examined the scratches and bumps the horses had received on their climb out of the ravine. Jess talked soothingly to them both, praising them for their good behavior, and apologizing for the slight injuries.

Mac assured her that even though the trek had been difficult, it had saved them several hours of hard riding—and from possible detection by the British.

Soon the sun was up and the air began to warm quickly. They came to a narrow but well-beaten trail and rode quite a distance, making good time. By midmorning they had left Charleston and Cornwallis's force far behind.

Stopping to rest the horses in the shade of some tall sycamore trees, they took long cool drinks of water from the canteens provided by the corporal. The morning sun had become hot, and the shade was a welcome resting place to stop and stretch their legs.

"How much farther?" Jessica asked after they'd rested nearly ten minutes.

"About five miles, I'd guess," Mac replied as he surveyed their surroundings. "The next few will be across some pretty open country just over that rise. Stay here; I'll go on up and take a look to see if any redcoats are crawling around down there."

Mac readjusted Ettinsmoor's cinch before mounting. As Jess awaited his return from the crest of the hill, Lady suddenly raised her head, checking the breeze with flaring nostrils. Jess slid to the ground from her rocky perch and patted Lady's neck.

"What is it, girl?" she whispered, looking around warily. She decided to mount, in case she must run.

Before she had settled into the saddle, a wild cry filled the air and several bronze-skinned men with paint smeared on their faces, arms, and chests jumped from the bushes. They carried tomahawks and feathered lances. One of the men grabbed for Lady's reins, but she reared, thrashing her forefeet and catching him with a deadly blow. Jess lost her grip and was thrown to the ground, landing on her shoulder and striking her head. Pain and confusion filled her, followed by a dark silence.

9

Jessica opened her eyes. For a long moment she couldn't remember anything. As she tried to sit up, a searing pain shot from her left shoulder to the top of her head. Suddenly it all came back to her in a painful flash.

She looked around her. Although the light was dim, she could see that she was lying in a dome-shaped shelter. She could hear voices outside, speaking a language foreign to her. A movement nearby brought her attention to an old woman whose gray hair fell in braids on either side of her leathery, wrinkled face. The woman said nothing, but put a cup of water to Jess's lips and helped her sit up enough to drink it.

Gripped by the pain in her shoulder as she laid back down, Jess had to wait for the pain to subside before thanking the woman, who made no effort to reply. Jess lay there for what seemed hours, trying to guess where she was, what had happened to Mac, and where their two horses were.

Her attempts to communicate with the woman were futile, except to understand that she was going to have to stay where she was. Jess didn't feel like trying to go anywhere anyway. Her head throbbed and she feared her shoulder had been dislocated in her fall.

The dim light in the shelter faded to darkness, and the woman went out briefly. When she returned, she carried a small oil lamp which cast an eerie glow in the hut.

Wishing desperately to communicate with the woman, Jessica tried repeatedly to prompt an answer to her questions, but to no avail. Finally, the woman gave her a drink of liquid with an unfamiliar flavor. Jess wondered if it might be some medicine for her pain. Immediately, however, she worried that it could contain poison. She soon began to feel herself sinking into sleep. As she closed her eyes, she imagined the appearance of a tall shadow at the doorway and Mac entering the hut and coming to sit down beside her. She wanted to speak, but the potion had taken effect and a curtain of darkness surrounded her.

Strange dreams filled her sleep. She seemed to float in and out of a thick fog. After an interminable time, a familiar voice began to echo through the fog and a sleepy hope sprang up inside.

Not knowing how long she had been asleep, she told herself as she roused that it had all been a nightmare. The pain in her shoulder jolted her, however, and the musty odor of the hut filled her nostrils. She dreaded to open her eyes again, and fought to quell the panic that rose in her. She found herself hoping that if she kept her eyes closed long enough, the Indian hut would disappear and she would be home again.

Suddenly a gentle hand touched her cheek, and that familiar voice persuaded her to open her eyes. She feared she was still dreaming. She gasped as she tried to sit up, and fell back, clutching Mac's hand.

"Mac," she said, choking back tears of relief. "Oh, Mac."

He stroked her forehead softly. "Shhhh," he whispered. "It's all right. Are you hurt badly?"

"It's my shoulder. I think it's dislocated."

"Let's see," he said, gently folding back the lapel of her jacket. She groaned as he pulled the jacket aside to examine her left shoulder.

"I'm afraid you're right," he said when he'd finished. "I'm going to try to fix it. It's going to hurt like anything for a minute, but it's very important you don't cry out." He handed her a thick piece of rawhide. "Bite down on this."

"They've given you a name, you know. Rea' na tani. It means 'Woman who rides the lightning.' They seem very impressed with you. And with that horse of yours."

"Where is Lady?" she asked quickly. "Is she all right?"

"Nervous as a cat in a pack of hounds, but she's not hurt. That's more than I can say for the two braves she laid low before breaking away from them." He took her right hand and placed it on his own shoulder. "Hold still now, and hang on to my shoulder."

She did as he said. Without warning, he thrust his shoulder against hers with excruciating force, jarring her dislocated joint into its proper place. She nearly bit through the rawhide and came close to fainting, but managed to keep from crying out. He quickly tore a piece of his shirttail, dipped it in a clay jar of water, and pressed it gently against her forehead. After a moment, he moved the wet cloth to the nape of her neck.

"Okay?" he asked softly, his dark eyes filled with concern.

She nodded and waited for the dizziness to pass. The pain was nearly gone.

Mac spoke a few quick words to the woman, and she reached into a reed basket. She brought out a long leather strip about three inches wide and handed it to Mac. He slipped it behind Jess's neck and created a sling by tying the ends together. Carefully passing her hand and wrist through the long loop, he said, "Try to keep your arm still; that ought to feel much better in no time."

"Thank you." She smiled gratefully, then asked, "Mac, where are we? Who are these people?"

"The Natiri," he explained, keeping his voice very low. "They're a band of Iroquois allied with the British. We're still alive because they think you might have special powers. The old woman is one of their medicine women. She's been watching you to make sure you don't stir up any magic against them."

"Why do they think I could?"

"I've heard that the Natiri are more superstitious than most. They see anything out of the ordinary as being a special sign from the spirits. The way Lady behaved for you and the fact that you're dressed strangely for a girl makes them think you're not an ordinary person. It seems that Lady struck out at one of the men and you were thrown. The minute you hit the ground, she turned and nuzzled you, trying to make you get up. They had fallen back, but thinking she was calmed down, they started to grab the reins. She kicked one of them, killing him instantly. One of the others jabbed at her with his lance and she reared up, struck him down, then took off. I was on my way back when she came streaking by me. She stopped when she saw Ettinsmoor and me, so I caught her and started looking for you.

"I found their trail, followed it to the camp and got close enough to hear one of the braves telling the chiefs what happened. He said Lady had lightning and thunder in her feet, and was so angry that you were hurt she killed one of their men.

"I took a chance and came into camp leading Lady. They were so surprised to see me with her, they stood back and gave me a chance to speak. I told them that I was one of your warriors and if they didn't let you go, you would call a whole herd of thunder and lightning to ride down on their camp."

"Are they going to take your advice?" she asked hopefully.

"Well, with you being injured like you were, they weren't fully convinced and decided to test your powers." He looked over at the old woman then back at her. "They figure the British will pay generously for a live medicine woman of their enemy."

"What happens when they learn I have no special powers?" she whispered uneasily.

Avoiding her questioning look, he glanced again at the old woman.

"Never mind," she said, closing her eyes. "I'm not sure I want to hear the answer to that." She opened her eyes again and asked, "What do we have to do to convince them?"

"Well, I've heard stories, but I'm not really sure what the test will be. The main thing is that no matter what happens out there, you mustn't say a word or let them see you're upset or afraid. If you do, it will be all over for us."

The blanket covering the entrance was suddenly whipped back and a painted brave entered. He directed gruff words to Mac, who nodded, then turned back to Jessica.

"Remember what I said," he reminded her.

She nodded and took his hand as he helped her to her feet. Her head swam and she leaned against him to steady herself.

"Mac."

He glanced down at her.

"Thank you for coming back for me."

"I had to."

She flashed him a questioning look.

"I don't know anyone else who can cook brook trout like you can." He grinned and squeezed her hand gently.

She took a deep breath and nodded.

The old woman rose and went ahead of them. Jess had to squint against the blinding sunlight. When she could finally see the scene before her, she wanted to draw back, but Mac's strong hand was at her elbow.

They had stepped into the midst of a crowd of curious, strangely clad people. The crowd parted as the trio passed. Jess nearly faltered when she realized Mac was no longer behind her. She remembered his words, however, and continued to follow the old woman to a place where three men sat on bearskin pallets.

The old woman motioned to her, indicating she should sit beside one of the men. Jess felt their careful scrutiny focused on her as she obeyed. When she turned to face them, however, they appeared completely oblivious to her presence.

The rest of the people had formed a large circle, leaving a wide center space. Two young men carried a large oblong panel that stood over six feet high and more than four feet wide. It appeared to be a mat of closely woven reeds stretched over a crude wooden frame.

Five braves took their places at the opposite side of the circle, each armed with a slender bow and two arrows. Jessica's heart began to pound when she saw Mac step forward to stand with his back against the reed panel. As she realized what was about to take place, she wanted to jump up and run out to tell them to stop. Remembering

Mac's warning, however, she gritted her teeth and presented an emotionless mask to her observers.

Mac's shirt had been removed; streaks of white paint were smeared across his face, arms, and chest. As the five bowmen took aim, she closed her eyes and held her breath. Opening her eyes immediately after the twang of the bows, she saw Mac standing perfectly still and apparently calm; five arrows surrounded him, imbedded in the mat. She breathed with relief until she saw the second round of arrows being strung.

Again the slender rods streaked through the air. This time, however, a murmur arose from the crowd; one of the arrows had grazed Mac's forehead.

She nearly jumped up to run to him but the old woman put a restraining hand on her arm.

"You must wait," she said in a harsh whisper, "Your magic weakens. We now see if it will give your man victory."

Jess was shocked that the woman spoke English. They apparently thought her "magic" could protect Mac. Praying desperately, she wondered what would happen next.

Mac had stepped forward away from the arrow-pierced wall. An elderly man, wearing a bearskin headdress with deer antlers attached, approached Mac; he called one of the bowmen to come forward. The young brave, who had apparently shot the arrow that had drawn blood, reluctantly joined Mac and the elder man. A brief discussion ensued, and Mac and the brave were each handed a tomahawk.

The young Natiri brave was as tall as Mac, and as muscular. His initial wariness, which Jess attributed to her reputed powers, was replaced by a ferocity that came into the Natiri's eyes as he and Mac began to circle each other.

Jess held her breath as the two struggled back and forth. She grimaced with each wild swing of the tomahawks. The men circled each other warily until at last the young bowman charged, knocking Mac to the ground. They wrestled back and forth in desperation until, in the end, the young brave had lost his weapon. Mac had suddenly gained the upper hand and was in the position to strike the blow that would end the fight and his opponent's life. A shout went up from the crowd as he swung the tomahawk. His stroke buried the tomahawk blade in the ground next to his opponent's head, missing by a slight margin; there was no mistaking the fact that he could have killed the young brave had he chosen to do so.

As he staggered to his feet, the circle of people murmured again. Jess, unable to contain herself any longer, jumped up and ran to him.

"Are you all right?" she gasped, choking back tears. Glancing about, she realized that her show of concern had placed them in a precarious position, and she whispered, "I'm sorry, Mac."

He said nothing, but closed his arm protectively around her, and drew her close to him.

The crowd gathered around them, then parted, allowing one of the chiefs to come forward. He spoke rapidly, and though Jess couldn't understand what he said, she could tell by the tone that it wasn't good.

"What did he say?" she asked with dread.

Mac didn't answer immediately. It was the old woman beside her who translated. "He is angry because the offender has not been properly punished as is our law, and also because he doubts if a weeping woman can really be Rea' na tani."

116

Jess looked up at Mac in surprise. "He's angry because you didn't kill that young man?" Mac nodded and she continued. "And now he suspects that I haven't any special power?" Again he nodded.

"What happens now?" Jess asked Mac. "What did he say?"

Mac translated the chief's tirade. "He says unless you prove you have power—power to control the killer of their warriors—our scalps will be handed over to the British."

It took a moment for the meaning of the chief's words to sink in, but then a grateful smile brightened Jessica's face. "Is that all?" she asked. "If I show them I can ride Lady, they'll let us go?"

"They'll at least spare our lives," Mac answered, watching the pressing crowd warily.

"Well," she replied with relief.

Mac frowned. "Ordinarily I'd say it's worth a try, but you haven't seen Lady. She's in such a state, she might not even know you. She's too dangerous for anyone to try to get on her now. Let me try to talk to him again." Mac spoke once more to the chief. Just when Jess thought he was convinced, the man broke into another angry tirade.

"Wait a minute," Jess interrupted, confronting the chief boldly. "Just wait a minute. Where is my horse? I'll show you I have power over her."

The old chief frowned, but took a step back.

"No, Jess," Mac insisted, grasping her arm.

She smiled bravely at him. "We haven't much choice. Where is she?"

The old woman led her through the crowd to a small enclosure of log rails. The filly paced back and forth frantically. Her neck and sides glistened with perspiration, her eyes stretched so wide with fear she looked impossibly wild.

117

Jess began softly whistling; Lady seemed not to hear.

"Jess." Mac caught her arm again. "You can't go in there. She's out of her mind with panic."

Jess didn't speak. She looked at him with silent resolve until he released her arm.

"Watch her," he said.

"Tell them to stand back," she ordered the old woman.

The crowd backed off and Jess moved forward. The frightened animal continued her frantic pacing and wheeling. Jess climbed into the corral through the rails, alternately calling and whistling softly. Suddenly, Lady stopped pacing and whirled around, apparently seeing the girl for the first time. Her ears lay back menacingly. She charged a few steps and stopped, swinging her head from side to side and pawing the dirt angrily before wheeling away to the other side of the corral. After a moment she charged again, stopping to rear up on her hind legs, flailing the air with her front hooves.

"Lady," she cooed. "Easy, girl. It's just me. Come on, precious, it's all right." She whistled again; this time, though the ground-pawing continued, Lady's ears pricked forward and twitched nervously, listening. Jess whistled again and moved forward. She stopped a dozen feet from Lady, who eyed her suspiciously. Finally, Jess stomped her foot and commanded Lady's attention. The horse lifted her nose into the air. Then suddenly, with a playful nod, Lady pranced quickly to Jess's side.

A gasp arose from the crowd as they expected Jess to be trampled. The gasps turned to low, awed mutterings when the horse stopped and allowed Jess to stroke her neck and velvety muzzle.

Jess led Lady to the rail, climbed onto the fence, and mounted the filly. After several turns around the small circle, she dismounted. She spent a few grateful moments praising Lady before coming out of the enclosure.

The people shrank from Jess as she approached; only Mac and the old woman walked toward her.

"Rea' na tani," the woman addressed her. "We see your great power. Do not be angry because we doubted. It is only the weak who weep among our people. It is not so with your people?"

"No," Jessica replied. "Even our God weeps, and he is almighty."

The old woman looked to Mac; he nodded.

"It is strange to my ears," she muttered, "but I doubt you no more."

The woman led Mac and Jess back to the chiefs and spoke with them. The first chief spoke, and two young men came forward quickly, carrying a bundle wrapped in a deerskin, along with Mac's shirt and hat. Handing the items to the old woman, they shrank back into the crowd.

The old woman came back toward the couple. "Gifts," she said abruptly. "Go now, if you wish." She spoke in a pleading tone.

Mac pulled on his shirt as he and Jess walked to where Ettinsmoor was tethered. He boosted Jess onto Lady's back, and they rode off at an easy pace without looking back.

Down the trail near where the ambush had taken place, Mac stopped, dismounted, and pushed over a large dead log to reveal a parcel wrapped in one of the blankets. It was the flintlock and powder horn. He had hidden them before riding into the camp the previous night.

Mounting again, they resumed their journey.

10

Stopping beside a small stream, Mac and Jessica dismounted wearily and sat down on the grassy bank. Jess took out her handkerchief, dipped it in the stream, and began cleaning the cut above Mac's temple where the arrow had grazed him. She finished cleaning the arrow wound, then gently dabbed the trickle of blood from the cut at the corner of his mouth.

Working so closely, she could feel his intent gaze on her face, and a blush crept up her neck and into her face. She cleared her throat self-consciously and asked, "Why did they make you wear their war paint?"

"Made a clearer target," he replied absently.

"Clearer?" She shuddered, still avoiding looking directly into his eyes. "They came close enough. If you'd been a clearer target . . ."

"The point is to get as close as possible without drawing blood . . . unless the target moves," Mac explained. "If he doesn't move and is hit, the person being shot at has the right to challenge, like today."

She turned to rinse out the handkerchief again. When she turned back, she said, "I'm glad you spared him."

"I'm not so sure I did him any favors," Mac replied grimly. He began washing the paint from his face. "He's been disgraced. May even be banished." He fell silent for a moment. "How's your shoulder?" he asked.

"I'm not sure. I think I'm still numb," she smiled. "How far are we from Hollow Creek?"

"We've missed our contact there," he said, drying his face on his shirtsleeve. "We'll have to catch up with the squad at Canely Ridge."

He stood. She followed him to the horses.

"Mac, I'm sorry I've caused you so much trouble. You were nearly killed and now you've missed your meeting at Hollow Creek, just because I was so stubborn and *had* to get the horses to Charleston. Then even that didn't go like it was supposed to. I wonder what Bradford will do now."

"I don't think you have to worry about Bradford Keene," he said. He tightened the cinch on Ettinsmoor's saddle. "And you needn't apologize for anything. You just saved our lives back there. Besides, I should have insisted you stay with Doc Barton."

"I would have gone anyway," she admitted. "Even if I'd had to hire Jake Sandy."

He looked at her for a long moment. At last he grinned, showing his white, even teeth. "That's what I was afraid of," he said. He cleared his throat. "We'd better get going. We ought to be at Canely Ridge in about three hours."

Without another word, he helped her into the saddle and they started out at an easy gait, not wanting to work the horses too hard. Lady had already worked herself into a state of near exhaustion; Jess kept careful watch on her.

Jess's shoulder began to hurt again and her head still ached dully; she was relieved when Mac finally reined in at the edge of a small stand of hickory trees.

"Is there time to rest?" she asked hopefully. She needed a break, but did not want to slow him down any more.

He assured her they would arrive at Canely Ridge several hours before dark, and could afford a little time.

"Where are we now?" she asked, scanning the countryside before them.

"I figure about ten miles northwest, as the crow flies," he said. He handed the canteen to her. "There's a small village not far from here called Ellensgate. Tory sentiment has been pretty strong over in that part of the country, from what I remember, so it probably wouldn't hurt to steer a couple miles east of there."

"Ellensgate?" Jessica said. "Lord John Keene's brother, Sir Gaston, has a large estate near Ellensgate. Oh, Mac, I wish you could meet him. He is the most wonderful old gentleman. He's the closest to a grandfather I ever had. He came to the colonies long before Lord John."

Her voice assumed a wistful tone. "When I was about three, I guess, Lord John sent Papa to help train some prize Arabians Sir Gaston had bought. Robbie and I had to go along because of a smallpox outbreak. Mother stayed behind because of Grandmother.

"We were there for three months and it was marvelous. He took a shine to me because I reminded him of his daughter, who was grown and married. He spoiled us rotten." She smiled. "And even sent a tutor for Robbie and me when we were old enough for school. I haven't seen him for nearly ten years."

"Is he still alive?" Mac asked.

"As far as I know. At least he was when Lord John died a year and a half ago. I'm sure I'd have heard if he died since then."

"Is he a Tory?"

"Sir Gaston?" she chuckled. "Good heavens, no! He has a title and a large estate, but he declared his allegiance to the new colonies without reservation.

"He may be Bradford Keene's uncle, but he's no Tory; he's never had much use for his nephew."

Mac thought for a moment. "Would you like to pay Sir Gaston a little visit?" he asked.

She looked at him quizzically. "That would be wonderful, but there's hardly time for visiting, is there?"

He looked up at the distant, tree-covered hills. "I think it would be a perfect time for you to spend a few days with him," he answered. "I could come back for you when this mission is finished, and take you back to your father and then home."

His words had a note of finality; he had made up his mind. Jess considered arguing. She was disappointed and slightly hurt that he wanted to leave her behind, but she told herself it was the only sensible thing to do.

She tried very hard to believe it.

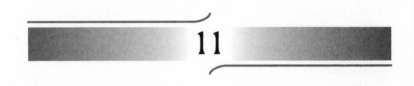

11

Mac and Jessica stood on the large portico of the Keene mansion, waiting for their knock to be answered. Jessica suddenly doubted the wisdom of the plan. It had been so long ago that she had seen Sir Gaston; perhaps he would not even remember her. The huge door swung open and a tall, immaculately tailored butler stood in the doorway. He glanced down his long nose at the two strangers.

Jessica realized how dreadful she must appear in Robbie's old clothes. After all they had been through, she imagined she looked like a waif who had just crawled out of the dustbin. She straightened her shoulders and raised her chin to firmly address the butler. "Please announce to Sir Gaston that Miss Jessica McClaren and her cousin, Mr. Jonathan McClaren, are here to see him."

The butler hesitated, studying them both for a moment. "The master does not wish to be disturbed. If you are hungry, you may go around to the kitchen and tell Cook I said to give you something." He started to turn.

"Sir." Jess spoke in a commanding tone. Fire danced in her eyes. "If you would be kind enough to relay the message to Sir Gaston, I'm sure he will want to see us. If he learns you've turned away his friends, he'll be very angry."

The man pursed his lips. "Very well," he said at last. "You may wait here."

When he had gone, she breathed a long sigh and looked nervously at Mac. He wore a slight, satisfied smile and nodded approvingly.

The butler finally reappeared with a smug expression on his face. "The master has no acquaintance with anyone by the name of McClaren. You'd better be on your way."

Jess was crestfallen. It had been too many years and Sir Gaston's memory evidently had failed.

"If I could just see him," she said pleadingly. Mac put a restraining hand on her shoulder and would have turned her to go; suddenly a husky shout sounded from inside the house.

"Poppit?"

She slipped past the surprised butler and stood just inside the door. Mac was as surprised as the butler was, but he stepped up quickly and placed a restraining grasp on the butler's arm as the man finally reacted by attempting to pull Jessica back.

She walked rather hesitantly toward the frail little man who leaned heavily on a cane of carved ivory and ebony.

"Is that really my Poppit?" he asked, peering at her intently. "Come here, my child."

"Grandpapa!" She hurried to his side and kissed his cheek.

He clasped her hand. "It is! It is my Poppit. When Charles announced you, I waved him away without thinking; your name didn't register until he had gone." He scrutinized her clothing. "What's this? Still wearin' Robbie's cast-offs?"

"Please excuse the way I look, Grandpapa. It's a very long story."

He raised his snowy eyebrows at her arm in the primitive sling. "What's happened? Have you been hurt, child?"

"I'm fine now, thanks to . . . uh, my cousin . . . Jonathan." She motioned for Mac to join her.

Sir Gaston warmly greeted the trail-worn pair. He took Jessica's arm and led them slowly back into the library. Motioning for them to be seated, he demanded an explanation of what had happened to Jessica.

She told him the story of their journey to Charleston, saying only that they had had difficulties with the horses and had been trying to make their way home when taken prisoner by the Natiri. She very carefully left out any reference to Mac's true identity and mission.

"You poor child. It pains me to hear of your father's accident and then all that you've been through. King George's boys would pay dearly if I were a few years younger."

He rang for the butler and ordered two rooms prepared with baths and hot meals.

Mac assumed his Scottish accent again. "Thank you for your hospitality, sir, but I must be on my way; I have some urgent business I must tend to. It was my hope that perhaps Cousin Jessica could stay here and rest from this ordeal until I return and make arrangements for a carriage to take her back home."

"Of course, my little Poppit may stay as long as she likes," Sir Gaston answered. "I shall insist she stay until she is fully recovered. As for your urgent business, young man, I suggest you postpone your departure until after dinner tonight. We have many misguided Loyalists in this

126

area. They've been quite uneasy of late, what with the Continental army's bands of rangers so active. They'll shoot any stranger first and ask his business later."

Mac started to assure the old gentleman that he would be very careful, but Sir Gaston held up a hand. "Why, just last night the powder store at Cadmon Corners across the ridge was broken into; a company of redcoats was nearby, and they captured most of the raiders at their camp on Canely Ridge."

Jessica looked quickly at Mac, but he betrayed no emotion. Sir Gaston continued.

"They say a squad of redcoats have been stationed there in case any couriers or other soldiers try to make contact. It seems there's one particularly troublesome patriot they've been itching to get their hands on. Now, my guess is that the raiders will probably regroup over in the Chalequah Valley, because the blooming redcoats would never think of looking for them in the midst of the Cherokee settlement. But, of course, that is just an old man's meanderings and I'm sure you're not interested in all of that."

The old man stared at the ceiling and stroked his chin. "I suppose anyone interested, though, might be wondering if the back trail that cuts over Jackson Falls into Chalequah Valley is still passable. From what I hear a good rider could make it in less than two hours even in the dark. But, there I go again." He turned his gaze to Jessica. "My dear, you look exhausted."

He rang again, and this time a pert little maid answered. Sir Gaston instructed her to show Jessica to her rooms and open up Miss Abigail's closets to find something suitable for her to change into. Jess excused herself and followed the maid.

As she was leaving, Jessica heard Mac answer Sir Gaston. "Yes, sir," he said. "I guess I might accept your invitation after all."

Jess felt relief that she and Mac would not be separated just yet. She had been dreading his departure ever since they arrived at Ellensgate, especially since they'd heard Sir Gaston's news.

She pondered over Sir Gaston's words; he seemed to know—or guess—Mac's business. His warning of the trap that waited at Canely Ridge had certainly seemed purposeful. But what did that mean?

She shook her head as if to clear her confusion. Her thoughts returned to Mac. He was quite capable of taking care of himself, of course, but she longed to go with him. Over the past week and a half in which they had worked together, braved the dangers together, and cared for each other's injuries, she had come to feel a part of his mission. The idea of helping him and contributing in some small way to the war effort had made the journey less painful. Now, although she knew it was a foolish thought, she was afraid for him to go on alone. She most dreaded the long hours waiting for his return, not knowing if he was safe and well. At least for the next few hours, she would know he was safe; he would be here with her.

She soaked in a hot, soapy tub, and afterwards ate a delicious meal of thick broth, cold sliced chicken, fruit compote, crusty bread, and fresh milk.

She was sound asleep within minutes of climbing into the huge canopied bed. It was the first time in two weeks she was able to sleep in a real bed, and with things apparently so well in hand, she relaxed into a deep refreshing slumber.

She awoke at seven-thirty, nearly three hours later. The maid, Molly, came in to help her dress for dinner. Jess was extremely pleased with the dress Molly brought her. Though a little dated in style, it was one of classic good taste. Made of deep rose-colored velvet, the shallow scoop neck was trimmed with champagne-colored satin; matching lace flared at the elbow-length, close-fitting sleeves. Jess was thankful that the front of the bodice was a panel of soft shirring because it would not require the uncomfortably stiff stomacher that was so stylish these days.

As Molly brushed Jess's hair into a glistening, dark chestnut-brown shine, she told Jessica about Abigail, Sir Gaston's only daughter, who had passed away several years earlier. Widowed two years before returning to the colonies, she had brought her sixteen-year-old son home to Ellensgate; Gregory was now grown and helped his grandfather manage the estate. Molly spoke of the young heir with admiration, saying he would most likely be dining with them.

Having finished styling Jess's hair in a becoming upsweep with a cascade of dark chestnut curls in back, Molly stepped back to appraise her work. Jess looked at herself in the mirror; she could hardly believe her eyes.

She had always considered herself rather plain. Her best features, she thought, were her gray-green eyes, although she had always wished they had been blue or brown. The color of the dress, however, made her eyes look more green than gray. Her complexion seemed to glow.

"You'll set 'em on their ears, Miss," Molly said with delight. Molly adjusted the sling she had fashioned from a matching satin sash, smiled broadly at her handiwork, then opened the door for Jess.

Jessica stood for a moment inside the library door before crossing the shining oak floor; her soft leather slippers made no sound as she walked. Sir Gaston looked extremely distinguished with his powdered wig, fine dark gray coat, white ruffled shirt, and matching dark gray breeches.

She assumed the young man standing next to Sir Gaston to be Gregory. He was tall like Mac and built much the same, but with blonde hair, blue eyes, and fine patrician features. His hair was tied in a queue at the nape of his neck. The dark blue of his well-fitted coat and waistcoat with a white silk cravat at the neck accentuated the blue of his eyes. He held his head with the air of an aristocrat.

Mac stood beside Gregory in a buff-colored suit she guessed must have been borrowed from the young Austrian. He looked surprisingly at ease in the high-collared white shirt, split-tail coat, waistcoat, and matching breeches. His boots had been polished to a shine, and he stood with his usual easy confidence.

Sir Gaston, finally noticing her, extended an arm to her. "My Poppit is a beautiful young woman," he declared with delight. He was astounded at how grown-up she was. It seemed such a short time ago that she'd been just a tyke. Hadn't it been the same with his dear little Abigail?

The two other men turned, and Jessica's pulse quickened as she saw the expression in Mac's dark eyes.

Mac was caught off guard by the lovely vision Jessica presented. He met her smile with a nod and did not bother trying to hide his admiration. Watching her come into the room, he found it a little unsettling to think of the rigorous journey this beautiful, delicate young lady had just endured. When she met his gaze again and lifted her chin slightly, Mac was instantly reminded of her determined spirit and gumption that he'd come to admire so much. His smile broadened.

Gregory suddenly stepped in front of Mac to stride forward and greet Jessica. The young man took her hand and, bending over it, kissed it lightly. Speaking with a slight Austrian accent, he introduced himself. "Gregory Starkheim the Fourth, at your service, Miss McClaren. It grieves my soul to hear of your capture and narrow escape from the savages, but it is no wonder they thought you a goddess. If you but say the word, I shall ride into their camp and show them the consequences of such despicable conduct."

"I'm very honored, Mr. Starkheim, but I hardly think that will be necessary." She laughed gently after catching her breath, sure that the young Austrian's affectation was meant to amuse her.

"Please come and sit down," Gregory said. "You must be completely undone after your injury and long journey."

"On the contrary," she answered. "I feel quite refreshed after such a long nap."

"Your cousin has been telling us what an excellent horsewoman you are," Gregory continued as he sat beside her on the settee.

Mac turned his attention to a piece of carved onyx on the mantel. Gregory continued. "I'd hardly expect such a delicate creature to be able to manage an unstable thoroughbred. But, I daresay, you excel in anything you attempt."

"Because she has a stubborn streak a mile wide," Mac interjected, without interrupting his examination of the onyx piece.

Gregory smiled uncertainly. "I daresay," Starkheim continued, "fortitude is a virtue lacked by too many these days; and I can tell by the depth of the green in your eyes that your soul must come as close to perfection as one can this side of heaven."

Jessica had had enough; she longed for the dinner bell to rescue her from Gregory's outlandish flattery.

Mac spoke again. "It's true," he said, "but what a temper! She even talks in her sleep."

"Ma—Jonathan!" Jessica protested.

Gregory stood. "Really, McClaren, I realize you're her cousin and you have traveled far under difficult conditions, but this steps over the bounds of propriety. I suggest you apologize immediately."

"I see no need to apologize for speaking the truth," Mac said, looking first at Jess then at Gregory. His expression reflected innocence.

To Jess's relief, at that moment the maid announced that dinner was ready to be served. While the two young men stood eye to eye like two rams about to clash, Jess took Sir Gaston's arm and walked out of the library toward the dining room. The young men followed silently, Gregory glaring disdainfully at Mac, and Mac looking pleased with himself.

"Grandpapa, you're very quiet," Jessica whispered.

"When one is too old to compete for a young lady's attention, he sits and watches, quietly trying to guess who will be the lucky one," he answered.

"Oh? And if this is true—I'm not saying I agree—but who do you think will be the 'lucky' one?"

"I wish I could say there was a chance for you to become my true granddaughter," he said. "But it's too late. The young Indian has already won your heart."

"Grandpapa! Where do you get such ideas?" She tried to keep from blushing, and glanced around to be sure Mac wasn't listening to their conversation.

"One only has to see your eyes when you look at him. It's a good thing he is *not* your cousin." Stunned by his comment, she turned to look at him, but his face was a mask.

Sir Gaston held her chair and they sat down to dinner. The meal was delicious. In those exquisite surroundings, Jess forgot the danger and stress of recent days.

Gregory dominated the mealtime conversation. He seemed to have an opinion about every subject under the sun, and seemed also to enjoy having an attractive female audience. Jessica caught Mac looking at her several times; the darkness and depth of his gaze troubled her.

After dinner, they adjourned to the formal drawing room for coffee. It seemed to Jess that they had hardly sat down before Mac excused himself.

"Thank you, Sir Gaston," he said, "for your hospitality. You've been most generous and kind. I'm afraid I must be on my way. Thank you for taking care of Jessica. Arrangements will be made to see that she returns home safely." He turned to Gregory. "Thank you for the use of the suit, Starkheim."

"Think nothing of it," Gregory answered loftily. "In fact, you may keep it. I've grown tired of it."

"Thanks," Mac replied, "but it's not exactly my style." He left the room.

When he came back downstairs, he was dressed in his buckskin trousers, faded blue homespun shirt, and buckskin jacket, which had been in the packs brought to them as they escaped from Charleston.

Mac stopped by the drawing room on his way out, and shook hands with Sir Gaston.

Sir Gaston addressed him formally. "It's been a pleasure having you here, my boy. I wish you luck and success in your travel." He hesitated before the last word as if he had nearly said something else. "Your horse has been saddled."

Gregory stepped next to Jessica and took her hand in his. "A pity you have to go, but you may be assured we will take very good care of Jessica."

Mac's face showed no reaction, but his fist was doubled and his knuckles showed white against his saddlebag.

Jess moved away from Gregory and took Mac's arm. "I'll walk out with you," Jess said. They walked out, crossed the portico silently, and descended the wide steps that swept down to the cobblestone drive.

It was a beautiful, fragrant summer night. The sweet scent of night-blooming jasmine floated on a gentle breeze. A half-moon glistened above them, accompanied by a million stars in a black velvet sky.

The clipping of Ettinsmoor's hooves sounded on the drive as the groom led the big stallion toward the steps, where Mac and Jess waited in silence. A soft glow from the windows fell across the portico and the drive.

Taking the reins from the groom, Mac checked the cinch.

Jess spoke quietly. "May I ask what you meant when you said 'arrangements' will be made to get me back home?"

He did not turn from his work. "I'll arrange for an escort with a carriage to come in two days to take you back to Barleyville and then on home."

"Oh. I see." Her face flushed. Endeavoring to control her voice, to sound unconcerned, she swallowed hard. "Then you won't be coming back this way?"

"You'll be well taken care of. There's really no reason to come back, is there?" He swung into the saddle.

134

She cleared her throat, and said, "Of course not. No reason at all." She reached up to shake his hand. "Mr. Macklin, take care and thank you." He clasped her hand tightly for a brief moment. Her heart pounded as she returned his gaze. He released her hand without another word and turned to ride away.

She hesitated a moment, then ran a few steps toward him. "Mac!" she cried.

He pulled up and turned to look back.

"Be careful," she called, fighting back hot tears.

He waved, then, and rode off, enveloped by the night.

She had dreaded his leaving, but she had not really been prepared for the feeling that now overwhelmed her. Only once before had she known the meaning of such loneliness—when Evan had ridden off to Savannah.

She listened to the fading hoofbeats and found herself praying fervently for his safety, and adding a wish that he would change his plans, return for her. She scolded herself for thinking such a foolish thought. He obviously was relieved to be rid of her.

"Jessica?" Gregory called from the steps. "Jessica, are you all right?"

She turned and walked slowly back to the house. She walked past Gregory and retired to her room.

The thin light from the half-moon dusted the road before him as Mac rode away from the estate. A tight knot doubled in his chest. The sound of Jessica's voice calling his name echoed in his ears. The vision of her filled his mind.

He hadn't said good-bye. He couldn't bring himself to say the words even though he told her he wouldn't be back. She'd even agreed with him that there was no reason to return. At least, that's what she said. Had the look in her eyes meant otherwise?

He suddenly wished they'd never stopped at Ellensgate. Remembering that if they hadn't, they might have been caught in the trap at Canely Ridge, he sighed in grim resignation. Canely Ridge. His mission—he mustn't forget his mission. Taking a deep breath, he glanced around him, checking the landmarks revealed by the faint moonlight. He told himself he ought to be relieved that he didn't have to worry about Jess's safety anymore. He'd be able to travel farther and faster without her. Trying to ignore the hollow sound of the hoofbeats of his solitary horse, he shook his head to refocus his thinking.

For a few moments he considered the information and documents he'd received in Charleston and was satisfied that the outcome would be very helpful to the war effort. It wasn't long, however, before his thoughts wandered back to Jessica. He was glad she was safe at last. Starkheim had assured him that he would take good care of her. The memory of seeing the young Austrian holding Jess's hand made him grit his teeth and spur Ettinsmoor to a gallop. He chided himself for becoming so distracted and let the big stallion have his head, carrying him away from Ellensgate, away from Jessica McClaren, and away from his heart.

12

Jess fell asleep quickly, but awoke again as the grand-father clock downstairs was striking the hour of twelve.

She lay in the dark, trying to shake the oppressive grip of her nightmare. She had dreamed of Evan; even wide awake, she could still see his blonde hair and smiling blue eyes. She felt as if his hand still grasped her wrist tightly, pulling her against her will away from someone. She had awakened shivering, glad that it had only been a dream.

This was the first time she had dreamed of Evan in months. The most disturbing thing she remembered was the gripping fear she had felt in her dream. Why? She had never feared Evan. He had been her champion, her knight.

She slipped out of bed. Taking the soft blanket folded across the foot of the bed, she wrapped it around herself and stepped out onto the balcony that extended the full length of the second floor. The night air was cool; she pulled the blanket a little closer under her chin. Looking out over the vast estate, she could see the dark outlines of the hills beyond in the muted light of the half-moon.

"Poppit, you should be sound asleep."

She turned to see Sir Gaston sitting at the end of the terrace, smoking a long pipe. Walking slowly down to stand beside him, she once again looked out over the countryside.

"He will be all right, won't he Grandpapa?"

"I'm sure he has a remarkable talent for escaping harm. What's troubling you, my pet?"

"Nothing," she said. She wondered what Sir Gaston really knew about Mac.

"You're hurt because he isn't coming back for you."

"Oh Grandpapa, that's silly, of course not. I . . . I just . . . well, I thought he might at least be gentleman enough to see that I get home safely."

Sir Gaston puffed silently on his pipe.

"What a ridiculous thing for me to say," she continued with a forced chuckle. "I'm certainly not his responsibility. I've already caused him a measure of trouble. Actually, I'm not surprised he's eager to be rid of me."

Sir Gaston remained silent and she sighed. Her voice softened almost to a whisper. "I suppose I thought he might *want* to come back for me."

"Ah, my Poppit, come sit down."

She sat down on the floor next to him, wrapping the blanket about her bare feet.

"Do you remember the last time you and Robbie visited me?" he asked. "Nearly ten years ago, wasn't it? You were here for your tenth birthday."

"Yes, of course." She smiled. "I'll never forget what a wonderful time we had, nor shall I ever forget the lovely pink dress and matching parasol you gave me. I can still see that gigantic birthday cake with all those huge sugar roses. I think Robbie got sick from eating so many of them." She paused. "I've really missed you, Grandpapa."

138

"Evidently not enough to write and tell me so," he grumbled.

"Why, Grandpapa, I wrote you every month for over a year and never heard a single word from you in reply."

"Jessica Gwyneth, I received one letter from you in all that time." He had only used her full name two or three times to reprimand her when she was little.

"I even drew pictures to make you laugh when I heard you were very ill." She was perplexed. "Bradford told me you were too ill for visitors and that Abigail was here taking care of you."

"Bradford!" The contempt with which he spoke his nephew's name startled her. "That explains a great deal," he said.

"What about Bradford?" she asked.

"He had the unmitigated gall to want to court my little Abigail. Adopted or not, he was all wrong for my little girl. I forbade him to ever see her again. He's had hard feelings for me ever since. I can't say I've felt kindly toward him, either."

Suddenly, as clearly as if it had been yesterday, a memory flashed across her mind's eye. She and Robbie had been playing hide-and-seek in the old gatekeeper's cottage when two people—Bradford and Abigail—had stopped there. She remembered the insistence in Bradford's voice, and the determination and fear in Abigail's voice as she told Bradford good-bye. They hadn't stayed long, and Jess and Robbie had never told anyone about it because they had been told to stay away from the old cottage and they feared they would be in trouble if their disobedience was discovered.

They sat in silence for a few moments, each deep in thought. Finally Sir Gaston spoke again.

"Forgive me, child," he said. "I thought you had forgotten all about me. I should have known better. I *did* know better. I knew you'd come back someday."

"How could I ever forget you? You've been as dear as my own grandfather. I can't imagine what became of my letters. If it hadn't been for Mac, we might have never straightened it out."

"Mac? I thought you called him Jonathan."

"Well, it . . . I . . . ."

He smiled and chuckled. "It's obvious you are not used to telling untruths, my dear. Lying doesn't come easily for you." He patted her hand and continued. "Mac is short for Macklin, not McClaren."

She stared at him in amazement. "How did you know that?"

"He told me."

"*He* told you?"

"Yes." He smiled as he puffed thoughtfully on his pipe. "I knew he was not a McClaren. You forget that I've known your family a very long time. Your father was an only child."

"Does anyone else know?"

"No. His secret is safe with me," he assured her.

"I'm so glad," she sighed with relief. "He is really a remarkable person, don't you think?"

"Yes, quite, and I think he would like nothing better than to come back for you himself."

"You're just saying that because you think it's what I want to hear," she said. "Well, it doesn't matter. Really. Besides, if he truly wanted to, he would. He's a very resourceful—and stubborn—man."

"You're right, my dear," Sir Gaston looked her in the eye. "And I think he has fallen deeply in love with you."

140

She stared at him. "What makes you say that?"

"When I first saw you two this afternoon on the landing, I knew by the look in his eyes that you held his heart. But he was shaken by your appearance at dinner."

"I . . . I thought he was pleased by the way I looked; especially after those old clothes I've been wearing."

"Pleased? I think he was enchanted. You looked like a princess. As the evening went on, he saw you in these surroundings and, if my guess is right, he began comparing what you two have just come through with what your life could be here. I'm sure he realized that someday this will all be Gregory's; he probably decided to step back, feeling he didn't have the right to stand in the way of your happiness."

Her brow wrinkled. "You're serious, aren't you? We've only known each other a little less than two weeks."

"Time has nothing to do with love, my dear. The first moment I laid eyes on my Genevieve, I knew I'd love her until the day I died. It took me six years to win her hand, but I knew from the first she would be mine."

"Could he really feel that way?"

Sir Gaston nodded with certainty.

"He should know I would never want to be the 'Lady of the Manor,'" she protested.

"My dear, the way you looked tonight, you could have been the princess over any court on earth. Gregory felt the same way—and I'm afraid he finds anyone less than the daughter of an earl a bit beneath his station."

"Forgive me, Grandpapa. Evan is very nice, but I'm afraid there could never be anything serious between us."

"Evan?"

"Gregory. I meant Gregory," she stammered. She paused. Her mind drifted to Mac again. "If Mac felt the way you say he does, he'd come back for me." Her voice trailed off.

"Patience, my Poppit. You must remember he has some other very important matters on his mind right now. But I'm betting he'll try to come back."

"Try?" she asked.

"Andrew Macklin has been very effective in harassing the British around here, and they would very much like to get their hands on him. So he may not be able to come back immediately. He's on the trail of the people responsible for the disappearance of a planter and his son over your way. Do you know of the Gallaghers?"

She nodded. "They were among the few big planters who had pledged support to the fight for independence. They were beginning to sway several others around to their way of thinking, but they suddenly sold out and were returning to Ireland." She remembered the look in Mac's eyes when the case of the Gallaghers had been brought up at the Bartons'.

"Mac and his superiors suspect foul play," Sir Gaston explained. "He evidently discovered something of importance in Charleston. It seemed to be very upsetting."

Jess noticed how animated Sir Gaston became as he spoke of Mac's mission. "I do what I can for the war effort, but I would be much happier riding next to young lads like Macklin. It's so right, Jessica. We must win."

She squeezed his hand. "If you were with Mac, I'm sure the British would give it up in a hurry. It's so good to be here with you again, Grandpapa, and I'm so glad you know about Mac. I don't know if I shall ever see him again, but . . ."

"Mark my words, Poppit, you haven't seen the last of him yet. Now, you must get some rest. Go back to bed now and try to sleep."

She placed a goodnight kiss on his cheek and returned to her room. Climbing in bed, the luxurious comfort of the down-stuffed mattress and fine linen sheets made her think of the past week and a half of nights sleeping out under the stars on the hard ground. At the moment, she would trade the warmth and comfort of her present surroundings to be back in the shelter of the ravine, sitting next to Mac with his arm around her, watching the rain drip steadily off the rock overhang. The discomfort of being rain-soaked and hungry was nothing to compare with the aching she felt inside now, wondering where he was and if she would ever see him again.

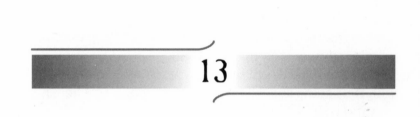

13

Jessica slept, but she awoke very early, as the morning sun's rays were just stealing over the far hills. The golden trilling of a thrush wafted through an open window. Listening a moment before opening her eyes, she tried to remember if it was her turn or Mac's to feed the horses this morning. Opening her eyes and looking about the room, she remembered that Mac was gone, and she wasn't sure she'd ever see him again.

She sat up slowly and noticed that Molly had laid out a charming dress of pale blue cotton, with tiny blue flowers embroidered on the large white collar and narrow cuffs.

The dress fit remarkably well, and she wished that Mac could have seen her dressed this way every day of their trip, instead of in Robbie's baggy old clothes.

Leaving her room, she found the house still quiet and she decided to stroll down to the stables to check on Lady.

Two of the young stable boys were already there, pitching hay to the impressive number of horses in the fastidiously kept stable. A young man entered and spoke a few words of instruction to the boys. About the same age as Gregory and Mac, he was slender, with sandy brown hair and blue eyes.

He approached Jess and tipped his broad-brimmed hat, introducing himself as David Wills, Sir Gaston's foreman.

"Her Ladyship is over here, Miss McClaren. She may be a bit smaller than most, but she is one of the best appointed thoroughbreds I've ever seen."

She smiled and followed him to Lady's stall. The stall next to Lady's was empty; Jess supposed it to be the stall Ettinsmoor had been stabled in the day before.

After a reassuring greeting for Lady, Jessica turned to the foreman saying, "She's a very special horse."

"I can see that, Miss, and you can be sure we'll take very special care of her. If there's anything at all you need for her, just let me know."

Jessica returned to the house for breakfast. She and Sir Gaston were just finishing their coffee when Gregory came down to join them.

"I saw riders coming up the road," he announced grimly as he filled his plate from the sideboard. "British escort and a large carriage."

Jess and Sir Gaston exchanged quick glances. They hadn't long to wait to learn who was visiting, for the butler was soon ushering them in. As Jess heard them coming, the color drained from her face. She recognized one voice—that of Bradford Keene.

Sir Gaston patted her hand. Bradford's voice could be heard before he entered the room. "Uncle, I'm afraid I must impose upon you," he declared brusquely.

He was accompanied by a British captain and a sergeant.

Bradford stopped when he saw Jessica. "What are you doing here?" he asked.

"It's a very long story," Sir Gaston said abruptly. "Tell me what *you're* doing here."

Bradford's thin face sharpened into a grim frown in response to Sir Gaston's tone. Dressed smartly in dark brown, he looked every inch the great plantation owner. In addressing those around him, his imperious manner indicated he fully enjoyed his status of wealth and power.

"Same old Uncle Gaston," he said with a sneer as he sat down. "Cheltenham Farms has been completely overrun by vile rebels. I just barely escaped with my life. The whole frontier seems alive with the blackguards. So here I am."

He turned to his companions. "Sit down, Captain," he said. "Captain Harcourt, this is my uncle, Sir Gaston Keene. Uncle, this is Captain Harcourt and Sergeant Smith. We'll be setting up headquarters here," he said matter-of-factly. "We'll begin interviewing the servants immediately after some breakfast."

"Headquarters? What's going on here?" Sir Gaston sputtered.

"We must interview the servants to weed out anyone not loyal to the Crown. They might also have news of rebel activity nearby. We will be taking care of some special projects for His Majesty from here."

Sir Gaston stared incredulously at his nephew. His face grew purple with rage.

"I'm well aware of your sentiments, Uncle; and it's only my regard for your age and title that keeps you from being arrested and shot for treason. That is why we feel it's necessary to check through the staff members.

"Don't worry, we won't be here very long. Cornwallis will soon make short work of these bands of rabble and I'll be able to return to my own home."

In a very short time, Sir Gaston's mansion bustled with nearly a dozen British soldiers, uniformed and in plain clothes.

Sir Gaston had ranted and raged until Jessica shepherded him to his room to rest. As she was coming out of his quarters, Bradford spotted her and came to stand before her, uncomfortably close. She stepped backward.

"Well, Jessica, now for your story." He stepped forward and closed the distance between them again. "What about my horses?" He glanced at her sling. "We received news of your father's accident. Were the horses delivered to the ship on time?"

"Yes," she answered—a little too quickly, she thought. "Yes, but they were stolen while we were arranging the paperwork and shipping. I must say the soldiers were not very helpful in recovering them. In fact, we were warned that Tarleton might have even been the one who had taken them since he was snatching up every horse in sight after losing most of his on the voyage from New York. My cousin's friends recovered them for us, but we were afraid to leave them in the vicinity for fear Tarleton would get them. The *Westwind* hadn't even arrived yet, which meant they would have had to stay there for two weeks before the ship would be ready to take them on board."

Bradford narrowed his eyes. "Where are they now?"

"Lady's down in the stable now," she answered.

"And Ettinsmoor? Where is he? You keep saying 'we.' Do you mean this 'cousin' your mother told me about?"

She frowned at him. "If you'll ask one question at a time. Ettinsmoor is with my cousin. He had an emergency to see to; but he will leave Ettinsmoor with Father. Sir Gaston insisted I stay here until my shoulder is better." She inhaled deeply, realizing Robbie must have had to explain the situation to their mother, and in turn they would have informed Bradford about who was helping her get the horses to Charleston. "Now, if you don't mind, can you tell me anything about Mother and Robbie? Are they all right?"

"I suppose," he answered. "He should have taken another horse," he said, still considering her story. "I could have your cousin arrested for horse thievery. Ettinsmoor is not an ordinary animal. He's too valuable to be used as a common saddle horse."

"If it hadn't been for my cousin, you would never have seen either one of the horses again," she answered. "Now, will you please tell me anything about Mother and Robbie?"

A slow smile curled his thin lips. "Jessica," he cooed. "Once the spirited little girl, now a spirited—and lovely— young woman." He sniffed.

"Your mother and Robbie appeared to be among friends when I saw them last. I must speak to your father about Robbie. He's keeping very dangerous company. If your father was not such a valued employee, I would be tempted to have your brother brought up on charges."

She bit her tongue to hold back an angry retort, then excused herself, explaining that she had to get some tea for Sir Gaston.

Bradford Keene and the British troops created a general upheaval throughout the house. Several servants were led away to detainment in town where the constable was a loyal Tory. By noontime, a dreadful gloom had settled over the house.

Jessica confronted Gregory outside the library as he was on his way to meet with his cousin Bradford. "Can't you do something? Your grandfather is so distressed, I don't know how much more strain he can endure."

"There's nothing I can do, Jessica," he said, lowering his voice. "I'm sure they won't be here long. Captain Harcourt mentioned something about reinforcements being on the way. They should be able to regain Cheltenham Farms without any problem."

His apparent disassociation with events surrounding them puzzled and angered her. "How do you think Sir Gaston will feel about that?"

He took her hand and avoided her penetrating gaze. "My grandfather is very dear to me; but he is a very old man. I will soon have the responsibility of this estate and I must do what I can to preserve it. I really don't see how this rebellion can succeed against the world's most powerful nation. We all have to make compromises sometimes in order to survive."

She pulled her hand away. "There are some compromises that cost too much. I don't think you have any idea the strength that can be mustered when certain ideals are at stake. I'm sorry for you, Gregory, but I'm more sorry for Sir Gaston."

"Sorry?"

"You have chosen what is convenient over what is right, and I'm afraid Sir Gaston will be terribly disappointed in his grandson. We are going to win, Gregory."

"Please, Jessica." He looked about them nervously. "Don't let Bradford hear you talking like that. He'll charge you with treason."

"You truly don't understand just what this is all about, do you?" she asked thoughtfully. "I guess I didn't really understand until just recently myself."

"I understand that you can suffer severe consequences for speaking so carelessly," he whispered. "Dear Jessica, we don't even have to be involved with all of this. We'll just bide our time; very soon Bradford will take his soldier friends and leave us in peace again."

She searched his face for the slightest indication that he might be able to understand, then sighed sadly and turned toward the stairway.

"Lunch is being served," he said stiffly.

"I'm not hungry," she replied without turning and hurried up the stairs.

Gregory watched her go with a frown. How could such a lovely creature be so stubborn and disagreeable. He shook his head in amazement, puzzled why she couldn't see the logic in trying to maintain a neutral footing between the two sides in this ridiculous revolution. If a neutral position wasn't possible, anyone with any sense could see the final outcome. The British would surely overcome the ragged little army of colonials.

He turned to walk out on the portico to overlook the wide fields of the estate. It was an impressive sight, he conceded, but nothing to compare with the splendor of the palace at Versailles, or the excitement of watching the stunning parade of lords and their ladies dressed in elegant style making their way to the Opera House on opening night in Paris.

Allowing his imagination to whisk him away to that world he longed for, he tried to picture Jessica McClaren on his arm as he escorted her to the special box reserved for his family. He could imagine every head turning to see such a handsome couple and Jessica looking up at him with an adoring smile, the same smile he'd seen the night before when she appeared at the library door. His pleasant dreaming was suddenly spoiled as he remembered that that smile of adoration had been directed at a roughian who preferred primitive buckskin clothing to a finely tailored suit.

"Mr. Starkheim." He turned to see one of the soldiers standing beside him. "Mr. Keene would like to see you in the library at once."

"All right," he answered with a sigh of resignation. He didn't go in immediately. After all, he reasoned, a peasant like Bradford Keene had no right to expect a Starkheim to jump and appear on demand. He'd go see what he wanted because he wasn't eager to antagonize Keene, but he would be in no hurry.

14

Jessica closed the door of her room and leaned heavily against it. She pondered her conversation with Gregory and wondered what would happen now. Would Bradford even allow her to leave if Mac did send a carriage as he had promised?

Her thoughts had never been far from Mac, nor from her conversation with Sir Gaston the night before. She began to worry that, if Sir Gaston was right, Mac might return for her after all. If he did, he would be walking right into the enemy's nest. The more she thought about it, the more she felt she must try to warn him.

A small tapping at her door interrupted her troubled thoughts; and she opened it to find a tearful Molly standing before her.

"What is it, Molly?" she asked.

"Oh, please, Miss McClaren, please come make him take his lunch. He won't talk, he won't eat. I'm afraid he will give up and die."

"I'll see what I can do." She patted the young girl on the shoulder.

Jess found Sir Gaston lying in bed, looking pale and terribly fragile.

"Now what's this about you not eating, Grandpapa?" she scolded.

"It's no use, Poppit. It's over," he answered weakly.

"Over? Nonsense, it's just beginning, and there are a lot of people who need your wisdom and courage to advise them and encourage them. Surely this isn't the same man who told me just last night that he would like to be in the thick of things?"

"There was a time," he sighed, "long, long ago that Bradford would never have dared darken this door. I would have tossed him out on his ear. Now, he marches in like he owns the place and I can't do a thing about it. I'm old, Poppit. I'm an old man."

"Well, Bradford evidently didn't want to face you alone," she said tucking a napkin in his nightshirt collar.

"How's that?" Gaston grumbled.

"He had to bring an escort of British soldiers, didn't he? Come now, no more talk about giving up. You must eat your lunch to keep up your strength." Leaning close, she whispered emphatically, "My goodness, the enemy has come to you. You can show them that Sir Gaston Keene is someone to be dealt with, and beat them at their own game. With your wits you can accomplish more than a hundred younger men could."

He studied her closely, considering her words. "But what about Gregory?" he frowned. "Didn't you see him? He didn't even raise his voice in protest. I've tried to overlook his attitude all these years. He's my Abigail's boy. I was sure some day he'd come to have a feeling for this place . . . for his grandfather. But it's clear he cares nothing for Ellensgate, nor ever will. He'll never lift a finger to protect the place. He's either a coward or a fool or both."

Jessica said nothing.

"He'd have me bow and scrape to these pompous Loyalists just to curry favor in case the revolution fails."

"When did Sir Gaston Keene start letting other men determine what he should do?" she countered.

His eyes widened, and Jess detected a flicker of response to her challenge. They sat quietly together for a few moments. Finally, Jess broke the silence.

"Grandpapa?" she said. "Do you remember telling Mac about the trail to the Chalequah Valley?"

Eyeing her suspiciously, he nodded and took a sip of broth she held for him. Avoiding his searching gaze, she continued. "I've been thinking about what you said last night. I'm afraid if you're right and Mac does come back, he'll be walking into a trap, so I've decided I should leave and try to find him first."

"Don't even consider that wild notion, Poppit. Just pray that Mac will see the British before they see him. Besides, do you think Bradford would allow you to leave?"

"He can't keep me here against my will."

"He took charge of my house," he barked gloomily. "No, my dear, if anyone leaves to warn him, it will be one of the servants—or Gregory. Put it out of your mind."

She sighed then, but the determination never left her face. He finished his broth, and she sat with him until he had fallen asleep. She waited until his breathing became slow and deep; then she kissed him lightly on the forehead and returned to her room.

She looked through Abigail's wardrobe and found a riding habit of dark hunter green with white ribbon piping around the collar and cuffs of the coat. She had just finished buttoning the white silk blouse, when Molly stepped into the room; she found the matching riding gloves of soft kidskin to complete Jess's outfit.

"Thank you, Molly. I would have changed into my own clothes, but I couldn't find them."

"Oh, dear."

"What's wrong?" Jessica buttoned her coat and smoothed down the heavy folds of her skirt.

"They're gone, Miss."

"Gone?"

"Yes, Miss. Gone. Burned. Sir Gaston gave orders. I'm sorry, Miss McClaren, but if you don't mind me saying so, these clothes suit you much better."

Jessica smiled patiently. "Oh, Molly," she said nonchalantly. "I understand we're not far from the Chalequah Valley. I have friends who live there. Do you know which way one would go to get there?"

"They're Cherokee, Miss," Molly exclaimed. "You're friends with the Cherokee?"

"Well, my cousin used to live there. I was just wondering if it was far. Being this close, I thought perhaps I would pay them a visit."

Molly stared in amazement. "Aren't you afraid of nothin'?"

Jessica laughed. "The Cherokee at Iron Mountain are Christians. It's quite safe."

"But most of the Cherokee want us out of this country. That's why they're helpin' the British." Clasping her hand over her mouth, she looked fearfully toward the door. Continuing in a whisper, she added, "How can you be sure you can trust *any* Indian?"

"How can you be sure you can trust any *white* man?" Jessica whispered and nodded toward the door.

Molly thought for a moment. "Well, I've never been to the Chalequah myself, but I know you take the post road off to the north. It passes the estate down by the river."

"Do you know of a way by Jackson Falls?"

Molly turned and began to hang up the dress from which Jessica had just changed. "The post road, that's as much as I know, but then I don't go nowhere but back and forth to Ellensgate." She closed the wardrobe doors. "Will that be all?"

"Yes, Molly. Thank you."

The maid turned to go but stopped at the door. "You might talk to Barnaby. He's one of the stable boys and he knows just about every square inch of this country around here."

Jessica nodded gratefully. "Perhaps I will."

"I'd think twice, though." Molly opened the door to leave.

"By the way, Molly, please don't mention this to anyone. It was only a thought and I wouldn't want to worry Sir Gaston about it."

"Oh no, Miss. I won't breathe a word of it. No one would believe it anyway," she said.

After Molly had gone, Jessica stepped out onto the balcony, which faced north. Down below on the grounds, she could see four or five soldiers standing at their posts. They were stationed on the inside of the stone wall around the gardens.

Off in the distance to the north, the dusty red ribbon of the post road wound its way toward the hills on the horizon. The countryside was a patchwork of varying shades of green in the brilliant afternoon sun, the dark green of loblolly and shortleaf pine blending with the brighter hues of new growth on large hickories and gray-barked beeches. She studied the scene carefully, then headed down to the stables to find Barnaby, the stable boy.

She was just passing the library when Bradford caught sight of her. "Jessica?" he said. "I must say you look very nice. Where are you going?"

"To give Lady a little exercise and get some fresh air myself." She held her chin high and looked him squarely in the eye.

"Well, in that case, just a moment." He called to one of the soldiers standing nearby and ordered him to saddle a horse and escort Miss McClaren on a short ride.

"That's not necessary," she insisted.

"Oh, but it is." Bradford smiled. "It just isn't safe for a young lady to go riding about by herself."

She turned to leave without acknowledging the man Bradford had ordered to escort her.

When she reached the stable, she looked about for the young Barnaby. A boy about thirteen years old came hurrying up to her, asking if she would like him to saddle a mount for her.

"Are you Barnaby?"

"Yes, ma'am," he answered quickly.

She told him she wanted to take Lady out for some exercise and followed the boy to Lady's stall. The soldier began saddling his own horse down at the other end of the stable.

"How do you feel about what's happened here?" she asked in a low voice.

He looked nervously toward the red-coated soldier. "Can't say, ma'am; I'm just a stable boy."

"Barnaby, I've only a moment," she whispered quickly. "I'm going to have to take the chance that you are more loyal to Sir Gaston than the British. I need your help."

He brightened. "What do you need?"

"Is there a shorter way to the Chalequah Valley than the post road?"

"There's the trail up to Jackson Falls. Takes half the time the post road does." He bent down and quickly drew a crude map in the dirt floor, telling her certain landmarks to watch for. He scuffed it out when he heard the soldier approach.

"This is our secret, all right?" she whispered. The boy nodded a silent reply.

"Thank you, Barnaby." She took Lady's reins and led her from the stall.

Jess ignored her escort as she rode across the meadows toward the river and back again. She tried to appear to be interested in little else other than the beautiful summer afternoon as she looked for the landmarks Barnaby had told her about.

Upon their return, she allowed Barnaby to care for Lady while she went on up to the house. Molly brought afternoon tea to her room, and Jess asked the little maid to explain to Gregory and the others that she would be dining with Sir Gaston in his room and then retiring early.

It was difficult to keep her mind on her conversation with Sir Gaston as she sat with him for dinner. Much to her relief, he seemed to be feeling stronger and more like himself. He apologized for letting Bradford upset him so much and thanked her for reminding him of who he was and what he could do.

Back in her room, she sighed with relief at not having been questioned about Mac and lowered the wick on the lamp until the room was dark. She quietly opened the door to the balcony and looked both ways to be sure it was clear; then, leaving the door unlatched, she laid down on the bed to wait until the house was quiet.

15

Jessica awoke with a start. Sitting up, her heart pounding, she was suddenly apprehensive, knowing she had something urgent to do. For a moment she wasn't sure where she was, until she noticed the balcony door standing slightly ajar, opened by the soft evening breeze. In a flash, she remembered everything. Laying aside the sling she had worn all day, she pulled on her jacket, and tiptoed to the door leading into the hall.

She listened intently for any sounds of movement; after a few moments of silence, she was satisfied that everyone had retired. She stole to the balcony door and carefully peeked out to make sure the way was clear. Remembering how as children she and Robbie used to climb down the large iron trellises that stood at either end of the portico, she planned to creep past Sir Gaston's room along the balcony to the trellis closest to the stables. Thankful that Sir Gaston's room was the only other room she would have to pass by, she slipped out onto the balcony and carefully closed the door behind her.

Holding her breath, she moved along the balcony until she reached the door to Sir Gaston's room. She peeked in through the windowpane of the French door. His bedside lamp was still aglow, and a book lay across his chest; he appeared to have fallen asleep while reading. Without making a sound, she hurried by his door and reached the trellis.

As a child, it had been a simple exercise to climb up and down the trellis. Now, however, her tender shoulder slowed her progress and her long riding skirt caught on several protruding edges on the way down the makeshift ladder. Her foot suddenly slipped; she clutched and clawed frantically. Her sore shoulder throbbed as she hung to the trellis with both hands. She scrambled to find a toehold, finally located one that would support her weight, and hung motionless, breathless, hoping the noise had not alerted anyone.

A few moments later her feet touched solid ground; she sank back against the wall to calm her racing pulse and steady her trembling knees.

The guards at the front seemed to be dozing as she passed; she made it to the stable without being detected. Reaching Lady's stall, she took only a bridle and led her precious horse out through the back stable door into a corral which was not visible from the house.

The gate was opened into the north pasture. Still leading Lady, she circled wide around the back of the estate. She reached the post road at last and climbed a large rock beside the road to lightly swing onto Lady's back.

Lady bounded forward, eager for a run. She rode faster than was safe down the dark road, but the dizzying speed helped Jess forget the danger of her mission.

She soon realized she would certainly miss her turnoff at such a speed, and pulled Lady to a slower pace. The trees along the road blocked out most of the moonlight and the stars, so she peered into the darkness for the trail.

A dark form suddenly dropped onto Lady's back, pulling Jess to the ground. They tumbled onto the soft carpet of grass and rolled down a small incline together. Jessica fought fiercely; she screamed and bit down hard on her attacker's shoulder. "Let me go. Let me go," she cried.

Her attacker was too strong for her, and quickly pinned her wrists to the ground. Her grunts and cries were suddenly interrupted by the sound of his voice. "Wait a minute," he said. "Jess? Jess, is that you?"

She stopped struggling and looked at the dark shadow above her.

"Mac?" she gasped, still panting from her exertion.

"What do you think you're doing?" he demanded.

"Mac!" She sighed with relief. "It *is* you. Oh, thank heaven."

He leaped up and pulled her to her feet. He wrapped his arms around her and held her tightly.

"I thought you were a courier." He pressed his cheek against her soft hair. "Are you all right? Did I hurt you?"

"I think I'm fine. Just a little shaken."

He released her and held her at arm's length. "What are you doing here?" he demanded. "You could have been shot."

"What are *you* doing here?" she countered. "You're supposed to be in the Chalequah Valley."

"I . . . well, I just thought I'd come back and see that you . . . uh, to see that you got home all right. I mean, as headstrong as you are, I figured someone ought to see that you didn't get into any more trouble."

"Headstrong?" she echoed.

"Yes," he said coolly. "I made a promise to your father to return you safe and sound."

She blushed. "I'm sure Sir Gaston and Gregory would have seen to my safe return."

"I trust Gregory about as much as I do the Larkins," he said. "You haven't told me why you're out here trying to get yourself killed."

She started to answer, but he suddenly pulled her into the shadows of the undergrowth along the road.

"Shhhhh," he said. "Riders coming." They lay motionless, hardly breathing.

The riders approached at an easy pace; there were two of them. "We'd better hurry or we'll lose her," one said.

"Where can she go? They've probably arranged a place to meet. There'll most likely be a fire. If we go slowly we'll catch them easily enough."

The men passed.

Jess turned to Mac. "Two of the men who came to Sir Gaston's with Bradford," she explained. She quickly told him about Bradford's arrival, and it suddenly occurred to her why her escape had been so easy.

"Oh, no. Here I was, coming to warn you of danger, and all along I was leading them right to you. I . . . . I'd been praying that you'd come back for me; then, when they showed up, I was afraid you'd be caught if you did."

He turned her face toward him, interrupting her with a tender kiss.

"Does that mean you're not angry with me?" she whispered softly.

He grinned broadly. "No more talk now," he said. "We have to leave."

"Where are we going?" she asked. He helped her to her feet again.

"After them. They're going to find a campfire all right, but about fifteen rebel muskets are waiting there. You can stay there with a few of the men at the camp while the rest of us do some cleaning up for Sir Gaston."

Mac led her to the place where he had tied Ettinsmoor. When Jess had been knocked from Lady's back, the filly had trotted away, but had found Ettinsmoor and now stood serenely next to the tethered horse. Mac untied Ettinsmoor, gathered Lady's reins, and handed them to Jess.

"You were crazy to come to warn me," he said sternly. "You shouldn't have tried something so foolish."

She half-smiled. "I'm not a child anymore."

"I'm well aware of that," he said. The moonlight bathed them in a mystical glow. She tried to think of something witty to say, but words failed her as they stood there a moment gazing at each other.

Mac took a slender leather string from around his neck. The moonlight reflected off a small silver circle riding along the strand. He placed it over her head and around her neck.

Jess inspected the silver circle in the moonlight; a finely-etched pattern adorned its face.

"It's lovely," she whispered.

"My father made it for my mother. When she died, she left it to me. I want you to have it," he said, his voice rich and deep.

She blinked at him, her gray-green eyes searching his face.

"Please," he said. "Keep it . . . as a favor to me."

Unable to speak, she reached up and softly touched his face. Closing his hand over hers, he lightly kissed her fingertips. "We have to be going," he said.

She nodded silently and he helped her swing up onto Lady's back. He mounted Ettinsmoor and led the way down the road, following the two British soldiers.

When they reached the camp, it was just as Mac had predicted; the two soldiers were bound, hand and foot. Their captors stood around congratulating themselves.

"Lieutenant Macklin," shouted a young buckskin-clad man. "Look who just waltzed into our party."

Mac dismounted. "Good work, Jim. They're from the new detachment we heard about. They've set up head-quarters at the Keene estate near Ellensgate. Bradford Keene has regrouped and settled in without his uncle's blessing. I think maybe we need to go over there and help clean house."

Mac circled his horse, and helped Jess dismount. He held her around the waist for a moment longer than necessary, searching her face in the light of the campfire. The adoration in her eyes was unmistakable. Remembering the others around them, he stepped back, letting her go.

Mac turned to the two men standing close by. "We'll wait here and ride over to the estate just before dawn."

Jess placed her hand on his arm. "Please, Mac, don't make me stay here. I must go back with you. Sir Gaston is not at all well. I must see about him."

"I'm afraid not. I don't want you getting hurt." Not giving her a chance to argue, he walked over to the campfire.

She watched him talking to three of his men as he poured coffee from a kettle on the fire. He was one of the tallest of the group and Jess couldn't take her eyes away

164

from his face, so serious now, concentrating on plans being made.

She became aware of someone standing next to her, and looked up to see a young Indian girl studying her in solemn silence.

The girl appeared to be about the same age as Jessica; from the look on her face, Jess judged that she was very unhappy about something.

"Hello," Jess said.

"Jessica, this is Little Sparrow," Mac said as he joined the two girls. "Little Sparrow, this is Jessica McClaren."

Jess took the cup he handed to her and smiled again at the pretty Indian girl. Her smile was not returned.

"Little Sparrow and her brother Bear Paw have come after their uncle, Quiet Bear, who has been riding with us. Their aunt is very ill and needs him to come back to the settlement."

One of the men by the fire called to him and Mac left Jessica and Little Sparrow by themselves.

A long moment of silence passed before Little Sparrow finally spoke, pointing to the silver ring that hung around Jess's neck. "I hope you are worthy. It was always thought he would choose someone from Iron Mountain."

Jessica glanced down at the ring, then shot a curious glance at the Indian girl. Little Sparrow turned and went over to the other side of the fire to sit just within the circle of its light. Jess had an uneasy feeling about the young woman, as if she viewed Jess as an enemy.

Mac returned to her side. "Is something wrong?" he asked.

"Huh? Oh, no. I was just wondering about Little Sparrow. She's very pretty, isn't she?"

165

Mac shrugged. "She's from the Iron Mountain settlement. We've known each other since we were children." More concerned with the matter at hand, he said, "You'll be all right here until I get back. How many men did you say Keene had with him?"

She smiled at his easy dismissal of Little Sparrow, and told him she had seen about twelve men altogether at the estate.

"With these two out of the way, that leaves ten," he said. "We'll be leaving in just a little bit. Now, promise me you will stay here until I get back."

He looked at her questioningly as he saw a sudden gleam appear in her eyes. "I'm not sure what you're thinking about, but don't. You're staying here and that's final."

"You might at least listen. It's really very simple," she argued.

Without rebuking her further, he listened warily as she explained her idea.

"It's not a bad idea, but you're still staying here."

"But Mac, there'd be very little risk," she protested.

Several of the soldiers standing nearby had heard the plan and were nodding their heads in agreement with Jessica. The one called Jim grinned at Mac and said, "You know, it could work. We'd have surprise on our side."

Finally, Mac, being outnumbered, and appreciating the merit of her idea, reluctantly agreed to give it a try.

Within the hour, Mac and Jess were once more headed toward the Keene estate, followed immediately by two of the young colonials riding the horses and dressed in the uniforms of their captives. Five others followed at some distance.

They soon reached the estate and rode in quietly. The moon was gone, and the first gray streaks of daylight softened the dark sky along the eastern horizon. In the uncertain light, the two guards at the gate hailed the two red uniforms as they rode by. Seconds later, the guards were dispatched quickly and silently by two of the following group that had dismounted and crept up on them as their eyes followed Jess and Mac's party.

Mac and Jessica dismounted and walked ahead of the red-coated soldiers, who pointed muskets at their "prisoners." The lights in the library blazed brightly even though it was only five o'clock. Mac whispered to Jess that Bradford and his men must be planning something special to be up so early.

Jess and Mac entered the house as subdued prisoners escorted by the two counterfeit British soldiers. The guard standing at the front door was distracted as he watched Jess and Mac, making it easy for one of the rebel band to quietly dispatch him before he discovered their trickery. They entered the library to find Bradford, Captain Harcourt, and two others studying a map spread out before them.

As they turned, Bradford's face lit up with a smile of smug satisfaction. "Jessica, my dear. How very thoughtful of you to bring back your *cousin*. I have been wanting to meet him for quite some time now." He turned his attention to Mac as he stood up. "Andrew Macklin, isn't it? What a stroke of luck. You have been a thorn in our side long enough. Now it seems we will finally be rid of you."

"Sorry to disappoint you, Keene, but not this time." Mac signaled the two men behind him. They stepped out from behind Jess and Mac and leveled their muskets at the four astonished men.

"Guard!" Bradford shouted.

His call was met by the grinning face of another American soldier. The plan had worked flawlessly and without one casualty. Within a short time all the members of the small garrison were held under guard in the large cattle barn, next to the stables.

Several of the members of the house staff had heard the commotion and greeted Mac and Jess joyously when they learned what had happened.

Jessica was giddily explaining the plan to Molly when Mac interrupted. "I still can't believe I let you talk me into it. You could very easily have gotten hurt if anything had gone wrong."

She smiled. "I think I was safer coming with you than I would have been back at your camp."

"You'd have nothing to fear from my men," he said.

"I was thinking more about an old friend of yours, not the men."

His brow wrinkled. He opened his mouth, but closed it again when another voice sounded behind them. "What's going on here?"

They turned to see Gregory coming down the stairs. "Jessica. Macklin. You're back." It was a statement, not a question.

They explained the situation to a frowning Gregory.

"I hope you realize what you've done," he said. "You backwoods bumpkins can't possibly defeat Cornwallis and the most powerful army in the world. They'll just come back and punish the rest of us for your deeds."

"You're partially right," Mac conceded. "We can't beat British regulars in a head-to-head battle, but we don't plan to fight on their terms. We'll do all right with our own strategy.

"But your Uncle Bradford is the reason we're here now. He is responsible for the deaths of two civilians. When his crime is made known to the other plantation owners in

168

this part of the colony, the Loyalist support will evaporate. Even if Cornwallis does make it this far, he will be a very long way from his supply line and reinforcements."

"Hear! Hear!"

They looked up to see Sir Gaston leaning heavily on the arm of Charles, the butler, at the top of the stairs.

"Grandpapa," Jess called. She ran quickly up the stairs to hug him. He winked. "See, I told you he'd be back," he whispered.

She took his other arm and helped him descend the stairs.

"How can we help, Macklin?" Sir Gaston asked. He shook Mac's hand; the sparkle in his eyes made him seem years younger. "Anything we can do? Anything at all? We owe you a great deal."

"Just don't give up the fight, sir," Mac answered. "Cornwallis is going to try to take the Carolinas and the only way we can keep him from succeeding is to harass his troops any way we can without becoming involved in a head-to-head battle. With Bradford Keene put away, we can make better progress. Help me convince your neighbors that we can win."

"That I will, my son. Now, I'm sure you and your men could use some refreshment. Charles, tell Cook to prepare an early breakfast."

"We have eight men, sir," Mac answered Sir Gaston's questioning glance.

"Eight? Only eight?" Sir Gaston slapped his knee. "Eight men! I'm beginning to think it can be done after all."

They were soon seated in the dining room, eating eggs and ham and crusty bread. Sir Gaston, seated at the head of the table, looked at his grandson, whose gloomy attitude was very apparent. Sir Gaston's face clouded briefly.

He started to say something, but turned to Mac instead. "What are your plans, now?" he asked.

"I think first, if she feels up to it, I'll escort Jessica back to Barleyville to see about her father and take them both on to Cheltenham Farms. I think it would be best to retire her from this business."

Sir Gaston smiled and patted Jess's hand. "You must take very good care of her, Macklin. She's a very special young lady."

"I intend to, sir," Mac said. He met Jessica's glance and held her attention for a long moment.

A sudden crash interrupted them; they both turned to see Gregory glaring at Mac.

"I'm so sorry," he said. "The glass was wet and slipped right out of my hand."

Jess looked from Gregory back to Mac. She reflected that it was probably a good thing they were leaving soon.

16

Jess and Mac left the next morning and started out on their three-day journey to Barleyville. Sir Gaston had insisted they take one of his carriages, and supplied them with enough food for two journeys. Two of the soldiers accompanied them, riding ahead of the carriage.

Word had been sent back to the camp to bring the two prisoners that had been caught earlier to Sir Gaston's estate, where they would be held with the others until a detachment could be sent from General Gates to take them officially into custody.

Mac drove the carriage; Lady and Ettinsmoor were tethered to the back.

After the experience they had survived together the past two weeks, they each found it difficult to face the fact that within a few days they would be parting. Jessica didn't want to think about watching him ride off, headed back to his army duties. Mac didn't want to think about leaving her behind. The inevitability of their parting left them both quietly reflective as they traveled.

The long periods of silence were not a wedge between them, but a bond; they enjoyed each other's presence, each one absorbed with the other's looks and gestures.

After a joyous reunion with her father at Barleyville, Jess continued westward with Mac to Cheltenham Farms. Rob McClaren was still very weak, so despite his objections, Jess took the reins as they began the last segment of their travels. Mac rode ahead of the carriage on Ettinsmoor.

That night, as they sat around the campfire drinking coffee, McClaren fixed his gaze on Mac. "Macklin," he said, "will you tell me what's been happening these past two weeks? Jessica has been very vague about a good deal of what went on."

Jessica and Mac exchanged glances, and she nodded, indicating her agreement for Mac to tell her father as much of the story of their journey as he thought was wise. She had been careful about saying too much about Mac's duties with the Continental army. She was afraid she might tell more than she ought to.

"It all started several months ago," Mac began. Jess listened closely, too. She craved to learn the details of Mac's activities. "You were probably aware of Ronald Gallagher's outspoken views in opposition to the Loyalists around these parts. Apparently, Bradford Keene promised to take care of the matter for General Clinton in return for a few favors, one of which involved safe passage to Charleston for the two thoroughbreds to be shipped to Duke Wilton in the West Indies.

"Michael Gallagher had written to Captain Miles of the militia, asking for help to find out who was behind some problems on the plantation—butchered stock and some ruined crops. Before Miles could get anyone over there, he received a message—supposedly from the Gallaghers—

saying they had given up, were selling out to Keene, and had decided to go back to Ireland.

"It was pretty suspicious, but there was no proof of any mischief. I was to try to find them, if possible, and help get them out of Charleston.

"They were found in an alley four days before we arrived. Michael survived long enough to write out a statement implicating Bradford Keene and two others" he turned to Jess "—the two men that chased us in Charleston. Those two are Clinton's men and have been in league with Keene for quite some time now. They made a fatal mistake this time. There were witnesses to the crime, one of whom was the shipping clerk we dealt with, Jess. Since the Gallaghers were not soldiers, they will be tried for murder."

"Ah, poor Ronald Gallagher," Rob McClaren moaned. "He was a good man. I thought it was more'n a mite peculiar when they left just like that. I'm not surprised Bradford had a hand in it, seeing as how the Gallagher place added a good six hundred acres of fertile land to Cheltenham Farms. What happens now?"

"The two henchmen will certainly hang; Keene will most likely join them on the gallows."

Mac then proceeded to tell McClaren about his daughter's ordeal with the Natiri Indians.

"She's a remarkable young lady, Mr. McClaren," he said.

The older man puffed on his pipe and nodded. Soberly studying his daughter, he said, "Well, my gal, it appears you have been on one very wild adventure. I should have listened to your mother and made you stay in the house with her and kept you away from the stables when you were little. If I had, you'd probably be bouncing a wee bairn on your knee instead of skulking around the forests on army business."

She propped her hands on her hips in mock indignation. "And just who do you think would have helped capture Bradford and his men if I'd been at home cooking and sewing?" She punctuated her words with a wink at Mac.

"Aye, aye, you're right. I surrender," her father declared with a grin. "But I think it's best we not share the entire story of your adventure with your mother. She'd faint dead away thinking about the danger her wee lass has been through." A serious tone entered his voice. "I'm very grateful to you, Mr. Macklin, for keepin' her safe and bringin' her back to us."

"I can't take much credit for that," Mac said ruefully. "If it wasn't for her quick wits and courage, neither of us would be here. She's been through more than she should have, but I couldn't have had a more valuable ally."

McClaren studied the admiring glances passing between his daughter and this young man. He couldn't recall Jessica looking at anyone the way she looked at Andrew Macklin.

Upon their arrival at Cheltenham Farms several days later, Mac and Robbie greeted each other like long lost brothers, and Jess looked at her brother with a new admiration. She regretted having underestimated him. Her mother looked very tired, showing the strain of worry about her husband and daughter while they'd been away.

Seeing her daughter arrive home in a carriage, dressed in a fine riding habit and escorted by an attractive young man filled Cara McClaren with curiosity. Afternoon tea was quickly laid out and Robbie and his mother began bombarding Jess, her father, and Mac with questions about their journey. Jess followed her father's advice, glossing over details, omitting parts of the story completely.

Mac asked his share of questions about the situation with the militia seizing the plantation. They were told that Robbie had been appointed as second-in-command under a captain from Pickens's militiamen. They had taken temporary control of Cheltenham Farms and its many resources. The news of Cornwallis's march westward made uncertain the length of time the rebels would stay at the plantation, but for a few days, they would be able to rest and plan their next moves.

Two days after their return, Jess was in the stable currying Lady when Mac came and stood for a moment watching her work. She hummed a happy little tune, oblivious of her audience until he cleared his throat.

"Has she recovered from her long trip?" He came nearer and began stroking Lady's glistening velvet-like neck.

"Oh, yes. She's just fine," Jess said.

"Jess." The tone of his voice struck a disquieting chord in her; she avoided looking at him, busying herself with the task of brushing Lady.

He spoke her name again, catching her hand to stop the brushing, and turned her to face him.

"Please, don't say it," she pleaded.

"I have to leave. I have to deliver some dispatches to Pickens. Then I'm to go on east." He paused. "I'm not sure when I'll be back."

She swallowed hard, searching his face for some reassurance.

"I *will* be back," he said softly, but with determination.

"But who's going to keep you out of trouble?" she asked. She tried to swallow the lump in her throat and smile at the same time.

"I'll travel so fast, trouble won't be able to catch me." He grinned.

She turned away quickly to hide the tears that welled up in her eyes.

"I'd like to take Ettinsmoor," he said. "I could use his speed."

She turned back to face him. "I'd have you take Lady herself, if I thought it would help you have a safe trip; but Ettinsmoor has more stamina. He's perfect for the job." She lowered her gaze. "When are you leaving?"

"In about an hour," he replied. He opened his mouth to say something else, but the sound of the stable door swinging open cut their good-bye short. One of the soldiers entered with a leather pouch full of dispatches for Mac to carry.

Mac bid her an unspoken farewell as he left the stable to prepare for his departure. A short time later, she watched with an aching heart as he rode away.

17

June turned to July; August arrived with no word from Mac. Robbie reassured Jessica, saying that when Mac was carrying dispatches, he would have little opportunity to write—or post—any letters. Still, she couldn't help worrying about him as news arrived that Cornwallis was marching his forces across the entire colony, establishing new forts to control the area.

The Continental army in the South no longer existed. With the defeat at Charleston, all the soldiers had been sent home after being made to promise they would never again bear arms against the Crown. However, frontiersmen and militiamen still raided and skirmished, waiting for aid from the continental forces to the north.

The news of General Gates's defeat at Camden in mid-August was extremely disheartening. Jessica overheard her father lament that with such incompetent men leading the forces coming to challenge Cornwallis, there seemed little hope for the South.

However, just as Mac had predicted, though the war news was not encouraging, it soon became apparent that the devotion of local Loyalists was weakening. In addition, more and more of those soldiers who had been at Charleston forswore their oath and slipped off to join the groups of rebels carrying on guerilla-type warfare against Cornwallis's forces.

Because of the increased hostilities in the South, the McClarens' plans to move to their own farm had been delayed indefinitely. They continued to keep the plantation operating as normally as possible until Bradford Keene's fate was decided—which, with the disruption in the court system due to the war, was expected to take a long time. Until that time, most of the vegetables and meat produced went to help feed the militia.

Through the long weeks following Mac's departure, Jessica busied herself with the everyday tasks at hand and tried to remind herself that Mac was very capable of taking care of himself. She had been tackling every extra chore she could find to keep herself busy enough to help pass the time quickly and keep from worrying about Mac. The house was spotless, and the laundry and mending hadn't had a chance to accumulate before she finished it. Lady was so well groomed she could have stepped into the show ring at a moment's notice. Jess had written weekly letters to Sir Gaston, and Dr. and Mrs. Barton. Still, she worried constantly about Mac.

One afternoon in those last dog days of summer at the end of August, her mother shooed her out of the house and told her to relax a little bit. Robbie had left with a load of supplies for the garrison at River Bend and would be gone for at least a week. Papa was working on his books and the stable boys had everything under control down at the barns. It was too hot to take Lady out for a ride so she walked down the lane toward the post road, as she had become accustomed to doing as each day passed and still no word came from Mac.

The late afternoon sun was intense, draining her energy. The humidity lay heavily like a thick suffocating blanket. The trees vibrated with the lazy droning of locusts, and it was too hot for the birds to sing. Seeking the shade of the huge magnolia at the end of the lane, Jessica sat down, leaning back against the tree trunk. The sleeves and bodice of her light gray cotton dress clung stickily to her form, and she thought about an icy cold bath in a swift running river. Brushing away the beads of perspiration from her forehead, she picked up a fallen magnolia leaf to use as a makeshift fan.

She closed her eyes, remembering the look on Mac's face as they said good-bye the day he had ridden away from Cheltenham Farms. She could almost hear the beat of Ettinsmoor's hooves over the hard drive. But the sound of hoofbeats she heard grew closer, not farther away. She quickly jumped to her feet. Standing and shading her eyes from the late sun, her heartbeat quickened. The silhouette of a man on a large horse appeared on the rise. He was tall, broad-shouldered and headed her way at a steady pace.

The horseman drew closer and waved to her.

"Jessica!" he called.

Her heart sank at the sound of his voice. *What is Gregory doing here?* she wondered.

He reined the horse to a halt and quickly dismounted. He wore a suit of rich brown and a hat with the brim folded up rakishly on one side and fastened with a long pheasant feather. Flashing a sparkling smile, he removed his hat and made a grand sweeping bow. Taking her hand up in his, he kissed it lightly.

179

"Jessica," he said. "What a pleasant welcome." His handsome smile changed quickly to a look of disappointment.

"Jessica, my dear. I do hope I'm not the cause of that crestfallen look."

"Gregory." She forced a smile. "Of course not. I'm just surprised to see you. What brings you all this way? Is Sir Gaston all right?"

"He's fine. I've just come on a matter of business for him." He explained that Bradford had been imprisoned at the Monmouth Court Stockade. Cheltenham Farms had been officially confiscated and would continue to produce supplies for the rebel militia. As Lord John Keene's only other relative besides Bradford, Sir Gaston was being allowed to recover any family treasures he might want. Local colonial officials did not want to antagonize a staunch supporter like Sir Gaston. Although the supplies produced by the plantation were essential, the value of artwork and furnishings of the house could not compare with the influence Sir Gaston could wield in rallying his fellow South Carolinians in the rebel cause. Sir Gaston had planned to send his trusted foreman, David Wills, but Gregory had insisted that he perform the task.

"To be honest, Jessica, I wanted the excuse to come so I could see you again."

She blushed; he continued, holding his hat in his hand. "I'm afraid I got off on the wrong foot with you. I'd like a chance to start over since the way is evidently clear now."

She wrinkled her brow in a bewildered expression.

Seeing her questioning look, he went on. "I mean I assumed, after Macklin and that Indian woman stopped by the estate last week, that you and he had gone your separate ways."

Jess's hand went involuntarily to the silver ring hanging around her neck. She could not have been more stunned if he'd struck her with the back of his hand.

"Oh dear, have I said something I shouldn't have?"

She took a deep breath and lifted her chin.

"No," she said. "No, of course not. Mr. Macklin and I haven't corresponded at all since he left." Her voice wavered slightly. "Did he appear to be well?"

"Oh, quite. He came to talk with Grandfather about something. They weren't there long, and we didn't speak, as I was busy with other matters. I see he is still riding a Cheltenham Farms stallion."

She was thankful that Mac was well and safe. She told herself that there was probably some very reasonable explanation why she had not heard a word for two months. Yet within the last week he had been just two days' ride away without coming by or sending word. Her brow furrowed darkly as she remembered the look in Little Sparrow's eyes that night at the rebels' camp; she felt a shiver creep up her spine in spite of the heat of the day.

"Ah, here come the wagons now," Gregory said.

She watched silently as two heavy wagons turned into the lane.

"Would you mind showing us the way, Jessica? This is my first visit here." He looked across the expanse of the plantation. "Mother always refused to come here for some reason."

"Yes, of course," she said, trying to fight off the sinking feeling in the pit of her stomach.

She gathered her skirts and, with Gregory's help, climbed up to the seat of the first wagon. They rode along the lane to the stables and proceeded to the main house.

Jessica stepped away from the wagons that were being unhitched.

"I must get back," she said, "and help Mother with dinner, Gregory. Would you care to join us?"

"Thank you, not tonight. I'd like to get settled in and get an early start in the morning." He turned to ride up to the main house, but stopped and looked back. "Would it be asking too much for you to come and help me with the inventory? I could really use some help."

The only thing she wanted to do now was be alone to contemplate the things she'd been told about Mac. So distracted by this news of Mac and Little Sparrow, she consented absently to help. Gregory waved happily as he rode off toward the mansion, but Jessica hardly noticed him leave.

That night she cried herself to sleep. In the dark early morning hours, she awoke from her recurring dream about Mac being pulled away from her by Little Sparrow.

Ugly ghosts of doubt taunted her. *He never really said how he felt about you,* she reasoned. *But words are not always necessary,* she countered, *and he did say he'd come back.*

The thoughts whirling through her mind left her wondering if she had overestimated the depth of Mac's feelings for her. It would only be natural that he would be drawn to someone with whom he shared a common background; he had grown up with Little Sparrow. The girl obviously cared about him. And she was very pretty, Jess admitted begrudgingly.

She tried to face the fact that she might never see Mac again. If he really cared for her, he would have contacted her one way or another. He had obviously taken time to contact Little Sparrow. The thought infuriated her and she turned angrily in her bed, punching her pillow briskly.

Why should she even care? She had managed quite nicely before she ever met Andrew Macklin and she would carry on very well without him. And her deep feelings for Mac aroused deep worries that she was being disloyal to Evan. She had only known Mac for a fraction of the time she knew Evan, yet there had been moments during their short time together that she felt as though they had always known each other. She had come to feel a strange permanence in their togetherness, though from the moment they met, she knew the inevitability of his leaving.

Mac never promised her anything. He never once told her he loved her, but she could almost feel—still—the touch of his lips on hers the night she had gone to warn him of the trap at Sir Gaston's estate. The look in his eyes when he told her he would return had been more convincing than a million promises. Yet, where was he?

The pre-dawn sky filtered gray light through her window; the slender slice of moon slipped below the western horizon. Mac had told her that the time always comes when one must put the past behind; perhaps that time had come. She fell asleep again, clutching the silver ring.

The next morning, after an early ride, Jess resolved that since Mac had apparently forgotten about her, she had been foolish to be so preoccupied with thoughts of him. She realized that it was not going to be easy to dislodge Mac from her thoughts, however. She needed something to keep her too busy to think about him. Remembering her agreement the evening before to help Gregory, she decided it would be just the thing to do, and she went up to the mansion. It was a large two-story structure of brick that had been made from the ground on which it stood.

It was very similar in design to Sir Gaston's home; the same architect designed both buildings. Ivy vines twined their way up the front elevation, creating a cool cover over the light red brick. A wide portico stretched across the middle third of the front with graceful columns upholding the second story balcony above it.

It was the last day of August, and although the day was already growing hot, a haziness in the atmosphere hinted at a change of weather.

Jessica wore the new dress her mother had made after her return from the excursion to Charleston. It was a pale pink flowered print with white ruffling at the elbow. The billowy skirt led the eye to white ruffling along the hem as well.

The windows of the mansion were opened wide and a slight breeze stirred the curtains as she entered the study. Gregory sat behind a massive desk. The study was lined with bookshelves; massive furniture was positioned about the room in a comfortable arrangement. This had been Lord John's study, and Bradford had changed it little since his death. The aroma of slightly spicy pipe tobacco, leather upholstery, and old books lingered in the room.

Jess used to love to come in here with her father when she was little. Lord John, a compact man with a large sandy-colored mustache, kept a small bowl of boiled sweets on his desk, which he always offered to the shy little girl peeking out from behind her father's legs. Even now, Jess could taste the sugary sweetness as she was flooded with a wave of memories.

Gregory looked up from the papers before him. "Good morning, Jessica. Don't you look lovely this morning." He stood and came around the desk to greet her. As always, he was impeccably dressed; a light gray coat and breeches complemented a white silk shirt with a short jabot.

"How are things progressing?" she asked.

"Dreadfully," he declared dramatically. "Look at this."

She followed him back around the desk. He pointed to a ledger filled with notations written in abbreviated forms.

"I can hardly make any sense out of these ink scratches," Gregory complained.

"Well," she said. "Let's look a little closer here."

She sat down and studied the page more carefully. After a few minutes, she lifted her head. "Yes, I see now. The descriptions are all abbreviated in a sort of simple code."

"Can you tell what's what?"

Studying a moment longer, Jess said, "It appears these initials here indicate the room . . . "

"You are so clever." He sighed with relief. "If it were not for you I would be lost. I must say it was most inconsiderate of Uncle John's secretary to leave such books and go get himself killed that way."

"I'm sure Mr. Gilet was not planning to break his neck falling off of a horse," Jess declared wryly. Gregory merely shrugged his shoulders and she turned her attention back to the books. "Let's see what we can make of this."

Jessica had always enjoyed a challenge, though, and the word puzzle before her was certainly that. They spent the rest of the morning translating the code on the first two pages of a twenty-page ledger.

A servant brought them chilled soup and croutons for lunch, and after a short break, they began working again.

It took the rest of the week to finish translating the entire inventory. The last day, they worked on it past eight in the evening. Jess finished the last item, laid down her quill pen, and shrugged her stiff shoulders.

Gregory looked up from his chair next to her. "No wonder you have a stiff neck," he said. "We've been at this for five straight hours. I'm famished, how about you?"

"No, I'm more tired than hungry," she admitted with a weary sigh.

"Please, Jessica. I knew we'd be finishing up tonight, so I had Cook prepare something special for us."

"You shouldn't have, Gregory," she replied as she straightened the ledger sheets. "I really am very tired."

He took her hand, pleading with his blue eyes. "I hate to eat alone. Besides, Cook will be very disappointed that all that work will be wasted."

She sighed. She was too tired to argue. They walked together to the dining hall with her hand tucked in the crook of his arm. She told herself that she should consider herself very fortunate to be the object of Gregory's attention. Working with him had not been unpleasant; and yet, the task at hand and all of Gregory's attentiveness had not been able to push Mac from her thoughts.

She felt Gregory's admiring gaze as they sat across from each other at one end of a long, formal dining table in a large rectangular room. She glanced about the room, taking in the gilded-frame mirrors hung along two walls above long buffet cabinets with ornately carved fronts. An elaborate silver candelabra sitting in the middle of the table cast a warm glow about them.

Gregory lifted his glass of wine. "To the lovely Miss Jessica McClaren, my undying gratitude for the hours of hard work in this overwhelming endeavor."

She smiled.

"Are you certain you won't have a little wine?" he asked.

She shook her head. "You'll probably think it's silly, but I hate to feel dizzy."

"I don't find it silly," he said. "You are the most level-headed young woman I have ever known."

A tiny smile curled her lips. "I daresay you've known too few women, then."

"Oh," he said. "I've known many. But none like you." The candlelight twinkled in his blue eyes.

They were interrupted by the maid bringing their meal.

"What's this?" he asked curtly, referring to the entree on his plate.

"It's Chicken Marengo, sir," the maid said timidly.

"I specifically ordered Tenderloin à la Madeira," he snapped.

"Sir," the girl answered, without meeting his gaze. "The supply wagon left today with all the butchered beef for the garrison at Ashton. Even if Cook had been able to catch them in time, it had already been salted."

He slammed his hand on the table, causing Jess and the maid both to jump. "I should have known," he said.

"Gregory, this looks delicious. Please don't be so upset," Jess said.

Anger flashed in his eyes as he turned to look at her. She saw his face soften, however. "Forgive me," he said, forcing a thin smile. "I'm afraid I still find it difficult to appreciate this rebellion. It can be such an inconvenience."

Jess held her tongue, but her nails cut into the palm of her hand as she clenched a fist, thinking that "inconvenient" would not have been a word she would have used to describe the war.

Their flaring tempers spoiled the ambience of their candlelight dinner for Jess, and though she kept up her end of the conversation, she grew more weary by the moment. When they had finished their meal, she thanked him and asked to be excused. Her assurances that an escort home would be unnecessary were disregarded, as Gregory insisted upon walking her down to her house.

The evening was lovely and cool; a hint of fall hung in the air as they strolled along the path that wound through the gardens between the mansion and the McClaren home.

"Well," Gregory said, "tomorrow we can begin packing it all up. I do hope you'll come up."

"I'm afraid not," she said as they reached the steps of the farmhouse. "I've been neglecting my chores here, and must catch up. Thank you anyway. Goodnight, Gregory."

He suddenly swept her in his arms and kissed her. She pushed against his strong embrace; he held her fast for a moment, then released her as suddenly as he had embraced her.

"I've been wanting to do that since the first time I saw you," he said softly.

She stepped back and glared angrily at him. "Goodnight, Gregory," she said; the words were spoken, not as a farewell, but as a command.

She did not return the next morning to watch the crating of the art treasures, but went riding instead. She was just coming out of the stable after her ride when Gregory appeared, carrying a bouquet of blue cornflowers.

He bowed deeply and handed the flowers to her. "I'll not apologize, because I'm not sorry I kissed you," he said bluntly. "But I do promise that if you will come up and help me keep an eye on the packing, I promise I will never do such a thing again. Without your permission, that is."

So surprised by his candor, she was uncertain of how to reply. Before she could answer, he smiled a rather teasing smile and said, "Of course, if by chance that kiss meant something to you after all and you would feel the slightest bit disconcerted to spend the day with me . . ."

She studied him for a long moment as she realized he had effectively boxed her in. If she refused to finish helping him with the task up at the mansion, he would think that she had been sufficiently affected by his kiss that she dare not trust herself in his presence. While returning to help oversee the packing would be what he had wanted in the first place, it would indicate that she gave no special significance to his kiss nor was nervous about being with him.

"I'll put these flowers in water first," she said firmly.

The next three days were spent packing priceless porcelain and china objects and crating up the Keene collection of Renaissance paintings.

Nothing further was said about that kiss, but Jess purposely kept a chair or desk between herself and Gregory at all times.

On the final day of packing, Gregory was overseeing the placement of the crates in the wagons as Jess finished with the paperwork. Collecting the original inventory ledger and the translated copy she had prepared, she started packing them in the valise Gregory had brought with him. Seeing a paper she had missed, she reached across the desk and knocked the open valise off the edge.

The case crashed to the floor and spilled its contents everywhere. Grumbling at her clumsiness, she began gathering up the scattered papers. She picked up an envelope and froze. The envelope was addressed to her, written in a hand she had not seen for years.

She hurriedly finished returning the other papers to the valise and stood at the desk, envelope in hand. It was sealed. She hesitated. Then, reminding herself that it did have her name on it, she opened the envelope to find a letter from Sir Gaston to her. It included the usual amenities and invited her family to come for Christmas, if possible. He was feeling well for a man of his advanced years and was keeping very busy. Her eyes came to rest on the last paragraph, and she read it twice.

"Mac was here today. He's on his way to Barleyville, taking a doctor friend of his home. The poor young lad has seen the last of his doctoring days, I fear. Even if he recovers from his wounds, he will never have the use of his left arm. The rout at Camden was terrible. Mac arrived three days after the battle and came across his friend and a small band of rebels who had escaped into the forest. He said if time and the tide of war permit, he will be coming to Cheltenham after his trip to Barleyville."

There was no mention of Little Sparrow. Of course, Sir Gaston might have withheld that bit of information to spare her feelings. Her heart fluttered briefly as she realized that Mac and Little Sparrow had not been traveling alone together as Gregory had suggested.

Gregory came striding into the room, mopping the perspiration from his face with a silk handkerchief, "It's too blessed hot for man or beast," he said. Halting several feet from the desk, he responded to her frown. "What is it, my dear?"

"The valise fell off of the desk, and I found this when I was picking up everything." She held up the letter.

His smile faded.

"Since it was addressed to me, I took the liberty of opening it. I hope you don't mind."

Recovering his poise quickly, he said, "Of course not. I must beg your forgiveness; I forgot I even had it. Grandfather gave it to me at the last minute."

190

He leaned forward and touched her hand. "Please, forgive me."

"Sir Gaston said Mac was taking his wounded friend home to Barleyville. You said nothing of anyone except Little Sparrow being with him."

"Oh, yes," he said nonchalantly. "He had two or three others with him, I believe."

"Gregory!" She was very angry with him and said in exasperation, "You made it sound as if Mac and Little Sparrow were the only ones traveling together."

He walked toward the window and looked out over the garden. "You're right, of course. It wasn't very decent of me, I'll grant you that." He turned and came back to stand beside her. "But I couldn't bear the idea of you throwing yourself away on someone like that."

She stiffened. "What do you mean 'someone like that'?"

He cleared his throat. "Well, he's neither here nor there; he's neither white nor red. He's in between. You can't want to be a part of that."

"Andrew Macklin is the bravest, most decent man I have ever known in my life. I don't see that anything else matters." The words tumbled out almost of their own accord and she wondered how long they had been milling around in her subconscious, waiting to be expressed.

"Jessica, please hear me out." He grasped her by the shoulders. "It was wrong of me to mislead you. I didn't want to hurt you. I told myself I'd make it up to you. I'd make you so happy, you'd forget all about Macklin. After all, the Indian girl *was* there with him. I wouldn't lie about that.

"Please, Jessica, try not to think too harshly of me." Placing his hand under her chin, he tilted her head up to face him. "It's not completely my fault, you know. I'll never forget the sight of you standing in the doorway that night, so lovely, so delicate. I've thought of little else since then. I'd do nearly anything to have you look at me the way you looked at him." His voice was low and strong, and his gaze was unblinking.

"Do you never give up?" she declared.

"Not in something so important to me. Please say you'll forgive me."

She studied him for a long moment, then finally sighed. "I suppose."

"Oh, Jessica, my dear." He pulled her close in a strong embrace. Having been on her guard the past three days, she quickly pushed him back.

"Jessie?"

They turned; Robbie stood in the doorway.

"Robbie!" she cried with relief. "Come and meet Gregory." She clasped her hands behind her back and nervously introduced the two young men.

They shook hands stiffly.

"It looks as though you're ready to leave," Robbie said in a no-nonsense tone. "Can I be of help?"

"Thank you, no." Gregory smiled broadly. "We'll be leaving at dawn, so I suppose I must bid you adieu now, my dear Jessica." He turned to her and kissed her hand. He nodded slightly to Robbie and left.

Jessica smiled at her brother. "Well, how was your trip?"

Turning toward her, his jaw tightened and his eyes flashed with silent fury.

"What's wrong?" she asked.

"We'll not talk about it here." He escorted her out of the study and out of the mansion. He marched along the path and stopped before reaching their house. Turning to face her squarely, he demanded, "What was all that about?"

"What do you mean?" Her own temper rose.

"Thank the Lord Mac didn't come back with me after all. He's off risking his neck in a desperate cause while you are playing pat-a-cake with a weaseling, rich coward."

"You've seen Mac?" she asked hopefully.

"Aye!"

He stood with his arms crossed and his jaw squared grimly.

"Is he all right?"

"Aye. Little it matters to you, apparently."

"Robert Ethan McClaren, how dare you say such a thing? Nothing went on between Gregory and me." Color rose in her face as she stood, hands on her hips, and matched her brother's indignant tone. "How dare you scold me, when I've not heard a word from Andrew Macklin in months—except to be told he's been galavanting around the country with some pretty Cherokee girl." She brushed away angry tears.

His voice softened, but his words still cut the air sharply. "I can't say I'm sure what you're talking about, but he had no girl with him in Barleyville. He was anxious to get back here to see you, but at the last minute he was ordered to King's Mountain. He didn't even have time to write a note. He asked if you still had that ring; when I told him you wore it, he smiled. He doesn't smile much, does he?"

"No," she said, suddenly quiet and touching the silver ring with two fingers. "Not nearly enough."

Seeing the faraway look in her eye, Robbie began to wonder if he'd misinterpreted the scene he'd stumbled into.

They walked on down to the house, calmly, without the slightest indication that only minutes before they had been snapping at each other.

Gregory left the next morning without seeing Jessica. She couldn't help feeling very relieved that he had gone. Being around him had been emotionally exhausting.

Still curious about the presence of Little Sparrow, Jess became confident that there must be some logical and innocent reason for her being with Mac. King's Mountain was not far, as the crow flies, to the northeast. Surely, he would soon be able to find time to make his way toward Cheltenham Farms.

The days continued to seem endlessly long as she waited to hear news of him. The only news, however, was discouraging information of British troops moving ever closer in their effort to control the entire colony.

18

September was always a busy month in the McClaren household; this year was no exception. The canning and meat preservation process consumed hour upon hour. There were candles to pour, soap to make, winter clothing to repair and clean or replace. All the bedding had to be turned out and freshened, and a general housecleaning done to prepare for the long winter months ahead.

News of a major British defeat at King's Mountain arrived in mid-October, a rare piece of good news from the war. Jess had tried to learn if Mac had been involved in the campaign, but she had not succeeded. One visiting militiaman was sure he had seen him riding northeast toward Philadelphia with dispatches right after the battle, and another had heard he had been wounded and captured before the battle began. Still another had been certain he was many miles away somewhere in Virginia. It seemed that few people really knew Andrew Macklin, though many had heard of his activities. Jess grew more and more exasperated at the unreliable rumors.

Two months after the victory of King's Mountain, a tenuous hope arose among colonials with the news that General Nathaniel Greene had been chosen to replace General Gates. By mid-December the hope grew into excitement, for under Greene's leadership, the militiamen and a small number of continental soldiers took a considerable toll on the British regulars.

With December also came the last-minute preparations for Christmas; the McClarens had accepted Sir Gaston's invitation to spend the holidays at Ellensgate.

The crisp December air was electric with the anticipation of the coming holiday. Jessica and her mother worked frantically, baking special treats and buying or making gifts. With money she had earned by training a Welsh pony to pull a neighboring plantation owner's pony cart for his children, Jess purchased some of her father's favorite pipe tobacco, a volume of Shakespeare's *Richard III* for Robbie, and two packets of flower seeds and a silk hanky for her mother. She embroidered Gregory's and Sir Gaston's initials on a fine linen handkerchief for each of them. She also knitted a woolen scarf, embroidered with Mac's initials, though she had no way of knowing if she would see him before the holidays.

The time to go to Ellensgate finally arrived. Since the shorter route over the gap was impassable due to heavy snowfall, they took the long way around by the post road.

During four days of steady travel, they struggled through muddy bogs two or three times without serious delay, and spent nights along the way with friends.

They were worn and tired by the time they arrived at Ellensgate, but it was nonetheless a joyous reunion.

The mansion was decorated with holly and pine boughs, candles, ribbons, and wreaths of fruits and nuts.

A huge tree, festooned with ribbons, baubles, and bows, adorned the main drawing room. In this room, before a roaring fire, they toasted each other with crystal cups of rich eggnog.

That evening, they all rode into the village for candle-light services in a tiny church. Jessica watched Sir Gaston with concern throughout the service; he appeared to have become even more frail. She was worried, too, that so much activity and excitement might be too taxing for him, but he seemed to thrive upon the merriment. He had even invited all his friends from the village to a New Year's Eve ball.

Christmas Day was filled with neighbors dropping in all day long to extend holiday greetings, exchange gifts, and share in the bountiful array of food specially pre-pared for the occasion. Gregory played the perfect host, although he commented to Jess that even this could not compare to the Christmas galas he had known in Paris.

Late that night, after the guests had gone, the last plum pudding had been devoured, and the last bits of Christ-mas wrappings put away, Jessica sat curled up before the fire in the library. The house was quiet, everyone else was asleep.

It had been a wonderful Christmas. Aside from the thinly veiled animosity between Robbie and Gregory, it had been the happiest family Christmas they had ever shared. But it had not been perfect.

She watched the flames lick hungrily about the wood in the huge fireplace and wondered where Mac had spent this Christmas. She had entertained hope all day that he might magically appear, but Christmas had passed and he had not come.

She turned the small card over in her hand and read it again. "This is not your only present, the best is yet to come. Your loving Grandpapa." The lovely emerald bracelet had been so much already, she couldn't imagine what else he could have meant. Sitting for a while longer she closed her eyes imagining Mac standing by the fireplace as he had that night six months before. As the months had passed without any communication from him at all, she had begun to wonder all over again if she had been imagining his attentions. Then touching the silver ring, she would remember that night in the moonlight, his words, the emotionless mask put aside, and the look in those deep brown eyes.

Weariness finally settled on her and she climbed the stairs to retire for the few remaining hours of night.

For the next week, Jess became involved in the preparations for the New Year's Eve ball. A string quartet from Jameston had been hired to provide the music. The cooks prepared the buffet, and the maids cleaned and polished everything that did not move.

Rob McClaren and Sir Gaston spent long afternoons locked in intense battles of wits over the chessboard. Robbie took advantage of the fine selection of books in the library. Gregory acted as tour guide, taking Jessica and her mother on scenic carriage rides throughout the countryside.

Mrs. McClaren watched with mixed emotions as the handsome gentleman paid gallant attention to her daughter. She was happy to see Jess enjoying herself, and should have been delighted that such a well-to-do young bachelor displayed such interest in her daughter; but something about Gregory disturbed her. Although Jessica didn't say anything, Mrs. McClaren could sense a wariness in her daughter whenever Gregory was present.

The day of the ball finally arrived. Jessica and Mrs. McClaren had both made new dresses for the occasion, and spent a long afternoon in preparation. Jessica's dress was a deep emerald green satin that made her skin look like blushed ivory, and gave her eyes a brilliant green lustre. The scooped neckline of the closely fitted bodice stretched from shoulder to shoulder and was accented by the delicate silver ring sliding along a green velvet ribbon. The flowing skirts rustled softly as she twirled in a circle for her mother. Mrs. McClaren, who looked ten years younger in her new lavender satin gown, smiled gleefully at her daughter. Jessica could not remember the last time her mother had been so excited and happy.

The night was clear and cold. The lavish buffet was in place and the musicians tuned up; chairs lined the ballroom.

People began arriving shortly after dark. The musicians played a jig to set the festive mood, followed by the strains of a popular minuet.

Jessica had never attended a ball before, and she blushed when Gregory asked her for the first dance. She declined his invitation at first, admitting to him that she had never danced a minuet.

He dismissed her reluctance with a wave of his hand. "I'll lead you through the steps. It will be easy for you."

"Just remember," she said nervously, "if I embarrass you before all your friends, you were warned."

"My friends are in Austria. What these people think doesn't matter one whit."

She blinked at him, surprised that after nearly ten years, he still considered only those in his native Austria to be his friends. She didn't have time to give it more thought because he swept her out onto the dance floor.

They made a handsome couple. Gregory cut a dashing figure in his dark blue split-tail coat, waistcoat, and breeches. His brilliant white shirt sported a wide ascot ruffling down the front. Jessica focused all her attention on following his steps, and did not notice the knowing looks and admiring nods people exchanged as she and Gregory danced.

The dance had nearly finished when a sudden draft rushed in from the outer hall. Murmurs and quiet gasps punctuated the music.

Gregory stopped and Jess looked up at him. A grim tightness appeared around his mouth; she turned to see the cause of his unpleasant expression.

Mac strode across the floor, clad in a coat made of red and ivory blanket wool over a suit of buckskin. He carried a hat of lynx fur. A similarly dressed young man walked beside him, obviously feeling very much out of place.

"Merry Christmas, Poppit," Sir Gaston whispered as he passed on his way to greet Mac.

She wanted to run to Mac, but her feet seemed rooted to the spot. He looked a bit leaner in the face, and tired; his eyes, however, still sparkled with vitality and intensity. He crossed the room to stand before her.

"Friends and neighbors," Sir Gaston called, halting the music. "May I have your attention." It was an unnecessary request. Everyone's attention had been focused on the two strangers from the moment they entered the room. "I want to introduce my very good friend, Andrew Macklin, and his fellow soldier, Jim Quidley. I'm delighted he was able to accept my invitation. We South Carolinians owe these young men and their fellow patriots a great debt of gratitude." Polite applause greeted the late entrants to the party, and after a few moments the music commenced again.

Mac and Jess gave no indication that they had heard Sir Gaston's words; their attention remained riveted upon each other's face.

"Hello, Jess," he said quietly.

Her voice was barely more than a whisper. "Hello, Mac."

"Well, Macklin," Gregory interrupted, "you know how to make an entrance, don't you? I'm afraid I no longer have the suit I loaned to you last time you were here," Gregory continued, "but I'm sure I have something suitable for you to change into."

"Don't worry yourself, Starkheim; we're not staying," Mac replied with a calm, confident tone. "I just stopped by to acknowledge your grandfather's invitation and pay my respects to him and the McClarens."

Mac noticed disappointment cloud Jess's gray-green eyes and started to say something when Gregory interrupted again. "I see you don't have your pretty little Indian friend with you this time," Gregory said.

Noticing Jess glance down at her hands to avoid looking at him, Mac wondered what Gregory might have been telling her. While he would have gladly cracked his knuckles on that smug Austrian jaw, he summoned the entire resource of self-control within him, and said simply, "No." He stepped closer to Gregory with a dangerous look in his eye and said, still very calmly, "If you don't mind, I'd like to speak to Jess alone."

Gregory hesitated, but decided he wasn't prepared for a serious confrontation. He nodded politely and stepped back, speaking to Mac's companion about the location of the punch bowl.

When he had gone, Jess looked up at Mac again. "I'm glad to see you're well, Mac."

"I see you're still wearing the ring. It does look better on a velvet ribbon than a rawhide string."

Her hand unconsciously went to the ring hanging around her neck on the green velvet ribbon.

"Have you come to reclaim it?" she asked, wishing she could know what he was thinking.

"No," he said quietly.

"I wish you would have written, Mac." She tried to sound very casual. "Robbie and I have been worried about you."

"I haven't had much time for letter writing," he said. "I wasn't sure what to write, anyway." He noticed several of the people dancing by looking askance at his rough frontiersman clothes, wondering why someone like him was talking so seriously to someone of Jess's obvious refinement.

Jess's words reclaimed his attention. "A simple 'I'm all right' would have been sufficient." She caught herself, realizing that she was wasting precious moments scolding him. "Are you allowed to say where you're bound now?"

He nodded. "I've been attached to William Washington's cavalry unit under Dan Morgan. Jim and I are to meet up with them this side of the Cowpens. Tarleton's getting ready to cross the Broad River and Morgan has chosen the Cowpens as the place to try to stop him."

She didn't want to think about what he was heading into. The name of Lt. Col. Banastre Tarleton was enough to raise the hair on the neck of any Carolinian; his cruelty and vicious military tactics had earned him the title of "Butcher."

They spoke about the Bartons and their son, Franklin, who would recover from the wounds he had sustained at Camden, although he had lost complete use of his left arm.

"Has Ettinsmoor been behaving himself?" she asked.

"He's a good partner." He finally smiled and her heartbeat quickened. "You look wonderful," he told her. "These clothes suit you much better than Robbie's old cast-offs. But they wouldn't be suitable for a river crossing, would they?"

There was the smile he had been waiting to see. The picture he would take with him forever, for this would be their last meeting. Her smile was suddenly gone and he realized she could tell he meant to say a final good-bye. He gripped his hat tightly, resisting the temptation to take her in his arms. "You belong here, Jess. This is what you're suited for."

She started to protest, but Gregory suddenly appeared, carrying two cups of punch. He handed one to Jess and kept the other for himself.

"Well, Jessica, my dear, have you told Macklin what a wonderful time we had working together at Cheltenham last September?" He turned his gaze on Mac. "She was remarkable. She did a marvelous job with the inventory records, and it only took us five days and one evening to accomplish it. I'll never forget that walk in the garden. Will you, Jessica?"

Jess cast a fearful glance at Mac. She saw him take a deep breath and let it out slowly, his patience nearly gone.

Gregory seemed quite pleased with himself about it. Jess turned to Mac to explain just as Jim Quidley came over and whispered something to Mac, who nodded in reply.

"We have to be going." He turned to Jessica and took her hand. "Jess, I hope you have a very happy New Year. Good-bye."

"Happy New Year, Mac. God be with you." She inspected the lines of his face and searched the dark depths of his eyes. Her throat tightened as he turned to shake hands and exchange a few words with Robbie on his way out.

As she watched him leave, her breathing quickened and her mind reeled. Gathering her skirts, she hurried after him in a flurry of rustling green satin.

When she came out onto the portico, he had already mounted Ettinsmoor. She planted her feet and called to him.

"Andrew Macklin!" she called angrily.

He turned Ettinsmoor back.

"How dare you?" she declared.

"You'd better get back inside," he said sternly. "It's freezing out here."

She stood as if rooted to the spot, her clenched hands poised on her hips in exasperation.

Mac dismounted and came to stand before her. "What's the matter?" he asked, bewildered by her outburst.

"How dare you decide what I'm best suited for? I'm not some porcelain doll to be put up in a glass case, and I'll thank you very kindly to stop telling me where I belong."

He stared down at her, completely baffled. "I only said what I thought would be best for you," he admitted.

She shivered with cold. "If you think this is best for me, then you know less about me than I thought." Her voice softened. "Perhaps *I've* been mistaken about how . . . how you feel." Little puffs of steam punctuated her

204

words. Her teeth chattered, and she folded her arms across her chest.

He touched her face lightly. "You're not mistaken," he said.

He held open one side of his coat and enclosed her in its warmth. "There are a lot of things I want to say, Jess, but there are some matters that need to be settled first. I couldn't leave you to face the possibility of another ordeal like the one you faced when . . . Evan didn't come back. It seemed best to leave you free."

She spoke in a whisper looking up into his dark eyes. "I didn't want to care about you. I didn't want to love you, but by the time I realized what was happening, it was too late. Perhaps it was too late the moment I first saw you."

Hugging her tighter, he pressed a kiss into her soft, fragrant hair, but he did not say the words she longed to hear. He finally released her. "Go back inside before you catch cold," he said. "Jim and I still have a few miles to cover tonight."

She searched his face, longing for him to say something more, then suddenly remembered. "Oh, wait a minute. Please. I have something for you." She hurried back into the house and into the library. She snatched up the gift she had made for him and quickly returned to where he stood, waiting.

"I made it myself," she said breathlessly as she handed it to him.

He opened it carefully, handed the ribbon and paper back to her, and held it up to admire it. He wrapped the scarf around his neck and said, "Thank you, Jess." He stepped backwards and started to turn. After a moment's hesitation, he reached out, took her in his arms and kissed her with a passion that warmed the frosty winter air. Jessica's eyes remained closed as he released her and turned away to swing up into the saddle.

Opening her eyes and looking at him through her tears, she said, "I love you, Mac."

He touched his forehead in a casual salute and turned his horse down the lane. He had not spoken the words she had wanted to hear, but the look in his dark eyes had said it all. She turned quickly, steeling herself against the wrenching pain of seeing him riding away once more. Only this time she knew with an inexplicable certainty that he would return to her.

She stopped short before entering the mansion. A figure darkened the library window. Gregory watched her with a grim expression. She gasped; for a split second, she had imagined it was Evan she saw standing there in grim disapproval. Shaking her head, she frowned at her skittishness and hurried inside.

Once back inside, she sought out Sir Gaston to place a kiss on his cheek and thank him for her Christmas present. He smiled with satisfaction and seemed very pleased with his role as Cupid.

Gregory joined them as Sir Gaston said emphatically, "Macklin is a good man, Poppit. You couldn't find better, rich or poor, if you tried."

Sir Gaston and Jessica glanced simultaneously at Gregory, whose blue eyes smoldered with anger.

Gregory haughtily excused himself. Moments later, he left the party.

Gregory stormed down to the stables on the pretext of checking the horses. Once he'd regained his composure, he returned to the house, using the rear entrance across the terrace. Passing the windows, he glanced in to see Jessica standing with his grandfather and her brother, Robbie.

A twinge of envy cast a dark look in his eyes as he wondered how a young girl from peasant stock could so easily gain his grandfather's approval as if she were his own flesh and blood, when it had always been so difficult for him.

Suddenly she smiled that radiant smile and his heart softened. *Who could resist such a smile,* he sighed to himself. He drew from his pocket the handkerchief she had embroidered for his Christmas present. Carefully running a finger over the neatly worked stitching, he smiled and began watching her through the window once more.

Staring at her with the grandeur of the ballroom surrounding her, he decided that surely there must be some royal blood flowing in that exquisite form from some lost generation along the line. Yes, he was sure of it and therefore it was his duty as a gentleman and heir to one of the great houses of Austria to save this fair young lady from making a terrible mistake. He must do everything in his power to win her hand and take her home to Austria where she would become his wife and learn the duties and privileges of a baroness. It would not be long before she had forgotten completely about this primitive place and especially Andrew Macklin.

His decision made, he squared his shoulders and retired to his room to consider his strategy for this noble challenge.

Mac fell in next to Jim and they rode down the drive toward the gate.

"My oh my, what a magical night," Jim declared with a wide grin.

Mac's mind and heart were still reeling, so he didn't hear his friend until Jim repeated the words. "Yessiree," Jim said louder this time, "a magical night. Have you ever seen the stars so bright?"

Mac glanced up into the star-filled heavens. Through the clear, crisp air, he saw the sky like an indigo blanket covered with millions of brilliant crystal lights. He had to agree, they'd never been brighter.

"I got a present once," Jim went on. "Course, it wasn't from such a pretty little lady."

Mac raised the end of the neck scarf to his nose and breathed in the delicate fragrance of lilac that lingered there reminding him of the wonderful scent of Jess's hair as he had held her close just a few moments earlier. Jim was reminiscing on about some long lost love, but Mac's thoughts were filled with Jessica. Her words declaring her love for him echoed in his brain, blocking out the sound of Jim's voice.

Suddenly a discordant note sounded as he heard Jim mention the name "Starkheim." Glancing over at his friend, he frowned slightly as Jim grinned and said, "Thought that'd get your attention. I wouldn't worry none about that high falutin' fella, though. For some strange reason that little lady seems blind to anyone but you."

"I'm just glad Robbie's there to keep an eye on that conniver," Mac admitted grimly.

"Yessiree, he's a smooth talker, that one. And all them fine duds . . . Could turn a girl's head, I s'pose."

Mac looked at Jim sharply, but could hear the grin in his voice as his friend said, "I guess the thing to do is get on over to our troops and get this war over with so you can get back to your lady while she's still interested."

With that Jim gave a boisterous whoop and shouted, "The lady loves him!" His horse bolted forward and Mac spurred Ettinsmoor to follow. Mac echoed the war whoop and the two soldiers thundered down the post road toward the rendezvous with their troops.

The joy swelling in Mac's heart made him feel like he could conquer the world. What was a mere army of thirteen hundred redcoats compared to the fact that Jessica McClaren just declared she loved him. There would be plenty of time to consider the war in the days to come, but for the moment, nothing could dim his happiness.

19

A light snow had begun falling silently outside a shelter of brush piled across two beams cut from saplings. The beams had been laid across the tops of two boulders, creating a roof for a shelter against the weather.

A horse stood several feet away, tethered in the shelter of a large pine tree. The animal had the size and contours of a thoroughbred, but his coat was thick and rough because of the winter cold. The horse's right foreleg barely touched the ground; a bandage wrapped around it held mosses and mud as a poultice against an injury.

A thin curl of smoke escaped the small fire inside the shelter. On a bed of evergreen boughs, a young man huddled in his ivory and red wool coat. He held his right arm close to his chest in a sling. His tanned face was pale.

He watched the horse from beneath the fur fringe of his lynx-skin hat. "Jess wouldn't like to see you standing out in the weather," he murmured. "When I feel a little better, I'll see if we can find better shelter."

Ettinsmoor made a low whuffling noise.

"It's your own fault." He winced as he moved slightly. "You and foxes . . . I swear. You're lucky I didn't shoot you on the spot."

Ettinsmoor whuffled again and shook his mane.

"All right, so you've gotten me out of some bad scrapes," he said. "I guess everyone is entitled to some weakness; but if you don't rid yourself of this fear of foxes, someone's going to get killed."

His arm and leg throbbed, and hunger gnawed at his empty stomach. He still had some beef jerky, hardtack, and a handful of walnuts, but he wanted to save them in case it snowed too hard, making it impossible to get to the river to fish. It had been a long cold day; Jim had ridden away before dawn that morning.

He began to drift off to sleep. The throbbing in his arm roused him, and he tried to remember the date.

The morning of January 17, 1781, he and Jim had been waiting with William Washington's 125-man cavalry unit. They were positioned out of sight, ready to be called into battle at the crucial moment. The little hill behind which they were concealed was one of two in that place where early cattle drovers had stopped to rest and graze their cattle on the way to eastern markets.

It was a level, lightly wooded area close to the Pacolet River, practically in the shadow of King's Mountain.

Couriers and agents were not usually involved in battle, as communication between forces was essential and they must be moving between the different groups with orders and maneuvering directions. However, with a group of just over eight hundred continentals facing thirteen hundred redcoats, every available man, musket, horse, and saber were pressed into service. So it was that Mac and Jim were to do double duty that day.

They had waited, listening to the militia, lined up in three waves, fire three volleys into Tarleton's advancing troops. The experienced continentals of J. E. Howard's Delawares and Marylanders had then charged with their muskets and bayonets ready.

Andrew Pickens's militia poured out from the cut between the two hills, and Kirkwood's regulars from Delaware struck at the right and rear of the redcoat forces.

British dragoons tried to turn Morgan's left flank, but Washington's cavalry drove the dragoons back. The British broke and ran.

Tarleton was in a blind rage at the rear of this fleeing band, trying to rally his dragoons for another charge, but Washington's men came smashing into their midst. A nightmare of slashing sabers, screaming horses, flashing black powder, blood, killing, and dying ensued.

Mac had seen Washington clashing with Tarleton himself, when Washington's horse went down. The continental officer survived the fall, but Tarleton broke away, escaping with only a small portion of his force.

When the patriot trumpets sounded recall, the battle ended; it had lasted less than an hour. Mac had always been impressed with Daniel Morgan, "the old Wagoner," as he was nicknamed, because he was a master strategist and leader of men. He had seemed to understand the curious blend of men under him and, unlike the incompetent Gates, had used each facet of his small force to its fullest potential. The Cowpens had been a crippling defeat for a British force much superior in number, supplies, and experience.

There had not been time to rest upon their laurels. Everyone knew that once Tarleton returned to Cornwallis, the general himself would come in hot pursuit with his vastly superior force.

Morgan, therefore, struck off toward the fords on the Catawba nearly one hundred miles away to rejoin General Nathaniel Greene. The Americans had captured eight hundred muskets, essential stores, and nearly eight hundred prisoners.

Mac and Jim Quidley had been ordered to hurry ahead to carry news of the battle to General Greene, who was waiting at the Cheraws on the Pedee River, 125 miles to the southeast.

The two men had come halfway, nearing the crossing of the Wateree, when calamity struck. Their trail cut through a wide stand of pines growing along the course of the river. Mac was in the lead, on Ettinsmoor, when suddenly a reddish brown streak cut in front of the big stallion. Ettinsmoor shied and swerved, smashing into a tree, causing Mac to break his right arm and a couple of ribs, and bruise his hip and leg so badly he could hardly stand. Ettinsmoor had also pulled a leg muscle of his own.

Jim helped Mac set the broken bone between his elbow and wrist; it was a clean break and easily—although painfully—set. He had then helped Mac construct the brush shelter and gathered enough wood to last several days; the shelter was only fifty feet from the river's edge, so Mac would have plenty of water. Following Mac's instructions, Jim had also gathered some mosses and mud to make a healing poultice for Ettinsmoor's injured leg.

Jim had fixed a bite to eat and rested a couple of hours before he left to carry the dispatches on by himself.

"Keep your powder dry, Delaware," Jim had called as he rode away.

"Watch your scalp, Irish," Mac returned.

The snow stopped again and the night sky began to clear. The temperature dropped. Mac added another piece of wood to the fire.

Since last June and the trip to Charleston, he thought of Jess every time he added wood to a fire—a lovely young lady dressed in an old suit of clothes three sizes too big for her, looking at him from under a floppy, wide-brimmed hat. He could see her steady, cool gaze and her quick smile. He could almost hear her quiet, gentle manner of speaking. He even smiled at the remembrance of her hard-headed determination.

He smiled, too, as he pictured her that New Year's Eve two weeks earlier.

He envisioned her look when Starkheim had mentioned Little Sparrow; he could only guess what that flattering conniver had told her. He only hoped he would someday have the chance to tell her the truth, if she needed to hear it.

Perhaps, when he told her about Little Sparrow, she could explain to him about what happened with Gregory at Cheltenham. The very thought of Gregory near Jessica made him turn over restlessly, which sent a sharp pain stabbing through his arm and down through his rib cage and right leg.

He had gone to Sir Gaston's party prepared to tell her a final good-bye. However, the vision of her loveliness and the look in her eyes as she watched him caused the memories of their time together to come rushing in on him and he couldn't imagine why he had planned to make that night their final meeting. Then as he had watched the way the people at the party looked at him, he remembered the reason. How could he even think of asking her to go through life with people staring at her?

She could have her pick of any young man she wanted; why would she settle for him? It wasn't a self-deprecating thought. He knew his strengths and weaknesses, and he knew he could stand equal to any man, red or white; but that was a man's way of thinking. He wasn't sure how a young lady like Jessica McClaren would feel about it.

Of course, he had thought he *did* know several months earlier during a strange encounter with Little Sparrow. Returning from the east, having just been assigned to act as courier for General Gates, he had been allowed time to stop at Iron Mountain to visit his grandparents. Upon arriving at Camden, he had found Gates's command cut to shreds. Franklin, being seriously wounded, begged him to take him home to Barleyville before he died.

It was then that Little Sparrow appeared on the scene. She had followed Mac from Iron Mountain. Her uncle, Quiet Bear, had encouraged Mac to court his niece, but he had not been so inclined. Little Sparrow had always worried him a little; even as a child she had been bitter toward whites because her family, like many of the Cherokee at Iron Mountain, had been pushed off their land. The bitterness had been fed by her parents and had poisoned her spirit, leaving her a cold young woman.

She appeared unexpectedly at Camden, soon after Mac had found Franklin so seriously wounded. That night at the campfire, she asked him bluntly if Jessica would be able to truly accept the fact that he was part Indian. Mac, absorbed in giving Franklin a drink, answered absently that he thought Jess would be able to accept that better than Little Sparrow would ever be able to accept his Scottish background. Little Sparrow had accompanied Mac's party as far as Ellensgate before turning back to Iron Mountain.

The mental journey through his memories helped to pass the long hours of the night as he fought pain and tried to sleep.

For the next two days, Mac rested, rising only long enough to move Ettinsmoor to another patch of dry grass and give him a handful of oats. Suffering from mild shock, Mac needed time to regain his strength. By the time he felt up to trying to find a more sheltered place, the snow had finally stopped, covering the forest with a light blanket of white.

The third day after the accident broke clear, with the sun shining in a brilliant blue sky. It didn't take long for the snow to melt away in faint mists of steam. With his right arm broken, Mac struggled to perform even the simplest task. He hobbled on his badly bruised leg to the river's edge and, after several clumsy tries, speared a sizable trout. After cleaning it, he skewered it on the stick and cooked it over the fire.

The task had taken him so long to accomplish that it was nearly dark when the fish was ready to eat. Just as he was preparing to take a bite, a sudden crash in the brush startled him. He reached for his tomahawk.

A young man suddenly broke into the clearing, staggering, swinging his arms wildly back and forth in front of him. Mac struggled to his feet, and lifted the tomahawk in his left hand. The intruder wore the red coat of a British regular.

"Who is it?" the soldier cried. "Help me, please. You have food? Help me."

Mac could see dark powder burns on the young soldier's face and realized that he was blind. Dropping the tomahawk, he grabbed the young man's arm with his left hand.

"Here. Here I am. Take it easy."

He clutched frantically at Mac's arm and said, "Please help me, sir. I could smell your dinner cooking. I haven't eaten for days." He sank to the ground and collapsed.

Mac dragged him closer to the fire and covered him with his blanket. Pouring some water from his canteen onto a handkerchief, he carefully dabbed the young soldier's face. The stranger slowly regained consciousness.

Mac eventually helped the stranger sit up to drink from the canteen; he then placed some of the cooked fish in his hands. Mac noted something vaguely familiar about him. He was hardly more than a boy, no more than seventeen. When the boy had eaten, he lay back and aimed his sightless stare toward the sky.

"Were you with the dragoons?" the boy asked.

"No," Mac answered. "Where were you when this happened?"

"I'm an artillery man. Just promoted last week. Sergeant Arnham put in a good word for me with his good mate, Sergeant-Major Effington. We were running along trying to get to the fords of the Catawba when we were hit on our flank by a band of militia. We swung our grasshopper around to meet their attack; she must've had too much powder in her, because there was a flash and a loud clap of thunder. The next thing I knew, I woke up and I . . . I couldn't . . . see. I must've been knocked aside. They passed on by me. I've been wandering ever since, trying to find our men . . . someone . . . anyone. Are you with the fusiliers, then?"

"No."

"Oh, no," the young boy moaned. He ran his hand through his dark brown hair. There were bramble scratches on his face and hands, and tears in his coat.

"Mother Cooke, your Richard boy is dead. You're one of . . . them . . . them rebels, aren't you?"

"Yes," Mac answered. "But just steady now, I'm not going to hurt you."

"What're you gonna do with me?" Cooke asked.

"Nothing for the time being. I'm a bit worse for wear right now, myself. I think we could both use a little rest before we think much about going anywhere."

"You mean you aren't going to shoot me or run me through?"

"Not likely," Mac answered. He helped the young soldier to sit and take another drink from the canteen.

"I've heard you Americans give no quarter to prisoners."

"It was Tarleton who massacred American soldiers under a white flag," Mac said grimly. "We don't harm wounded boys who stumble into our camps, half starved. Just lie back and rest easy."

The boy lay back and pulled the blanket up over himself. He turned his head from side to side at every sound.

"I'm the only one here, soldier," Mac said. "My horse is picketed over to the right there. The river is just off to the left about fifty feet. I'm sure you can tell where the fire is by the heat of it. It's been dark about an hour, I'd say, so you may hear a wolf or two or a coon chattering, but they're only the forest creatures about. They won't come near the fire.

"The sky is clear, no moon, but plenty of stars." As he continued to describe their surroundings in his calm, low voice, he could see the young soldier begin to relax, little by little.

Before long, the boy fell asleep. Mac slept lightly, wondering if the young soldier would be the object of a search. It seemed doubtful, if he had been wandering for days

218

and his regiment had been in pursuit of Greene. That meant it would be up to Mac to decide the boy's fate . . . a boy about the same age as his brother, Roger, had been when he marched off to Savannah.

They stayed at the campsite for the next four days. Mac's leg was nearly well and he was able to get around better. He speared more fish, snared a rabbit and a squirrel, and found some nutritious, edible roots. With the ample supply of food, Private Cooke began to regain his strength. He was soon feeling well enough to walk around the camp aided by a walking stick Mac had given him.

Mac revealed nothing about his identity other than to instruct the boy to call him Mac. He realized, however, that the soldier looked familiar because he was the one who had almost searched him the time the redcoat sergeant had stopped by their camp when Jess and he were on the way to Charleston. Sergeant Arnham was now stationed at Fort Winnsboro, about twenty miles to the southwest. Cooke had been stationed there, but had grown bored with the tedious routine of the fort. He had longed for the excitement of battle and had pestered his sergeant until he was finally transferred to an artillery company.

The snow was holding off, though a gusty north wind chilled the air. Their camp was well sheltered from the wind, so they were fairly comfortable. Another two days of recovery time would probably be sufficient, and then Mac needed to be on his way.

Not having any idea where his fellow rebels would be, Mac had decided that the only thing he could do with the young redcoat would be to take him over to Fort Winnsboro. It should be simple enough; he would take him to within sight of the fort and point him in the right direction, while staying out of sight himself. The sentries would see Cooke and come out to help him into the fort, where he would be back with his old company.

When he told Cooke of his plan, the young soldier ducked his head, blinking back tears of gratitude.

They broke camp and began walking southwest. Ettinsmoor's leg was nearly whole again, but Mac didn't want to risk straining it before it was completely healed, so the two men walked along on either side of the horse. Cooke held on to the saddle for guidance.

They reached Winnsboro the next day about midafternoon. Mac stood at the edge of the forest and looked across the wide open area surrounding the palisades of the fort. The wind had subsided, and the early February day was chilly, but clear.

"The sun's shining bright, so they won't have any trouble seeing you," Mac said. "You'll be crossing about two hundred yards of open field. It's mostly short dry grass—only a few rocks here and there. There's a creek bed running off to your right, but if you keep walking straight so you feel the sun square on your face, you won't go near it.

"Well, that's about it, lad," he said, drawing in a deep breath of the brisk air. "Good luck to you, Private."

"Mac, I don't know how I can ever rightly thank you. I just want ya to know I'm glad I'm out of the fighting so there's no chance I'd ever be firing in your direction. My mother will be ever so grateful for sending her only boy back home to her." He groped for Mac's hand and gripped it firmly.

"Go on, now," Mac said. "Remember what I said about the sun."

He turned the young soldier in the right direction and the boy started out haltingly, swinging his walking stick back and forth, searching the path before him.

Mac watched from the cover of the trees as Cooke made his way slowly across the open field. He was doing fine until, suddenly, before he had gone quite halfway, he stumbled. He fell down, his walking stick flying from his hand. He lifted up on his hands and knees and began groping desperately for the stick. Soon, having become totally disoriented, he began calling for help.

Mac watched apprehensively as Cooke finally stumbled to his feet and began walking again, directly toward the icy, swift-running stream.

Mac hesitated only a moment before leaving the protective cover of the trees. "Cooke, stop," he called, running up behind him.

"Go back. They'll see you, Mac," Cooke called, turning toward the sound of his voice.

It was too late, they had been seen, not by the sentries, but by a returning hunting party which bore down on them from about a hundred yards away.

"What's happening?" Cooke demanded as he clutched at Mac's coat sleeve.

"They've seen us," Mac answered grimly, knowing it was futile to try to run.

"Don't worry," Cooke said nervously. "Sergeant Arnham will speak for you. You'll see, it will be all right."

The moment they entered the gates, Cooke began calling for Sergeant Arnham.

"What's the ruckus here?" came the gravelly voice of the old sergeant making his way through the crowd. "Cooke? Well, I'll be." The sergeant winced and rubbed his chin in frustration at Cooke's condition. "How'd it happen, boy?"

Cooke quickly explained, including the part of the story of Mac's lifesaving help.

"Mac?" The sergeant pondered a moment, studying him curiously. "McClaren, isn't it? Of course, I remember you, lad. On the road to Charleston, it was."

Mac nodded a bit hesitantly and shook hands with the sergeant. As Sergeant Arnham was thanking him for bringing the young soldier in, someone began pushing through the crowd around them.

"McClaren, my eye," a gruff voice said. "That's Andrew Macklin. He's one of Washington's agents."

Mac turned to see Malcome Waite, an old adversary from the early days of the war. They had been acquainted in Lexington, and had chosen opposite sides from the very beginning.

Though Cooke objected loudly, Sergeant Arnham studied Mac's face for a moment. When Mac didn't dispute his accuser, Arnham stood silently by as Mac was roughly escorted to the guardhouse.

Someone grabbed his hat as a trophy. As he was pushed into a cell, Waite stood in front of him.

"I always knew you'd come to the end of a rope," he said. "You sure won't be needing this then, will you?" Grabbing the scarf Jess had made, Waite yanked it away. Mac caught it with his right hand, but Waite knocked against his broken arm and grabbed it away. Mac clutched his arm and lunged after the thief, only to be pushed back by two guards.

The door clanged shut and the group filed out, laughing at the prospect of another hanging.

222

Mac found himself in one of two barred cells in a small, rough log cabin with a low beam ceiling and dirt floors. The only furniture was a rough-hewn cot spread with one moth-eaten blanket.

Just after dark, a noise drew his attention to the single window in the cell.

A whispered voice spoke his name.

Mac looked out through the bars and saw Private Cooke standing in the shadows.

"I'm sorry," the young man said dismally.

"Move along, soldier," came a low warning from a guard coming around the corner.

Mac watched the young man feel his way along the wall and wondered what the coming years would hold for Cooke.

He lay back down on the cot and closed his eyes, thinking he'd probably been in tougher spots, but he couldn't remember when. The irony of the situation didn't escape him. He had lived with the possibility of capture and execution for his activities for the Continental army for five years. This capture, however, had been the result of helping a British soldier.

A cold draft swirled in through the barred window; he pulled his coat collar up around his ears. Without the woolen scarf that Jessica had made for him, the chill seemed more penetrating. He closed his eyes and the memory of her face, the touch of her hand, the sound of her voice brought him comfort and pain at the same time. His arms ached to hold her close once more, to hear her speak again. He began to pray for her and for some miracle that would allow them to one day be together again.

That night in the darkness of that cold cell, in that state between sleeping and waking, he could almost hear the strong, deep voice of his Grandfather Macklin reading the Scriptures, as he had after every evening meal, in his thick Gaelic accent: "Even the youths shall faint and be weary, and the young men shall utterly fall: But they that wait upon the Lord shall renew their strength; they shall mount up with wings as eagles; they shall run, and not be weary; and they shall walk and not faint." Isaiah 40 was one of Mac's favorite passages. As a boy, he had imagined being taken up by the wings of an eagle and soaring over the forest and fields; he thought those wings would certainly come in handy right now. He finally fell asleep, satisfied that whatever came, he would be given the strength he needed to face up to it.

In the morning, Sergeant Arnham paid him a visit.

"So you're not really a McClaren, heh?" Arnham said, leveling a steady gaze at Mac through the bars. "I never have appreciated being made a fool of. I just can't believe Rob McClaren's little girl would be mixed up in this business."

"She wasn't in it by her choice," Mac said, meeting the Sergeant's direct look. "She felt especially bad about lying to you, but she was just protecting me—and you too, really."

"How do you figure that one?"

"How do you think Rob McClaren would feel about the man who arrested his daughter for harboring a spy?"

He studied Mac for a long time. "Doris Cooke begged me with tears in her eyes to take care of her son. The young fool couldn't stand the quiet life of the fort. He wanted to be in on the action. So I finally gave in, thinking the artillery group would at least keep him out of the front line. He's been like a son to me; and whether you're a McClaren or no, I'm grateful to you for saving his life."

He turned and left.

The third morning of his captivity, Mac looked out of the barred window at the wide blue sky above the palisade walls. Malcome Waite came strolling by.

"Thanks again for the scarf, Macklin," he taunted. "It'll keep me nice and warm while we go help General Cornwallis catch Greene up on the Dan. Sorry I can't stay around for your little party."

Mac gripped the bars of the window in anger and was quickly reminded of his broken arm.

Five days later, just after dark, Sergeant Arnham paid another visit.

"Afraid your time's up, lad. Things aren't going well for the general. Your militiamen and General Greene have led him on a mighty costly goose chase. Tempers here are riding high and they're looking for a scapegoat. Looks like you're it." The old sergeant stretched forth his hand to Mac. "Just thought I'd come over and tell you good-bye."

Mac hesitated. "Remember what I said about Jess McClaren. She wasn't at fault."

"I'll remember, lad. Now won't you shake my hand in parting?"

Mac took his hand. The older man turned away. Mac's hand had closed around a slender metal object. Without even looking, he knew it was the key to his cell door.

"One thing, Macklin," the sergeant stopped and turned again. "Private Cooke has been making sure they're taking good care of your horse. I think he's down there right now, so you don't have to worry about him. His leg seems to be fine. God have mercy on you, lad. The hangman will be waiting for you in the morning. Good-bye."

Arnham left with the guard. Mac heard him say, "How about a couple of hands of rummy, Otis?"

"Well, I don't suppose a couple of hands would hurt. It gets pretty dull just sitting here."

"Right. I'll go get my coin pouch; you go get the cards."

"But Sarge, I can't leave here," the guard said.

"Five minutes won't hurt anything. He hasn't given you any trouble yet, has he? Go on. I'll meet you back here in five minutes."

Mac heard their footsteps fade. He quickly worked the key in the lock. The area out front seemed to be clear as he ducked out the door and around to the side. During his stay, he had learned that the stables were around the back of the guardhouse and close to the rear gate. He moved silently from one building to the next, keeping to the shadows. All the men appeared to be in the dining hall, leaving the grounds nearly deserted.

He could see the lantern in the doorway of the stables and heard voices. He crept to the wall around the corner from the stable door.

The two in the stable were arguing; Mac heard Cooke's voice.

"I'll bet two shillings I can saddle the American's horse," the private said.

"Yer on," the other man answered quickly. "This will be the easiest two shillings I ever won. That horse is so jumpy, he'll never let you do it."

"Just hand me the bridle and stand by with the blanket and saddle."

Mac waited in the shadows, listening. Voices drifted from the dining hall across the parade ground. The men were beginning to come out. He wasn't going to be able to wait any longer, if he was to make it at all. Quickly ducking around the doorway, he crouched down behind the first stall. Cooke had Ettinsmoor out in the center aisle with the bridle and bit in place. He was just getting ready to throw the saddle blanket on when Mac tossed a pebble across to the other side to divert their attention.

"What was that?"

"Nothing," Cooke said. "Watch this." He gently swung the saddle blanket across Ettinsmoor's back.

"I heard something over there."

"Why are you so jumpy? Where's the saddle?" Cooke asked impatiently. "You trying to beat me out of my two shillings?"

"Naw. Here's the saddle. Didn't you hear about those Indians over at Fort Harris? They sneaked in and scalped two livery boys and took five horses."

Cooke hefted the saddle in place; Ettinsmoor sidestepped nervously.

"Watch him. I told you."

"Whoa, boy." Cooke reached for the cinch and looped it through the rings, pulling it snug.

"There is someone there," the other soldier said, pulling out his pistol.

He walked past Mac's hiding place and Mac stood to knock him out from behind. However, his aim with his left hand was off and he came down on the man's shoulder. The soldier whirled and shouted. Mac grabbed for the gun. They struggled, and a loud crack sounded as the gun discharged.

Mac went reeling backwards from the force of the shot that ripped into the left side of his chest.

The soldier ran outside. "He's here, the prisoner's here."

Mac staggered to his feet and reached for Ettinsmoor. "Cooke, can you help me up?" He gasped for breath, fighting to remain conscious.

The young soldier helped him climb into the saddle. "The back gate is open," he said. "It's around to the right just behind this building."

"Thanks, lad. Tell Arnham that Jess and I will name our first boy after him."

He doubled over from the pain, but he managed to guide Ettinsmoor out the stable doors and around to the gate.

Once through the gate, he slumped forward, giving Ettinsmoor his head and disappearing into the night. Musket shots rang after him in the dark, but no one pursued.

Through the red haze of pain, he felt suddenly euphoric. He felt as if he were flying. "Eagle wings," he whispered with a smile.

20

Jess gazed out the drawing room window of the farmhouse at Cheltenham. A late March wind whipped a cold rain in driving sheets across the gardens between their house and the mansion.

She clutched a blood-stained woolen scarf in her trembling hands. Jim Quidley stood before her. She could hear his voice, but she was having a hard time focusing on his words.

"I thought you might want to have it back, Miss," Mac's friend said. "It sure didn't belong with that dead Tory I found it on."

"But you didn't actually see Mac."

"No, ma'am." He paused, not wanting to say what he feared. "He prized that scarf, Miss McClaren. He was a good man, and I was proud to ride with him."

"Thank you, Jim." She turned away and went to her room.

Robbie invited Jim to stay for dinner and spend the night in the bunkhouse. He gratefully accepted the invitation.

"Can you tell us what happened after you left Mac? We've heard several different stories, but no one seems sure."

Jim took the cup of coffee offered by Mrs. McClaren and stood by the fire. "Well, if you heard that we whipped them good there at the Cowpens, you heard right. After Mac was hurt, I went on to meet up with General Greene. The general hurried us on over and we met up with Morgan again—none too soon, either, 'cause Cornwallis was hot on his tail. We met them redcoats there at Guilford Courthouse and our boys took a terrible toll on them. I've heard people talking about it like it was a British victory, but that's just because General Greene didn't press in to crush them. The general is a man of uncommon principle, and he couldn't see the need for a slaughter when they were whipped already. Them redcoats paid a terrible price that day, and Cornwallis has started retreating through Virginia." He paused and sipped the hot coffee. "It's just like Mac's been saying all along, without the Tory support Cornwallis was expecting, he's having to fall back. Last I heard he'd marched all the way back to Wilmington for reinforcements."

Jim's words ran out and he took another drink. "I should have stayed there with him till he was feeling better. But he wouldn't hear of it. When they first teamed us up, you know, I wasn't too sure about it—what with him being half Delaware. But the truth of it now, I don't expect I'll ever have as good a partner again."

They finished their coffee in silence, and Robbie glanced at the door to Jessica's room. Recalling those difficult days after the news had come about Evan, his heart ached for his little sister. He wished he could leave with

230

Jim in the morning so he wouldn't have to watch Jess endure another heartbreak.

Jim left the next morning, but Robbie stayed to carry on his duties at Cheltenham Farms.

Now that the Carolinas were virtually free of British control, life at the plantation had settled down to a less frantic pace. They were still producing supplies for the Continental army and militia, but with the forces moving back toward the north, only those forces dealing with the remaining British garrisons were supplied directly.

Ever since that grim day when Jim Quidley had brought Mac's scarf back to Jess, she had found it increasingly difficult to concentrate on the tasks at hand. She nurtured a hope that as long as nobody had actually seen what had happened to Mac, there was still the possibility he was alive.

In an attempt to find out the truth, she had written letters to the Continental Congress in Philadelphia, to General George Washington's headquarters in New York, and to General Greene, whose location was constantly changing in his increasingly effective campaign against Cornwallis.

Robbie had cautioned her that she was unlikely to receive answers to her letters. Although she was well aware that he was right, she waited for word with stubborn hope.

As the days passed, Jess resumed her practice of taking long walks down the lane to the post road. Her family was very concerned about her and tried numerous ways to cheer her.

It was different this time than it had been when the news had come about Evan. She was heartbroken then, but she had also been angry, not only about the terrible toll of the war, but with Evan himself for taking the entire matter so lightly, for throwing away their future by following a mere whim. To him, going to Savannah to join the militia had been a grand new adventure that would allow him an opportunity to prove himself in battle. She couldn't help wondering if he had ever come to recognize the full implication of what he was doing; or had he known all along, and simply chose to speak of it lightly?

In any case, she knew Mac was firm in his convictions and aware of what he was trying to accomplish; he was willing to sacrifice his life for freedom. Jessica's heart was swelled with admiration for Mac's courage, but it didn't make it any easier to imagine losing him.

One cold, blustery day toward the end of March, she wrapped herself in a heavy cloak and walked out into the chill dampness of early afternoon. Low, dark clouds scudded across a leaden gray sky. The wind nipped sharply at her cheeks and nose as she walked slowly along the lane leading to the town road. The trees stood starkly bare. As the chill began to penetrate her heavy woolen cloak, she decided to head back.

The sound of rapid hoofbeats carried on the wind. Her pulse quickened. She held her breath. A rider appeared on the road, galloping at breakneck speed. She peered intently in an effort to recognize the rider, but the form bending over the horse's neck was unfamiliar to her.

The rider reined to a jolting stop and fairly flew out of the saddle. "Miss McClaren?" he called breathlessly.

"Mr. Wills," she said in surprise, recognizing his face.

"You've got to come quick. It's Sir Gaston." The young man bent over with his hands on his knees, trying to regain his wind.

"Let's go up to the house and let you warm yourself and catch your breath," she said. David Wills wore a grave expression.

Once inside by the fire, the young foreman from Ellensgate gratefully took the cup of hot coffee Mrs. McClaren offered.

"Sir Gaston is very ill," he explained. "He's been calling for you. He insisted you be brought right away, before it's too late. It's a hard ride, but coming through the gap, I made it in two days. Will you come, Miss?"

"Of course I will," she said, heading toward her room. "Let me put a few things in a bag, and change into my riding clothes."

At that moment Robbie came in from a trip to town, still walking with a slight limp as a reminder of his injured leg. As he warmed himself by the fire, his parents related the information about Sir Gaston.

"Robbie," Mrs. McClaren asked with concern, "do you think it's safe for her to go?"

"I'll ride along," he assured his mother. "She'll be all right."

"Wouldn't you like to rest a bit, lad?" Rob McClaren asked the young Wills.

"No, sir. Thank you. We've got to get right back."

Within the hour the three were on the road to Ellensgate. David had been given a fresh mount and Jessica, not wanting to subject Lady to the rigors of the difficult ride, rode Ajax, a sturdy gelding.

The hamlet of Ellensgate lay on the other side of a narrow range of low hills. The weather appeared to be clearing somewhat as night fell, and they made camp in a small clearing at the foot of the mountain trail. A few stars began to twinkle through the thinning cloud layer, and soon the cold light of the three-quarter moon broke through.

To their relief, the next day dawned bright and clear, although quite brisk. They rode at a steady pace, stopping for an occasional short rest and camping that night just fifteen miles short of the estate. Jess wanted to push on, but her brother and David convinced her that it would be foolish to try to follow the mountain trail through the gathering fog in the dark.

They awoke to a cold wet morning. The fog that had descended upon them the night before still lay in a heavy blanket of silence over the forest. The dampness penetrated through their woolen clothes, adding discomfort to their weariness.

After a quick breakfast of coffee and pan cornbread, they began the last stage of their journey. The dense fog slowed them, but by midmorning, the sun had burned its way through and they were able to travel faster. They arrived at the estate around noon.

David knocked on the huge door and they waited expectantly. It was opened by Charles, the butler. He stepped aside and silently motioned for them to enter.

They walked into the large entry hall and stood for a moment. Jess heard sobbing somewhere in the back rooms of the house. She shot a desperate glance at Charles. He started to speak, but was interrupted by a small sorrow-filled voice.

"Miss McClaren."

Molly descended the stairs toward them. Her face was pale and drawn in tight little lines as she tried to speak.

"Miss McClaren," she said. "He's . . . gone. He just couldn't hang on any longer. He passed on this morning. He wanted . . . he wanted me to give you this." She choked back tears as she pulled an envelope from her apron pocket.

Jess took the proffered envelope with a trembling hand. She clutched her brother's arm and leaned heavily against him. He led her to a chair, where she sat down, afraid to trust her weakened knees.

"At the last," Molly continued, "he seemed to gain his old strength back and asked for quill and paper. He wrote with a frenzy, he did. Then he just sank back against the pillows as if he'd put all his energy on that paper. He smiled a little and apologized to you for not being able to wait any longer. He blamed himself for not sending for you sooner. Then he just closed his eyes so peaceful." She buried her face in her handkerchief and hurried down the hall to the servants' quarters.

David clutched absently at his hat. "I thought we'd make it back in time . . . I'm sorry, Miss."

"He wouldn't blame you," Jess reassured him. "You did all that anyone could have done."

He nodded silently and left by the front door.

"May I see the letter?"

Jess looked up and saw Gregory coming from the library. She searched his face. The coldness she heard in his voice was magnified in his eyes. She ignored his question and slipped the envelope into the deep pocket of her cloak.

"I'm so sorry, Gregory," she said. She walked over to him. "I wish I had known sooner. I would have come to help."

He nodded and after a wary glance at Robbie, he turned his full attention on Jessica.

"Please don't think ill of me," he said, "if I appear relieved rather than grief-stricken. Grandfather suffered so these last two months; I am satisfied that he is at last free of pain.

"I'm sorry you made your long journey for nothing, but I am very glad to see you again. Charles will show you to your rooms, and I'll have Molly bring you both a bite to eat." He gazed into Jessica's eyes, and kissed her hand.

"We'll visit later," he said.

21

Jessica and Robbie hugged each other in the hall outside their rooms.

"Are you all right, Jessie?" Robbie asked, still holding her close.

She nodded.

"That Gregory is a mighty cold fish, if you ask me," he added.

"Robbie," she scolded gently. "He's probably just in a bit of shock."

"I don't think much could shock that one." He released her from his embrace with a comforting pat on the shoulder. "Well, go on now and get some rest. I'll see you in a wee bit." He opened her door for her, then went into the room across the hall.

Jess removed her cloak and let it fall across the small settee by the window. The envelope slipped out of the pocket and she stooped to pick it up. She read the name, "Poppit," scrawled on the front, and stinging tears rose in her eyes. Clutching the envelope to her breast, she sank down on the side of the bed and gave in to her sorrow. Sobs wracked her body, and tears streamed down her face.

When her heaving sobs finally gave way to soft sighs, she wiped her eyes and carefully opened the letter.

The writing was bold and energetic. Sir Gaston's very essence seemed to leap from the page as she read the words through tear-filled eyes.

"My dearest Poppit," it began. "I'm sorry I couldn't wait for you, but it seems the Lord is in more of a hurry to take me home than I thought. Don't weep, my dear little Poppit, for when you read this, I'll already be marching in glory with a new strong body.

"There are some important matters I must entrust to you, my dear. First of all, do not show this letter to Gregory until my barrister, Smythe, has arrived to read my will.

"I'm afraid you were partially right about Gregory. He is not a coward, nor is he a fool. He is, however, singularly cold and selfish. He will no doubt be very unhappy when he learns that most of the land around the estate is going to my staff. The stock I'm leaving to the Continental army.

"I am leaving the house to Gregory, which I'm certain he will sell quickly and return to Austria, to his father's family. Good riddance, I say. This new country needs men like Macklin and women like you, who will devote their energies to building it and caring for it during these tender years.

"The bulk of my assets—including my two French shipbuilding companies and the jewels that have been in our family for three centuries—I leave to you.

"Smythe has been instructed to take care of the sale of all or part of the stocks and jewels, if you wish. It will make a handsome nest egg for a young couple just starting out.

I ask only that half of the proceeds go to the treasury of the Continental Congress to help finance the growing war debt. It will be a staggering weight for our young government to manage and perhaps my small contribution will be of assistance. It's nothing more than Nathaniel Greene is doing by undertaking the burden to supply his troops using his own funds.

"One last thing, my pet: I've also made certain that the papers for Lady Heather Star show your name as proper owner and the papers for Ettinsmoor show Andrew Macklin as owner. Call it my wedding present to you both.

"Now, he's calling me, my dear, and I don't want to keep him waiting. Please don't weep, I feel glorious. Your loving grandpapa, Samuel Gaston Keene, of Ellensgate, South Carolina."

Joy and sorrow mingled in her tears. Sir Gaston was gone, but she rejoiced in his passage into eternal life and peace.

She carefully folded the letter and slipped it back into the envelope. She was troubled by Sir Gaston's assessment of Gregory, but her spirit was buoyed by the news that Lady and Ettinsmoor actually belonged to her and Mac . . . if Mac ever returned, of course. The thought of him pierced her heart anew, and she began to weep again.

The rigors of travel and her grief over Sir Gaston's death had drained her, and she lay back across the bed in a state of exhaustion. She slipped the envelope under her pillow, and quickly gave in to her weariness.

When she awoke, late afternoon shadows were lengthening into early twilight. She hadn't meant to sleep at all, let alone for the three or four hours she had let slip by. The cold north wind was wrestling through the branches of the huge oak tree outside her window, causing a steady tapping against the glass panes.

Another gentle tapping at the door brought her to her feet. It was Molly.

"Master Starkheim is having tea in the drawing room and would like for you to join him." She lowered her head with a slightly embarrassed smile. "He didn't mention Mr. McClaren, but surely he's invited as well."

Jessica managed a knowing smile, remembering how Molly had admired Robbie during their Christmas visit. "Thank you, Molly, I'll ask him."

Jess crossed over to knock on her brother's door, smiling again as the young maid scurried shyly away down the hall. When Robbie answered and she mentioned the invitation, he told her he was not anxious to try to make polite conversation with Gregory over tea, or any other time for that matter. He had found a good book on the shelf in his room and would be very content to read quietly until dinner.

Jessica returned to her room to freshen up. After patting her face with a little water from the basin on the dressing table, she smoothed her dark chestnut hair into place. Then, taking a deep breath, she headed downstairs to meet Gregory.

Gregory stood by the fireplace, tending the cheery blaze. He looked striking in a dark gray coat and breeches with a white satin cravat showing above the lighter gray waistcoat. She was reminded of the first time she saw him on the night she and Mac had come to the estate nearly a year ago. He seemed different now, perhaps older, and much more serious.

Watching Jess as she entered the drawing room and sat down, Gregory was reminded of the vow he had made to win her hand. Even in her sorrow, she was poignantly beautiful. The past two and a half months, with his grandfather so ill, he had been very busy managing the estate. Seeing her now, he cursed the labors that had kept him from his campaign to make her his own. But she was here now, and very soon he would be prepared to return home to Austria.

He offered her a cup of tea, then poured a cup for himself.

"I must say," he began, "you're every bit as lovely as that first night you walked into my life. I'm so very glad to see you, Jessica. I wish it had been under more pleasant circumstances, but I am really delighted you came. I think about you so often."

"I only wish I could have arrived in time to see Sir Gaston before . . ." she said. Tears welled in her eyes again.

"I'm afraid Grandfather refused to believe he was so seriously ill until the very last moment. He was such an obstinate man—and so unrealistic at times." He sat down close to her and stirred his tea absently. His admiring gaze never strayed from her face.

"I think Sir Gaston had an excellent grasp of reality," Jess countered. "He had wonderful insight into the way things ought to be. I think he was always aware of the things that fell short of that, but he was never discouraged by it. He was always ready to do whatever he could to make things better."

Gregory chuckled. "Ah, dear Jessica. You and Grandfather were cut out of the same cloth. Hopeless romantics." He sensed her irritation and quickly added, "Of course, it is a charming quality. I'm afraid toward the last, however, Grandfather misinterpreted my pragmatism as something less than admirable; he died feeling rather unhappy with me. If he had recovered and regained his health, I daresay we would have been reconciled." He cleared his throat. "I'm sure he mentioned that in his letter to you."

She sipped her tea thoughtfully. "Not really," she said. "I'm so sorry you didn't have the chance to straighten everything out."

He sighed as he continued to watch her face closely. She returned his gaze unblinkingly. At last, he smiled and looked away.

"Enough of that," he said. "Let's talk of more pleasant things. How is everything at Cheltenham Farms?"

"Running very smoothly considering the difficulties of the war and all. Have things quieted down around here now that the British are in full retreat?" She was grateful for the change of subject.

He nodded. "I understand the Kensingtons' plantation and McWhatley's mill have been confiscated by the new local officials."

"Yes, I've heard that most of the Loyalist property in the colony has been confiscated, and that most of them are preparing to leave the country, if they haven't already."

"They've had little choice," Gregory grumbled. "However, I'm free to do as I choose, and I choose to depart this ungracious land and return to civilization, in Austria, to assume the title left to me by my father."

"Has it been that distasteful to you, Gregory?" she asked.

He stared into the firelight. "I've never been able to forgive my mother for isolating me here in this wilderness away from my friends, the royal courts of the continent, the beauty and grace of the cultural centers of the world. It's been like living in a primitive wasteland without food or drink for the soul."

"I'm sorry, Gregory. Perhaps if you could have just tried to see the beauty and grace here, it wouldn't have been so difficult."

He returned his gaze to her face and his expression softened. "The only thing of beauty and grace I've found here walked into this room nearly a year ago, looking like a princess, her arm in a sling, the unfortunate but courageous victim of this primitive place."

She blushed and shook her head. "I'm not a victim, Gregory. On the contrary, I feel very blessed to have been born in this country. I love it here. Mac says we have the opportunity to create something here unlike anywhere else in the world."

He raised an eyebrow with an impatient sigh at the mention of Mac's name. Showing her a mirthless smile, he asked, "And what do you hear of Macklin these days?"

She touched the silver ring on the ribbon around her neck. "I haven't seen him since New Year's Eve. He's apparently . . . missing."

Gregory's smile spread briefly, then disappeared. His expression grew solemn. "Dear Jessica, I've just realized the lateness of the hour. I'm afraid you'll have to excuse me. I still have some arrangements to make for the service in town tomorrow. If I don't hurry, I shan't make it back in time to enjoy dinner with you."

He kissed her hand and excused himself.

Jessica had forgotten Sir Gaston's wish to have his memorial service in town at the church he had built for the village. Gregory had found it rather odd that his grandfather should insist upon being buried in the church cemetery instead of on his own estate, but Sir Gaston had himself provided the land adjacent the church property for a village cemetery, convinced that church-affiliated cemeteries were inclined to better preservation through the years. His wife and daughter had also been buried there.

Returning to her room, Jessica saw Molly coming out of the door. The young girl appeared nervous and upset, and scurried down the hall with hardly a word to Jess.

Jess entered her room, and went to the wardrobe to take out the one dress she had brought with her in order to change from her riding clothes for dinner. She dreaded the prospect of dinner with Gregory.

She laid the blue dress of linsey-woolsey across the bed, which had already been turned down. She smiled at Molly's thoughtfulness, thinking how strange it was to have someone taking care of such things for her. She stopped smiling, though, as she remembered Molly's manner in the hall. She reached for the pillow, hesitated, then lifted the down-filled case slowly, peeking under it. The letter was not there.

Sitting down on the edge of the bed, she thought she knew who had taken the letter, but wasn't sure why Molly was acting so suspiciously. A knock at the door startled her; she rose from the bed and opened the door.

Robbie stood in the hall, with his hands stuffed in his pockets.

"I thought I'd take a walk. Do you know when dinner will . . ." He trailed off, noticing her perplexed expression, and asked, "What's wrong Jessie?"

"Come in," she said, pulling him in quickly and looking up and down the empty hallway. She closed the door and led him to the other side of the room. She told him about the letter, its contents, and sudden disappearance.

"Well, we both know who's responsible," Robbie declared with certainty.

244

"But why?" Jess asked.

Robbie shrugged. "If Sir Gaston didn't change his will to indicate the things he wrote in the letter, then that is the only evidence of his final wishes. If that be the case, it's no wonder the letter is missing. Let's go down and just see what Mr. Starkheim has to say about it."

"Wait a minute," she said, grasping his arm. "We can't do that."

"We can and we will," he insisted.

"No, we can't," she replied with determination. "First of all, he's not here—he went into town. Secondly, the will has evidently been changed already; Mr. Smythe is coming out to read it sometime very soon. So maybe we're wrong."

Robbie leveled a penetrating glance at his sister. "Who else would want to know the contents of that letter? Who else would stand to lose if they could guess what might be in it? It might not do him any good, but he stole something that belonged to you."

She soberly considered his words as she fingered the silver ring on the ribbon around her neck.

"You can't just let it go," he insisted.

"Why can't I?" she countered. She turned to look out the window. "It doesn't really matter. The letter said that ownership of Lady and Ettinsmoor was already transferred to Mac and me. I don't care about anything else. Gregory can have the rest."

"That's all well and good, Jess. I understand how you feel and I think we ought to head on back home right now. It would be a lot easier that way, except for one thing."

"What's that?" she turned to face him.

"You would be ignoring Sir Gaston's last wishes if you walk away from the responsibility he entrusted to you. He wanted to leave something to this country, Jess, and he evidently didn't want Gregory to get his hands on those companies and stocks because he didn't have confidence that his wishes would be carried out. What you do with them is entirely up to you, but remember, Sir Gaston trusted you to make the right decisions."

She fell silent for a few minutes. Finally, she bowed her head resignedly. "All right. I'll talk to Mr. Smythe and see what he has to say about it."

"Good. As soon as the funeral is over, I'm all for heading home right away. Now that Sir Gaston is gone, I have no desire to hang around."

Jessica nodded; she admitted to herself that she, too, would be very glad to leave the estate and get back home. Without Sir Gaston, Ellensgate was a very cold place.

Gregory had not returned from making funeral arrangements in town by the time they went down for dinner—much to Jessica's relief. Molly's reluctance to be in the same room for more than a few seconds at a time became painfully obvious as the young girl could not face Jessica during dinner.

After a quiet meal, they returned to their rooms to turn in early in preparation for the difficult day that lay ahead. Jess spent a restless night; she lay awake most of the time, watching the passing moon cast silhouette patterns across the floor and the wall opposite the window. She finally drifted off into a fretful slumber two hours before sunrise.

22

The sky had begun to brighten with the first light of the new day when a gentle tapping at her door woke Jessica from disturbing dreams.

"Come in," she called sleepily.

Molly peeked through the slightly open door. "May I speak to you, Miss McClaren?"

"Yes, of course. Come in." She sat up. The chill of the morning air made her reach for the blanket lying across the foot of the bed and pull it around her shoulders.

Molly entered, nervously wringing a handkerchief and trying to avoid Jess's gaze.

"Miss McClaren . . ." she began.

"Yes, Molly? What is it?" Jess asked gently.

"Miss McClaren . . . I've done something terrible." Bursting into tears before she continued, the girl buried her face in her handkerchief.

"Please don't cry, Molly. I'm sure you couldn't do anything that was terrible."

"Oh, but I did," she insisted tearfully. "And I can't eat or sleep on account of it."

"Whatever it is, I'm sure you had a very good reason for doing it," Jess said.

"I . . . I was so foolish. He told me if I'd bring him that letter to look at, he'd give it right back. I didn't think it was quite right that he wanted your letter, but he sounded so nice, so kind. Then when I gave it to him, the look on his face frightened me. He looked at me as if I was nothing, just a piece of furniture, maybe. He told me to leave while he read it and that he would let me put it back before you returned to your room after dinner.

"I left the room but I peeked back through the crack in the door and watched him read it. I'll never forget the look on his face as long as I live. He turned almost purple. When I saw his face, I knew he'd never give the letter back and I was too afraid to ask him for it. Then he left the house and didn't come back until real late last night." After pouring out her story she drooped like a wilted flower. "Can you ever forgive me? I'm so ashamed and so sorry."

"Of course, I forgive you, Molly," Jess said. "Please don't worry about it, everything will be all right. No real harm has been done."

Relief showed on the young girl's face. "I'll do anything I can to make it right," she said. "I'll tell the constable. I'll tell Sir Gaston's lawyer. Please let me help."

"I doubt that will be necessary. Thank you for offering your help, though. Now, I'd better get dressed. I fear it's going to be a rather difficult day. Do you know what time we are supposed to be at the church?"

Her face clouded suddenly. "The church? Oh yes, the service will be at ten o'clock." She scurried from the room, closing the door softly behind her.

After Molly had gone, Jess began to dress. She chose the only black dress in Abigail's wardrobe. It was rather plain, with a wide pleat down the middle of the back, gathered at the waist and flowing down the length of the full skirt. The high neck buttoned with tiny gray pearl buttons, as did the narrow cuffs at the wrists. When she'd finished dressing, she began to look for the matching gloves in the dresser drawer where accessories were kept. She found the proper gloves, and also discovered a small brocade-covered book.

It was a diary, written in a fine, delicate hand. She turned the pages without thinking. "Abigail's diary," she said out loud. She stood transfixed before the open dresser drawer.

"Father was so right about Bradford," one entry read. It was dated June 22, 1764. "How could I have ever been so foolishly in love with him? We met today at the old carriage house and he begged me to stay with him. Oh! He is so selfish and wicked—to think that he would ask me to abandon my husband and child to be with him! Joseph has been so good to me, I could never do such a thing. I shudder to think what would happen if Bradford knew about Gregory. I will be glad to be away from here and back by my Joseph's side."

The next date to catch her eye was October 6, 1772—the year Abigail had returned to care for her father. "My darling Gregory is so unhappy. I feel I've done him a terrible injustice, taking him away from his friends and Joseph's family. I pray he will forgive me and come to love this wild land as Father and I do. Without Joseph, this is the only place I really feel I belong now.

"October 10, 1772. Bradford came by today. I have long dreaded the time when we would meet again. However, he seems to have completely dismissed our past relationship and apparently regards me with the same disdain he holds for Father. What a relief.

"November 15, 1772. I found Gregory destroying a letter belonging to Father. It was from the little McClaren girl. Gregory is jealous of Father's affection for the girl. He has promised never to do such a thing again, so I have said nothing to Father. It would only upset him and he is still so weak. I fear the move from Austria has been more difficult for dear Gregory than I had imagined."

Flipping further toward the end, she stopped again. "January 2, 1775. The New Year's festivities are over. The last of the guests have returned to their homes. I do not envy the Carlisles' long journey to Charleston. Poor Gregory—after three years, he still pines for our home in Austria. I don't suppose he will ever be able to adjust to this new world.

"September 3, 1775. I shall not see the yuletide season this year. I grow weaker with each passing day. Thankfully, Father is nearly recovered. Gregory could learn so much from him. I do regret taking my dear son from his world and making him so miserable. Yet for myself, I'm thankful to be here. For all of its hardships, it is my home and I'm glad I shall be laid to rest here."

It was the last entry. Jess carefully closed the book. She stood before the dresser and turned the diary over in her hands. She now knew what had become of her letters to Sir Gaston. Beneath Gregory's outward appearance of admiration dwelt a deep-seated jealousy of the affection his grandfather had felt for her. Perhaps that had been the real reason behind the disappearance of the letter from Sir Gaston.

Gregory seemed an enigma to Jess. She could almost picture him as a tragic character from a Shakespearean play. Beneath a cool, aristocratic exterior lay a turmoil of jealousy, egotism, and pride in his social station, conflicting with a deep insecurity and a need for attention and affection.

She was reminded of that first evening she and Mac had come to Sir Gaston's. The two young men standing at the fireplace were both the product of two worlds. Although Abigail Keene Starkheim was English by birth, she had totally embraced the colonies. Her marriage to a titled Austrian, whom she met while attending school in Europe, gave Gregory a heritage as diverse as Mac's. The major difference between the two young men was that Mac had grown up with a deep appreciation for both facets of his ancestry. He was the synthesis of the old and new worlds; Gregory had never accepted life in the colonies, but clung desperately to the old aristocracy of his father's land.

"Oh, Mac," she whispered, "how desperately I wish you were here."

If Gregory was as angry about the letter as Molly had said, Jess couldn't help wondering what he might do. He may have endured colonial life for the sake of the large inheritance he anticipated; perhaps he imagined himself returning to Austria with land and ships and jewels. What would he do if Sir Gaston's will deprived him of that dream?

Jess deliberately returned the diary to its place and closed the dresser drawer. She spoke to her reflection in the mirror.

"Jessica McClaren, how in the world did you manage to get involved in this situation, anyway?"

"Talking to yourself?"

She jumped and turned to see Robbie sticking his head in the door, "You didn't answer my knock."

"You scared me to death," she said, placing a hand over her heart.

"It's time for breakfast," he said. "Are you all right?"

She nodded and took her brother's outstretched hand. As he escorted her out the door, she briefly told him about the diary and her speculation of Gregory's aspirations in regard to the inheritance.

Gregory did not appear at breakfast. Robbie mentioned that Gregory had made no plans for the usual gathering of friends and neighbors to come by after the funeral to offer their condolences. Jessica was not surprised, knowing what little regard Gregory felt for the people in the community. She was about to explain this fact to Robbie when Gregory finally joined them, looking very poised and distinguished in his dark mourning suit.

As they prepared to leave for the church, Gregory appeared appropriately solemn and, as always, charming and considerate. He offered his arm to Jessica as they left the house and helped her into the waiting carriage.

Gregory filled the ride to church, not with memories of Sir Gaston, but with tales of his travels in Europe as a boy. Jessica nodded courteously, but she heard nothing he said.

23

The funeral service was well attended. Sir Gaston had been a very popular man throughout the countryside. His influence had touched many lives and nearly everyone in town turned out to pay their last respects. Harold Smythe, Sir Gaston's lawyer, approached Jessica and Gregory after the graveside ceremony.

"According to your grandfather's wishes," he said, addressing Gregory, "I will be coming out to the estate tomorrow morning around eleven o'clock. See you then, Miss McClaren."

Gregory touched the brim of his tall beaver skin hat and bid Mr. Smythe good-bye.

The carriage ride home was very quiet. Little was said until they reached the estate. Gregory's expression seemed to brighten then, and he said, "Jessica, I haven't shown you the new horses yet. Why don't we change and go for a ride? I think it would be good for both of us."

"I don't think so, Gregory. Not today," she answered.

"At least come to the stables and see the new horses," he insisted. "They are really something. Please. We'll have time before lunch."

Robbie scowled at them both. She finally relented, knowing how horses always seemed to comfort her. Gregory leaned forward to tap on the driver's box and instruct him to drive directly to the stables.

Taking Gregory's hand, Jess stepped down from the carriage in front of the long whitewashed building. She felt a sudden chill as she looked up at him. His smile had lost its charm.

Robbie stepped down and followed as Gregory led them into the stables. He directed them to the first three stalls on the right, where three outstanding thoroughbreds stood.

Robbie and Jessica were appropriately impressed. When they had spent sufficient time admiring the horses, Gregory said, "Rob, would you mind going on up to the house to tell Charles that we will be ready for lunch shortly? I'd like to have a few words with your sister in private."

Robbie was about to say he did mind, but Jessica nodded, assuring him there was nothing to worry about. Still reluctant, he said that he would be expecting them to follow *very* shortly. After Rob had gone, Gregory studied his new horses for a moment, then turned to Jessica.

"I know this is probably not the appropriate time to discuss such matters, but I'm afraid we might not have the opportunity to talk later. Perhaps you'll forgive me if I speak boldly." He took both of her hands in his and pulled her gently toward him.

She knew that many girls would happily change places with her now, standing here, capturing the full attention of this handsome, charming young man. She reflected soberly that she wished it were some other girl.

"Jessica, you know that nothing in the world would have made Grandfather any happier than to have you and me get together. He would have loved to have you in the family. I . . . I would love to have you in the family. I know we haven't spent a great deal of time together, but the times we have spent together were wonderful. My father and mother knew each other only two weeks before they were married—it was almost scandalous, really—and they were happily married for fourteen years. I could make you very happy."

"Gregory, please." She stepped back. "Not now. Please don't ask me now." Tears rimmed her eyes again.

He was silent a long moment, studying her face. An expression of regret flickered across his face. "Yes, of course," he said. He released her hands. "You're right it is not the proper time to discuss such things; but keep in mind what I said, will you?" He smiled again and tucked her hand in the crook of his arm; then he led her out of the stables and back toward the house. "Maybe we can take that ride in the morning," he said.

24

The next morning as Jessica and Robbie lingered over their last cup of breakfast coffee, Jessica told her brother she was going for a ride with Gregory. He objected strenuously, saying he would not let her go without him along.

"Robbie, don't be silly. We won't be out of sight of the house."

"Jess, it may not have occurred to you, but he knows you're going to inherit the bulk of this estate. He may not want anyone standing in his way."

"You mean you think he might try to harm me?" She knew by the furrows in his brow that he was indeed worried for her safety. "Well, just to put your mind at ease—he wants to marry me, not murder me."

"What? When did he say that?"

"Yesterday, down at the stables."

"You refused him, of course."

She didn't answer immediately.

"Jessie," he objected. "You're not actually considering his proposal?"

"No, of course not. I just couldn't reject him outright."

Robbie sighed. He turned in his chair and gazed out the window. "You know," he said slowly. "Gregory at times reminds me a bit of Evan. Don't you agree?"

Her eyes opened wide. She stared thoughtfully at the gleaming silver cream pitcher sitting in front of her plate. Finally, she spoke softly. "You know how much I loved Evan, Robbie." He turned again to face her. She continued. "Ever since we first came here, I've had dreams about him. Not pleasant dreams. Maybe Gregory does remind me of him. At first I thought I felt guilty because I had been so angry with Evan for throwing his life away, but then there was Mac."

She hesitated. Robbie said quietly, "You felt like you were betraying Evan by falling in love with Mac?"

She shrugged. "Evan was so dashing and brave, so alive. When he was killed, I thought I'd never be able to love anyone ever again; but Mac . . . I found my feelings for Mac growing even deeper and stronger than I had ever felt for Evan and I hadn't thought it possible. Am I terribly fickle? Have I betrayed Evan, Robbie?"

He patted her hand. "Ah, Jessie, don't fret so. You know Evan was the sort of lad who would be more upset to have you pine away for him than to see you find someone to love and make you happy.

"He was my best friend, but he had the spirit of a will-o'-the-wisp, Jess. He loved you desperately too, but his dreams were bigger than life. Who knows if he would have ever been able to settle down to a normal existence? Maybe he realized that better than anyone. At any rate, he loved you too much to have you waste your life wearing black for his benefit."

"But the nightmares, Robbie. In the nightmares he's always pulling me away from Mac and . . . he frightens me."

"Don't you see, Jessie? It's Gregory, not Evan. You're just getting the two of them all mixed up in your dreams."

Until this moment she had not realized how deeply disturbing the nightmares had been and how comforting it was to be able to get them out in the open, to examine them and dispel their hold over her. She smiled gratefully at her brother. "You make it sound so simple. Why couldn't I see that before?"

"Sometimes we can't see the things that are most obvious. Just like Gregory. It's obvious he's not to be trusted, and you must promise me you'll be very careful around him. The fearful feeling in your dreams is probably just your good sense warning you about Gregory.

"I've not said it before because I wasn't aware that you were so troubled, but Evan would approve of Andrew Macklin. He would want you to be happy. He would warn you about Gregory too, I think." He frowned and paused.

Gregory suddenly entered the dining room. "Did I hear my name mentioned?" he asked cheerfully.

"Oh," Jess answered airily. "I was just telling Robbie I was going out riding with you."

"Are you ready? I've just come from the stables; Jamie has saddled our two best thoroughbreds."

Jess glanced at her brother and smiled reassuringly. "I'm ready." She pulled on her riding gloves, walked behind Robbie, and patted his shoulder.

"Thank you, Robbie," she said. "I promise I'll be careful."

She and Gregory were halfway to the stables when they heard Charles calling.

"Sir. Sir, could you please come back for a moment? It's quite urgent, I'm afraid."

"All right! I'll be right there," Gregory called back impatiently. "Jessica, why don't you go on down and get acquainted with the mount I've chosen for you? I'll be along shortly."

She headed toward the stable, Robbie's words still turning in her thoughts. It was a beautiful early spring morning with the sun shining brightly in a cloudless blue sky. An energetic mockingbird trilled through his song variations; a soft breeze brushed her cheek. Closing her eyes just a moment to savor the fragrant air, she heard a whisper.

"Jessie, live."

Catching her breath, she whirled around. "Evan?"

Only the soft breeze stirred about her. No one else was near. Her pulse raced; she told herself her imagination was running away with her. And yet, looking up at the blue of the sky, she could almost see the blue of Evan's eyes there. His eyes were smiling, and the soft warm breeze caressed her cheek as if he'd touched her.

"Robbie's right." Was it another whisper of the breeze?

"Evan," she whispered wistfully. A warmth filled her heart and at last she felt peace there. Robbie was right, and she finally knew it with her whole heart. Evan would not wish to hold her to his memory, shutting out the life she could share with Mac . . . if she should ever see him again.

The breeze diminished until it was a mere breath of air; she touched her cheek. Evan would always hold a special place in her heart and memory, but she realized now that she was free to love again, free to live.

Still in deep contemplation, she continued to walk toward the stable where the horses stood quietly at the tether rings. She stood there for some time, silently reflecting on the direction of her life.

One of the saddled thoroughbreds stamped restlessly, drawing her attention to the present. It was almost like awakening from a dream. No one seemed to be around, although Jamie, the groom, was supposed to be minding the horses.

"Jamie?" she called through the open stable door.

"Right here, Miss." He scratched his head as he came down the center aisle between the stalls. He was a middle-aged man, of slight build with prematurely gray hair and gray eyes. He wore a bewildered expression.

"Is something wrong?" she asked.

"I could have sworn I heard a crash back there, but nothing is out of place." He shrugged and shoved his hands into his pockets. "What do you think of Doubloon?"

They went back outside and she patted the large bay's neck. He snorted nervously; she spoke softly to calm him.

"Here's the mounting block, Miss." Jamie brought the stepping block out for her and placed it next to the horse with the lady's sidesaddle.

"Here comes Mr. Starkheim now."

She turned and saw Gregory striding toward them.

"Go ahead, Jessica," he said. "Step up and take a turn around the yard. His gait is as smooth as silk."

Jamie offered her a hand as she stepped up on the box and took the reins. As she settled onto the saddle, the horse suddenly let out a shrill whinny as if in pain and bolted forward. She pulled back on the reins and grasped the upper pommel of the saddle, hanging on for dear life.

Doubloon leaped twice, then jerked forward and broke into a wild gallop; he dashed across the lawn and down the gently sloping hill toward the river.

It was all Jess could do just to hold on. Pulling with all of her might, she sawed on the reins, but the horse refused to pay attention to the bit. She struggled to keep her seat; with each jolt over the uneven ground, she slipped closer to being thrown.

Another rider suddenly appeared beside her on a horse that matched Doubloon's speed. A strong arm reached out, encircled her waist, and lifted her off Doubloon's back. The arm around her waist held her tightly until he reined to a stop and gently lowered her to the ground. She lowered her head and closed her eyes to control the light-headedness that had overtaken her.

Suddenly she heard her name.

Catching her breath, she looked up into two dark brown eyes.

"Mac?" she cried. Her dizziness returned and her knees nearly buckled.

He caught her arm and pulled her to him.

"Mac!" she cried again, throwing her arms around his neck. She held him tightly, as if he were the only thing keeping her from falling to the ground in a heap. As their lips met in a long tender kiss, they were oblivious to the world around them, not even noticing the commotion of the crowd approaching them. Still embracing, they studied each other's face with delight.

"It really is you! I knew Jim was wrong when he thought you were dead. Where did you come from?" she asked in amazement, still slightly out of breath.

"I arrived at Cheltenham Farms two days after you left. Your father told me about Sir Gaston, and I was just riding up when I saw that bay take off with you. Are you all right?" His voice sounded like music to her ears, and she could not tear her gaze from his dark eyes. He looked a little tired, but even more handsome than she had remembered. He no longer wore buckskins, but a dark blue coat and waistcoat, with cream-colored shirt and breeches. His attraction lay not in his appearance, however, but in the character reflected in his eyes.

Gregory suddenly jolted to a halt next to them. "Jessica," he said, panting. "Are you all right?"

"I'm fine," she said. "Thanks to Mac." She answered without looking away from Mac's face.

Robbie and two stable hands came running. Robbie marched over to Gregory. His eyes blazed. "How could you let her ride a half-wild animal like that?"

Gregory blinked dumbly at Robbie. His face was pale; he appeared genuinely upset by what had just happened.

"I don't understand it," he said. "Doubloon's the gentlest of the new three. I never thought he might behave like that."

Robbie and Gregory glared at each other for a long moment.

"Mr. Starkheim," said Jamie, the groom. "Look at this." He had caught Doubloon's halter and held the still trembling thoroughbred. One of the other hands, who had helped him subdue the animal, was holding something in his hand.

"It was sticking through the saddle blanket," the stable hand explained. "It was a mighty painful jab when the lady sat in the saddle."

Gregory took a long, wicked-looking thorn from the boy's hand.

"Someone was very careless with that blanket," he said, "and didn't shake it properly before saddling him. Let's get back up to the house and I'll have a word with the stable boys right away." He turned to Jess. "Jessica, you may take my horse," he said.

"She will ride with me," Mac said. He picked her up at the waist and set her on Ettinsmoor's back. He swung up behind her and slipped his free hand around her waist. He guided Ettinsmoor back toward the house at a leisurely walk.

"Are you sure you're all right?"

"I am now," she said with a smile.

"What's going on between Robbie and Gregory?" he asked.

She told him about Sir Gaston and the unusual situation with the inheritance problem. They arrived at the house before much else could be said; several of the house staff met her at the door and insisted upon bringing her some tea to calm her. She and Mac and Robbie were sitting in the drawing room when Gregory joined them.

Coming to stand before Jessica, he took her hand. "Are you certain you're all right, my dear?" he asked with concern.

"Yes, I'm fine," she said, withdrawing her hand and glancing up at Mac.

Gregory followed her gaze to meet a very grim expression in Mac's eyes. Nodding slightly to Mac, Gregory moved to a small table holding a crystal decanter. He poured himself a small snifter of brandy. "What a surprise, Macklin," he said. "What news of the war do you bring us?"

Mac related the latest war news, telling them that Cornwallis was now at Wilmington, North Carolina, trying to regroup after the tremendous losses he had suffered at Guilford Courthouse. Mac smiled and said that Cornwallis was having a difficult time trying to rally local Tory support. The Articles of Confederation had finally been ratified the first of March, showing a solidification of American resolve and proving that the colonies were able to compromise and work together in establishing a new, albeit fragile, government. With this development and the encouraging military successes against British forces, Loyalist support throughout the South was waning rapidly.

Gregory stood and lifted his glass. "Macklin, it appears you were right. I salute you and your fellow rebels, and propose a toast to your continued success and final victory."

Mac and Robbie stood and joined in the toast with their cups of tea.

"Aye," Robbie added, "and the sooner, the better."

Jess studied Gregory's face carefully, and she started a bit when he turned to her suddenly.

"Don't forget, Jessica, my dear, Harold Smythe will be here shortly. He seemed anxious for you to be present for the reading of the will. Now, if you will excuse me, there are a few matters I must see to."

After he had gone, Robbie made a discreet exit as well, smiling at his sister. He was certain that his absence would not be noticed.

"How are you, Jess?" Mac asked when Robbie had left.

Jess stared into his eyes for a long moment before answering. "I'm fine now. Just fine."

"You certainly are." He smiled, completely captivated by the sight of her once more.

"I've been so worried about you," she confessed. "What happened to you after Jim left you?"

He shrugged. "I've been a bit under the weather."

"I suppose it would be asking too much for you to stay a little longer this time?"

"Well, as a matter of fact, they've sent me home for a rather extended recuperation. Seems I ended up on the wrong end of a pistol. Good old Ettinsmoor managed to walk into a detachment of our militia before it was too late."

She clutched his hand. "Was it a serious wound?"

"The doc said if the lead had been at a different angle and an inch closer, I'd be with my ancestors now; I figured you must have been praying for me," he said.

"I haven't stopped for a moment," she declared. "Even after Jim Quidley brought your scarf back." His brow furrowed, and she explained about Jim bringing the scarf to her; Mac promised to tell her someday how he came to lose it.

"I'm sorry about Sir Gaston," he said, shifting the conversation away from himself. "He was quite a gentleman."

She suddenly remembered where she had stopped in her earlier account of the past thirty-six hours. She filled in more details and told him about the stolen letter. "I really don't care about any of that now. The most important thing now is to take you to Cheltenham Farms and make sure you get the rest and healing you need. I suppose I must wait until Mr. Smythe comes, but as soon as possible, we will leave for home."

"I'm all for that. The sooner we're away from here, the better I'll like it. I'm not sure I appreciate the way Starkheim looks at you and keeps calling you his 'dear.' In fact, there's a little matter about you helping him with inventory at Cheltenham Farms I would like to hear about."

She smiled at his apparent jealousy. "I think I'd like a small rumor about Little Sparrow cleared up at the same time. Besides, you needn't worry about Gregory; I think the only person he really cares about is Gregory."

He cocked his head and furrowed his brow again. "Robbie doesn't seem to take it quite so lightly."

"He was afraid Gregory might try to get me out of the way so all the inheritance would go to him, but I think that's silly. I'm sure he had nothing to do with that thorn in the saddle blanket. Didn't you see his face?"

"I think it would be better if you save your horseback riding until we get back to Cheltenham. I intend to see to it that he doesn't get you alone anymore." He smiled, but his eyes were filled with concern. "By the way, I have something for you. Wait here."

He was gone several minutes. When he returned, he carried a small bundle.

"I was at Iron Mountain last week," he said. "I had already told my grandparents about you, and they want me to bring you to visit as soon as I can. My grandmothers sent this to you."

She opened the bundle, wrapped in a doe-skin pouch, to find a beautiful shawl of fine cream-colored Scottish wool embroidered with a delicate pattern of flowers and leaves. Her mouth opened wide in wordless appreciation.

"It was my Grandmother Macklin's wedding gift nearly fifty years ago. She had Grandmother She-wan-ikee stitch some Delaware patterns on it to symbolize the blending of the two cultures."

"It's magnificent." With tears brimming her eyes, she stood and draped it around her shoulders.

He told Jessica how, in telling his grandparents about her, he had also related his misgivings about asking her to marry him, aware of the prejudice against Indians she might have to face.

His grandfather had told him a story he had not heard before. Apparently his parents had faced the same misgivings before they were married; they decided to part for a while to see if it would be best to go separate ways. They had each been so miserable without the other that they decided the disapproval of strangers would be much easier to bear than life without each other.

He looked from the intricate shawl to her gray-green eyes. "It suits you, Rea' na tani."

He took her in his arms, and for a few long moments their past fears and present surroundings seemed to melt away.

After a moment, Mac whispered her name.

"Hmmm?"

"What's Sergeant Arnham's first name?"

"What?" She looked up at him in bewilderment. "Uh, let's see, I think it's Abercrombie . . . no, that isn't it."

"Thank goodness," Mac said.

"Aloysius, I think . . . yes, it's Aloysius. Why?" Her face registered confusion and curiosity.

"Oh, never mind. Maybe they'll all be girls," he said, a note of dismay in his voice.

Before she could ask him to explain, Charles entered and announced the arrival of Mr. Smythe.

25

A portly gentleman in his late fifties stood behind the massive desk in the library. Gregory introduced Mr. Smythe to Robbie, Jess, and Mac. The lawyer came around the desk and offered each of them a firm handshake.

"I'm so happy to meet you, Mr. Macklin," he said. "Gaston spoke very highly of you. As you will soon see, his words were only a slight indication of his regard for you both." He returned to his former place behind the desk. "Please sit down and we will begin."

As she sat down, Jessica noticed Gregory direct a dark look toward Mac before nodding politely and moving to stand behind her chair.

Jess listened with apprehension, wondering what Gregory's reaction would be when Mr. Smythe reached the portion of the will directing the distribution of Sir Gaston's wealth. Each of the servants was well cared for; out of the corner of her eye, Jess observed Gregory's hand clenching into a fist as Smythe read the news that the bulk of the land surrounding the estate was to be turned over to those workers who had tended the fields so long and so well.

Smythe read on. "To my grandson, Joseph Gregory Starkheim the Fourth, I leave the main house and adjacent buildings.

"The cattle herd shall be turned over to the Continental army to provide for the troops. All horses, except Gregory's own sorrel stallion, Zenith, shall also become property of the Continental army cavalry.

"To my Poppit, Miss Jessica Gwyneth McClaren, I leave the controlling interests in my two shipbuilding companies in Calais, France, and the Keene family jewel collection. I do ask that half of any profits or proceeds from the sale of these companies and/or stocks shall go to the treasury of the Continental Congress to be applied to the retirement of the debt accrued in the war for independence from England. The only other stipulation I place on this is that she must see to it that my grandson, Gregory, is never allowed to get his hands on any part of it. She may do whatever she sees fit with these properties, for I trust her judgment implicitly; I am certain Andrew Macklin will be a worthy advisor in any of these matters."

Jessica winced at the huge responsibility being settled upon her shoulders. Any thoughts she may have entertained of turning it all over to Gregory had been dispelled by the strict limitations put forth by Sir Gaston.

"Miss McClaren, do you understand what I've just read?"

She nodded.

"Very well," he continued. "I also have the ownership papers for the two thoroughbreds, Lady Heather Star and Ettinsmoor, in my office.

"I'm sure you will want to take some time to consider what you will do now, so I will call back in a couple of days to see if I can be of further assistance." Turning to Gregory, he continued, "I think I may have a prospective buyer for the estate. I'll let you know for sure when I return. Good day."

He packed his paperwork and walked out, giving Jessica a nod as he passed her.

After a few moments of heavy silence, Gregory spoke. Still standing behind her chair, he spoke in a very controlled, calculated manner.

"Congratulations, Jessica. Evidently, Grandfather considered you as a member of the family already. If you'll excuse me, I have a few questions for Smythe." He left the room quickly.

Robbie grinned as he came over and patted Jess on the shoulder. "Well, just as I said, it didn't do him any good stealing the letter, did it?"

Mac tilted his head curiously, studying her expression. "What's the matter, Jess?" he asked.

"I still can't help feeling sorry for him. After all, he was Sir Gaston's only grandson. I just don't feel right about it." She looked up at him and placed her hand in his.

"I'm sure Sir Gaston had his reasons," Mac said thoughtfully.

"Perhaps." She stood and walked to the window. Gregory stood beside Mr. Smythe's buggy, waving his hand angrily in the air.

"Mac, do you think we could go to see Mr. Smythe this afternoon?"

"This afternoon?" Robbie interjected. "Shouldn't you take a little time to think this thing through?"

"I can't wait. I need to find out why Sir Gaston changed his will. We'll go in and settle everything today, so we can go home tomorrow."

Mac touched her shoulder, and she jumped. He studied her face with a worried expression.

She forced a smile. "I'm sorry. I just want to get this thing over with and get home." She drew her new shawl closer about her, gaining a measure of comfort from its warmth.

26

Jessica and Mac sat in Mr. Smythe's office, listening to him explain the reason for Sir Gaston's change of heart concerning his grandson.

"Please don't worry yourself, Miss McClaren. Sir Gaston was indeed thinking clearly when he made the change in his will. He was a wise gentleman with strong convictions about honor and truth. He found out that Gregory had been most deceitful.

"Evidently, Gregory had long been in league with Bradford Keene, supplying him with information about the rebel activities in this area. He pretended to be oblivious to the war and tried to convince Sir Gaston to remain neutral concerning such things.

"Sir Gaston overheard a conversation between Gregory and Charles, the butler, about how pleased they were that Colonel Tarleton was in charge of the forces near Cowpens.

"He later found out that Gregory had somehow recognized you and sent a messenger to Bradford Keene, telling him about you, Mr. Macklin, informing him that you were leaving and would probably be back. Bradford came to

Ellensgate to capture you and establish a center of operations from which he could influence other Loyalists in the area."

He sat back and thoughtfully puffed on a large cigar. "I think if Gregory would have just come right out and declared himself a Loyalist, Sir Gaston would have been able to accept that. He would have at least respected his convictions. But Sir Gaston regarded Gregory's duplicity as treachery, and came to see his grandson as an unprincipled opportunist.

"Now, perhaps, you can understand why Sir Gaston wrote his will as he did. I trust you will understand that what I've told you is in the strictest confidence."

Jessica was speechless; she nodded.

Mac shrugged. "The British are in retreat," he said. "I doubt that Starkheim can do any more damage. He will probably be leaving with the rest of those Loyalists returning to England and Europe, so there would be little point in turning him in."

"Thank you, Mr. Macklin. Now, Miss McClaren, is there anything else I can help you with?"

She took a deep breath. "I have absolutely no idea how to run a shipbuilding business, nor do I have any desire to learn. Mac suggested I follow Sir Gaston's example and allow those people who have been in charge to continue running the companies. Since he asked that half of the profits or proceeds from the sale of the company be given to the new government, I suppose the best thing would be to allow the company people to buy out Sir Gaston's interest at a price they feel is fair."

Mr. Smythe studied her face thoughtfully for a moment, then smiled broadly. "A most admirable position, Miss McClaren," he said. "I'm sure the boards of directors of both companies will gladly accommodate you. It will take several weeks to work out the details and get it all in writing, of course."

Disappointment showed in Jess's face. "Of course," he added quickly, "I'm sure the bank in town will be happy to advance a substantial amount if it's money you need now."

"Oh, no," she said. "It isn't the money. I . . . I just thought we could have it all settled today so that we can go back home tomorrow."

"Oh, well, yes, I can see where it might be a bit awkward with Gregory. Since it will take some weeks to complete everything, why don't you go on back to Cheltenham, and when everything is ready, I will come for your signature on the necessary documents. My wife and I have always loved that valley in the spring. The azaleas are usually quite abundant about that time."

"Thank you, Mr. Smythe. I appreciate your understanding."

Mac and Jess stood to leave, but the lawyer stopped them.

"What about the jewels? There's quite a valuable collection, you know. It's been in the Keene family for over three hundred years, I'm told."

"I'd almost forgotten," she said. She glanced questioningly at Mac. "I must think more carefully about that."

"Very wise, my dear," Smythe agreed. "All right then, I will take care of the rest and see you at Cheltenham Farms in about a month."

It was growing dark as Jamie drove them back to the estate in the light brougham. Jess watched the pale light linger briefly in the western sky after the sun slipped behind the Appalachian silhouette in the distance. The

274

air had grown much cooler with the coming of dark and she pulled her woolen cloak tighter under her chin. She had changed from her riding clothes to her blue linsey-woolsey dress before leaving to see Mr. Smythe and had left her new shawl wrapped safely in the doe-skin bundle at the estate. Thinking about it now, she looked up at Mac and smiled.

"Cold?" he asked.

"A little." She nodded. "Thank you for coming with me, Mac. I don't know what I would have done without your advice and encouragement."

"You would have done fine. You would have thought of the same thing if you hadn't been so worried about being fair to Gregory. Sir Gaston knew what he was doing leaving things in your hands, but I don't think he realized what a spot he was putting you in."

She sighed a little. "About Gregory," she said. "When I think about how he betrayed you, and can still talk to you as if nothing ever happened, I'm really sorry I ever mentioned Ellensgate and got us into this whole thing. We should have kept riding that day and never come here."

"Don't start apologizing for things you have no control over," he said. "If you'll remember rightly, had we gone on to Canely Ridge, we would have walked into a trap. Just think about the happiness you brought to Sir Gaston. If it hadn't been for you, he would have lost all hope when he discovered Gregory's activities. You gave him someone to rest his dreams on." He put his arm around her and cradled her head against his shoulder. "If it's anyone's fault, it's mine. I should never have allowed you to leave Dr. Barton's to go to Charleston."

She was quiet for a few moments, trying to imagine what would have changed had she stayed at the doctor's.

She finally said, "But then I never would have gotten to know you. If I had to choose between being safe and going through what we have together, I guess I wouldn't change anything. Especially if it meant giving up being with you."

"Jess," his voice was deep and soft. He smiled down at her, marveling at her words. "I don't know why the Lord chose to bless me with someone like you, but I'll be forever grateful." He leaned down to kiss her. The crack of a musket shot rang out suddenly, shattering the moment. The carriage jolted to a halt. Another shot sounded, accompanied by a gruff shout.

"Get down from there!"

Jamie jumped down from his seat and Jessica gasped as one of the highwaymen knocked him down with a blow from his pistol handle. Mac leaned forward, shielding Jess from the view of another rider approaching the carriage. The man put his hand on the door and leaned over to peer inside. "Sorry to spoil your evening, Jessica . . . ah, yes, and Macklin, too."

She sat forward and looked around Mac.

"Bradford?" she asked in astonishment.

"Surprised to see me? Thanks to your friend here, I have spent the last ten months in the prison stockade at Monmouth. It was only late last night that I was released—much to the surprise, I might add, of the guard posted by my quarters. Who would have ever thought Gregory would have the gumption, let alone the intelligence, to arrange such a thing?

"Just sit back and relax now. We will be in charge of the rest of your journey." He pointed his pistol at Mac. "I said, sit back, Macklin, or *your* journey will end right here. I'm sure you wouldn't want Jessica to hold your lifeless body all the way to her destination. That would be quite dreadful for her, don't you agree?"

Jess glanced up at Mac. The fury blazing in his eyes made her place a trembling hand of restraint on his arm. Gritting his teeth, he slowly settled back. Bradford gave a signal and the carriage started off with one of Bradford's men driving. Jessica clutched Mac's arm and buried her face in his shoulder. He put his arm around her again and let out a long sigh of frustration.

27

They pulled up ten minutes later in front of a deserted-looking cabin. Jess recognized it as the old gatekeeper's cottage at the back of the estate, the very place she and Robbie had been playing as children when they overheard Bradford and Abigail saying their good-byes.

One of the two men with Bradford opened the carriage door and roughly ushered them into the musty-smelling little house. A single oil lamp flickered dimly from a table in the middle of the room.

Robbie sat at the table, bound and gagged. Jess started to rush to him, but a rough hand caught her arm in a tight grasp. Mac angrily knocked the man's hand away from her, but his effort was met with a thudding blow to the back of his head from Bradford's pistol.

"Mac!" Jess screamed as Mac crumpled to the floor. She longed to kneel beside him, but the man who had grabbed her arm pushed her into a chair next to Robbie. Her brother glared hatefully at their captors and struggled against his bonds, but to no avail.

"Gently. Gently, Oscar," Bradford advised mockingly. "Tie her securely, but be gentle with her, please. She's an heiress, you know. Besides, they have a performance tomorrow and can't be too mussed."

Jessica looked at him with contempt. A smug smile spread across his face. Mac stirred, and the other man dragged him to another chair in the room and tied his hands behind his back.

"You can't possibly get away with this," Jessica declared hotly.

"On the contrary, my dear Jessica. We have a rather fool-proof scheme. Fortunately for me, Gregory had no choice but to invite my help. You see, with you out of the way, I am the only other living relative of Sir Gaston. Since he so strongly excluded Gregory from his will, I am the only one who can claim those things he left to you. Unfortunately, my little accident was spoiled this morning when Macklin saved you. He has been most troublesome."

"So it was you," Jessica exclaimed.

"That's right, my dear. Gregory had nothing to do with the thorn in the saddle blanket. A few of Gaston's servants can be quite easily bought. I think Gregory has some strange notion of spiriting you off to Austria. He seems to think if he can show you the beauty and sophistication of the continent, you will soon come around and fall in love with him, forgetting this wilderness and, of course, Macklin there." He laughed derisively. "Have you ever heard such romantic drivel?"

The two men had finished binding Jess and Mac to their chairs and came to stand beside Bradford. He directed them to wait outside. As they left, in the dim light, Jess suddenly recognized them as the two men who had been chasing Mac and her in Charleston.

Bradford turned and stood in front of Robbie, removing the kerchief that had silenced him.

"You see, I'm not totally evil. You may have these last few hours to visit with each other. You needn't bother yelling, though. No one has come this way for years. There's even enough oil in the lamp to last for perhaps another thirty minutes or so. Oh, and the house staff isn't expecting you back for dinner. They've been told you'll be dining in town with Harold Smythe.

"Tomorrow, Jessica, you and Robbie will return to the house, pack your things, and appear to be returning to Cheltenham. Gregory will graciously insist you go by coach. Of course, you will come back here instead." He smiled confidently.

"What makes you think we won't tell someone at the house about your plan?" Jess asked.

"You will tell them Macklin had to return home suddenly and borrowed a horse from Smythe. I will be sitting here next to him with this pistol next to his heart. If you don't do exactly as I say, I will kill him."

She bit her lip, and looked at Bradford with unmasked loathing in her eyes.

Bradford chuckled to himself as he turned and walked out, closing and latching the door from the outside. Leaving the carriage to be used the next day, the three kidnappers rode away on horseback.

Robbie swore under his breath and struggled against the binding ropes. Jess fought to hold back stinging tears.

"What are we going to do?" she asked Robbie.

"Courage, Jess. We'll think of something. Look, he's coming around."

Mac stirred. "Mac? Are you all right?" she asked. She gritted her teeth, frustrated at not being able to help him.

Mac groaned against the stabbing pain in the back of his head. He blinked his eyes repeatedly in an attempt to clear his vision.

"Where's Keene?" he asked.

"He's gone, for the time being," Robbie answered. "But the snake's coming back soon. I'm sorry, Jess. I went down to the stables to investigate your accident, and these scoundrels must have been waiting for me inside the stable. I woke up in here. Gregory's telling them at the house that I went into town to meet you two for dinner with Smythe."

Jess turned to Mac. "Those two men with Bradford were the ones chasing us in Charleston."

"That explains how Gregory recognized me. Remember, he wasn't at the estate when we got there. When I started checking around after we stopped here the first time, I found out that those two had been spotted in Ellensgate on several occasions. They must have come here straight from Charleston instead of going to Cheltenham Farms, and reported to Gregory about you and me being together."

"I had wondered about that when Mr. Smythe was telling us his story." She turned to her brother. "Did they hurt you, Robbie?"

"Not much, just a knot on the back of my head and a headache to last until next week," he answered as he turned his gaze to the lamp on the table. "If there were some way to break that lamp chimney, we might use the broken glass to cut these ropes."

"Mac, what about your knife?" Jess asked hopefully. "Didn't you have one hidden in your boot?"

"Not in these boots," he answered in disgust. He didn't confess that his buckskins and moccasins with the knife scabbard were packed away because he had wanted to look his best for his reunion with Jess. "Robbie, can you stand up enough to blow out the flame?" Mac asked.

"I don't think so."

Each of them tried to stand; each failed.

"As soon as the flame goes out," Mac said, "we'll see what we can do with the lamp. If we knock it over before then, we'll be in bigger trouble than we are now." He scooted his chair closer to the table.

"Let's hope it goes out before they come back," Robbie said.

They watched the flame as it danced along the top of the wick, until finally it seemed to tire and diminish in brilliance. It seemed like an eternity, but at last the room was encompassed in darkness.

"I'm going to try to turn the table so the lamp will fall behind us," Mac announced. They sat in darkness and listened to Mac rocking his chair and banging into the table. Finally, a terrible crash proclaimed his success. They heard more chair rocking and another heavy thud.

"Mac?" Jessica called, straining to see through the thick darkness.

"I'm okay," he said breathlessly.

The next few minutes dragged as Mac maneuvered his chair across the stone floor. In a moment they could hear the tinkling of glass.

"Be careful," Jess said. Moments later, they heard a triumphant grunt.

"Got it," Mac said. The scrambling noises continued until suddenly Jess felt him standing behind her, working quickly to untie the knots in the cords binding her wrists. A few minutes later, they were all free.

They listened at the door. When they were satisfied that no one approached or lingered outside, Mac and Robbie synchronized their efforts, and kicked at the middle of the door. The old wooden latch splintered, and they stepped into the fresh air of the cool spring night.

28

"How far are we from the main house?" Mac asked.

"About half a mile," Robbie answered. "Jess and I used to come down here as children when we were visiting Sir Gaston."

"They left the carriage," Jess said.

"They would be able to hear it coming," Mac said, "long before we could get there. If we can reach the house without being discovered, we will have a better chance of overpowering them."

Robbie agreed with Mac. "Aye, that's right. Come on. There's a shallow draw over there that comes up along the stone fence in back of the house."

Mac took Jess's hand and started to follow Robbie.

"Wait," Jess called, stopping in her tracks. "We ought to go after the constable."

"There isn't time," Mac said. "If they come back and find us gone, they'll get away."

He started forward, but she pulled back on his hand. "Let them," she declared. "They'll be caught eventually, but I don't want to take the chance on you getting hurt."

Clutching his arm, she drew close to him. "I couldn't bear it if anything happened to you now. Please, let's just go for help."

He put his arms around her and smiled. "Nothing's going to happen to me now, Jess. We've come through too much to let anything spoil our future together. Don't you see? You aren't safe until Keene and Starkheim are put away; we're not going to give them the chance to escape."

"Aye," Robbie said. "Mac's right, Jess."

"But there are at least four of them and only two of you," she protested.

"If we can get inside the house without being seen, we'll have surprise on our side, which will help even the odds a bit," Mac said.

"But there may be more," she insisted. "Bradford said he had paid someone to put that thorn under the saddle. Some of the servants could be helping Bradford and Gregory."

"She does have a point," Robbie agreed.

"Well, let's at least get up there and see what the situation is," Mac said. "We're not accomplishing anything here."

"Mac?" Jess hugged him desperately, unable to put into words the terrible dread that filled her.

He held her tightly and kissed her forehead.

Robbie patted Jess on the back. "Let's go," he said softly. He led them to the draw sheltered by overhanging elms and sycamores. They moved quickly and quietly, stumbling over tangled roots and outcropping rocks in the dark. Robbie suddenly stopped; Jessica nearly ran into him.

"What's wrong?" she asked.

"I just remembered why Sir Gaston stopped us from coming down through this draw."

"Why?" Mac asked.

"The place used to be crawling with copperheads and timber rattlers."

"Now is not the best time to be telling me that," Jess warned.

"Would you rather take your chances with the snakes on the ground or the ones at the house?" Mac encouraged. "As cool as it is, the ones down here probably won't even know we've passed by. Let's go."

They started again, but moved more cautiously now. Each step through the thick layer of dead leaves, grass, and rocks, Jessica dreaded putting her foot down. She tried to ignore the vivid childhood memory of watching in horror as one of the field hands was treated for being bitten on the leg by a huge timber rattler. She had been taken away from the dreadful scene and had heard the adults later saying the poor man had died.

A slight breeze rustled the dead leaves, and Jess could almost imagine scaly, coiled forms with their flickering forked tongues lying in wait along the embankments of the draw as they passed by. A gust of wind sent a flurry of leaves past her, causing her to hesitate a moment.

She pushed herself toward the shadowy form of her brother moving ahead of her. Suddenly she stepped on a bare tree root; it gave way, sending her lurching forward. She landed on her hands and knees, and before she could get back to her feet, something slithered across her hand.

She cried out, expecting to feel the sharp fangs pierce her hand.

"Jess? Are you all right?" Mac helped her to her feet.

She grimaced, clutching his arm. "Something just went over my hand."

"Come on, Jess," Robbie called quietly. "We're almost there."

"Thank the Lord," she said, hoping her heartbeat would slow down and stop pounding so loudly in her ears. She had begun to think they would never reach the house, but at last they caught sight of the lights shining through the trees. Another five minutes of walking brought them to the stone fence at the foot of the garden, along the terrace.

"Wait here," Mac whispered. "I'll check to see where everyone is."

He slipped away silently before Jessica had a chance to say anything. They watched nervously as he moved like a shadow toward the French doors opening onto the terrace. Robbie touched Jess's arm, directing her attention to the eastern horizon.

"We'd better make our move soon," he whispered.

Just above the trees and rolling hills, they could see the full round disk of the moon beginning its climb into the cloudless, star-filled sky. While they waited for Mac's return, they quietly discussed how they should proceed.

A shadow suddenly appeared on the top of the wall and dropped silently next to them.

"Bradford and Gregory are there along with two henchmen," Mac reported. "Jess, how did you get out of the house the night you came to warn me?"

She thought for a moment. That night seemed so long ago.

"I climbed down the trellis at the end of the balcony," she answered.

"Just like when we were tykes?" Robbie asked with a surprised grin.

She nodded.

"Tell Mac your idea," he said.

"While you two are getting your guns, I can run down to the stable and find David and Barnaby—they can be trusted. We can send Barnaby for the constable, and David and I will slip up to the house to help you two."

Mac shook his head. "Out of the question. You stay right here until we call for you. I'll not have you getting hurt."

She squared her shoulders. "I refuse to sit here doing nothing but worrying about you two when I can go for help."

Mac studied her face, now touched by moonlight. She glared defiantly at him. After a moment, he smiled and turned to Robbie. "Has she always been this stubborn?"

"From the day she was born," Robbie declared with a nod.

Mac finally sighed. "You make your way down to the stable and get David, while Robbie and I climb up to the balcony. We'll get our guns from our rooms and wait until you've had time to get back to the house before we confront them. But be careful; it would be best not to talk to anyone other than David and the boy."

She nodded. Quickly kissing them both, she let them boost her up over the stone wall and began hurrying across the garden terrace.

They gave her time to make her way around the back of the house before they headed for the large iron trellis at the end of the balcony.

Jess hurried along the stone wall to the far end of the house. The stables lay nearly a hundred yards down a slight incline of rolling lawn. She would have to hurry across a wide expanse of open area to reach the cover of a small stand of willow trees about a third of the way. From there she would be shielded from view of the house by a large hedge of azalea bushes. Checking to see that the way was clear, she held her breath and darted across the lawn.

The rustle of her petticoat and skirt sounded like a blaring alarm to her, and she was certain she would be discovered. She reached the slender willow trees and, leaning against the trunk of one of the trees, stopped a moment to catch her breath. A moment later she was off again, staying in the dark shadows that were now cast by the rising moon's brightness.

Only a few feet farther and she could see a slender line of light under the closed stable door. She prayed fervently that the only person inside would be David. Taking another deep breath, she started across to the door. A sudden shout froze her in her tracks.

"Who's that?" the voice said.

She turned slowly. A man came forward, brandishing a pitchfork. As he drew closer, she suddenly recognized him.

"David," she cried with relief.

"Miss McClaren? What the . . . I thought you were in town. You all right? You look awful."

She quieted him. "We need your help," she whispered. The scraping of the latch on the stable door cut her short; she grabbed his arm and pulled him into the shadows beside the building. They waited as one of the young stable boys came out and headed down the walk toward his living quarters. After he had gone, Jess peeked cautiously around the corner.

"Was anyone else in there?" she asked.

"No. Everyone else has already gone to bed. What's going on? Mr. Starkheim told us that you and Mr. Macklin and Mr. McClaren wouldn't be back tonight. He said you were staying in the village."

"I don't have time to explain everything right now but Robbie and Mac and I were kidnapped by Bradford Keene and two of his men. We managed to escape from the old gatekeeper's house. Robbie and Mac are up at the house right now getting ready to confront them, but we're out-numbered; we could use your help."

"Yes, ma'am," he said enthusiastically. "Maybe that will kinda make up for not getting you back here in time for Sir Gaston. Besides, I wouldn't mind planting a good one on Keene for my own reasons." He doubled up his fist and smiled with grim pleasure. "Just a minute," he said and ducked quickly into the stable. A minute or two later he returned, brandishing an old pistol. "This might come in handy."

"I was hoping to send Barnaby for the constable."

"I'm afraid he's already turned in," David answered as he loaded the pistol. "Besides, it doesn't sound like there's time to be waiting for the constable."

They hurried up the wide walkway toward the house and, staying to the shadows, reached the steps leading up to the front portico without any trouble. They tiptoed up the steps and hurried across the wide porch to press flat against the brick wall on one side of the library windows. Muffled voices drifted from inside; David risked a quick peek.

He ducked back against the wall suddenly.

"What's the matter?" Jess whispered.

"Something must've gone wrong. They've got your brother and Mr. Macklin in there right now with guns in their backs."

"Oh no. Now what?" she asked fearfully. "Do you think we could somehow cause a distraction long enough for Robbie and Mac to overpower their guards? They'll be waiting for some sort of help to come."

"Maybe. Wait a minute, Keene and Starkheim won't know I have any idea what's going on. What if I knock on the door and ask Gregory to come down to the stable because of some problem with his stallion, Zenith? That'll get him out of there and alert your brother and Macklin that we're here to help. When Gregory comes out, we'll hold the gun on him and use him as a shield to go back into the library, then make the guards drop their guns."

"That's a good idea," she agreed. "Let's hurry, though."

Peeking through the small leaded glass panes alongside the front door, they could see the entry hall was empty and the door to the library was open. David began banging on the door, and Jess stepped back to hide in the shadows.

In a moment Charles appeared and David, sounding very upset, requested to see Gregory at once.

"Master Gregory can't be disturbed," Charles replied.

"Just tell him it's about Zenith. I'm sure he'll want to know." David insisted.

Charles told him to wait, closed the door and they watched through the narrow leaded windows as he went into the library. In a few moments, Gregory came to the door.

"What is it, David? What's wrong with Zenith?" he demanded.

Glancing past Gregory to see the hallway was clear, David grinned and raised his pistol. "Nothing really, we just wanted to join your little party in there. Now, let's go back in and figure out what Lieutenant Macklin thinks we ought to do with you fellows."

Gregory raised an eyebrow in surprise at the sight of the pistol. When Jessica stepped forward out of the shadows, a strange look came into his eyes, and he bowed his head slightly in a silent salute of acquiescence. They followed him inside and just as they were about to enter the library, Charles stepped out into the hall.

"I say, Miss McClaren. David, what do you think you're doing?" the butler demanded.

"Step back in there, Charles," David ordered.

The butler did as he was told, and they followed. The men inside the room had been alerted to their presence, however, and the moment Gregory passed through the doorway, one of Bradford's men who had been standing just inside the library door grabbed David's wrist and knocked the pistol from his hand. Gregory turned and smiled at Jess, causing a shiver of dread to race up her spine.

29

The man ordered them inside, waving his pistol toward Jessica to follow David into the library.

Her eyes met Mac's as she entered. "I'm sorry," she said.

"Don't feel bad, Jess. We didn't fare well, either. Thanks to Charles."

"Really, Jessica, you and your friends are becoming very tiresome," Bradford declared impatiently. "Charles, close the door. We don't want anyone else in on this."

"Now what, cousin?" Gregory asked, referring to the additional problem of David's presence.

"Nothing's changed," Bradford snapped. "We just have a new driver. This young man will merely join his friends at the bottom of the ravine along the mountain road. It will be even more convincing that way."

Jessica was reminded of their driver earlier that evening. "What happened to Jamie?"

"Oscar hit him a little too hard," Bradford replied as he came around the large oak desk.

Jessica felt a little dizzy, thinking about the poor man who had just happened to get in the way of Bradford's plans.

Bradford's lip curled into a wicked smile as he stopped in front of Mac. "This man and your brother," he said, addressing Jess over his shoulder, "were mainly responsible for the loss of Cheltenham Farms, not to mention ten wretched months I spent in that hideous prison stockade; but I'll not be denied my portion of Gaston's estate."

"How can you expect to gain the inheritance?" Robbie asked. "You're a fugitive!"

"Quite simple, really. All I have to do is reach England with the paperwork we will obtain from Mr. Smythe's office. He received an urgent message from Boston and he is leaving the first thing in the morning. That will get him conveniently out of the way until we are safely departed from here. I'm sure the British courts will look quite kindly upon one of their loyal subjects in such a matter; I should have no trouble at all in claiming everything."

Gregory had moved over by Jess; he placed his hand comfortingly on her shoulder. "Jessica, my dear, don't worry. No harm will come to you. You will stay out of sight until it's time to sail for home . . . for Austria."

"Gregory, you're a fool," Bradford scoffed. "She'll never consent to go with you. It's too dangerous to let her live. She'd give us away the first opportunity she had."

Gregory wheeled around to glare angrily at Bradford. "She wouldn't. I'd see to that. In time, she'll come around. Once she sees Europe, once she's away from this . . . wilderness. She can't help it if she's never known anything better."

"Enough!" Bradford shouted. "You're not only an imbecile, you're mad. Look at her. Look at her face." He walked to Jess and grabbed her by the jaw.

"No!" Gregory shouted. He knocked Bradford's hand away, sending Jess reeling backward. He swung at Keene and landed a savage blow on his chin.

The room exploded into havoc.

Everyone had been watching the drama intently. The sudden and unexpected attack on Bradford was the opportunity Mac and Robbie had been waiting for. They turned quickly and knocked the guns from their guards' hands. After landing several well-placed blows, the guards were subdued.

The scuffle pushed Charles against the lamp table, knocking it to the floor. Hot lamp oil splattered on the floor and heavy window drapes. Within seconds, the window was encircled by fire. It quickly spread along the Persian carpet toward the other draped window.

Gregory saw the flames and shouted to Mac. "Get her out of here!" He and Bradford continued to fight furiously.

David had retrieved the two guns knocked from the guards' hands; he handed one to Robbie as Mac hurried to Jess's side. She had fallen backward, striking her head against the front of the desk. She was stunned by the blow, and was just trying to get to her feet when Mac came to her side.

Mac helped Jess to her feet and shielded her from a shower of sparks as one of the heavy drapes fell, igniting the papers on the desk. Within seconds, the room filled with heavy smoke. Bradford and Gregory locked each other in a mad, desperately hateful struggle.

Jessica began choking on the smoke as Mac led her from the room. Once out in the hall, the heat was less intense.

The rest of the house staff came rushing from their quarters, screaming and hurtling past the library and out the front door. Jess and Mac followed the servants toward the door and safety. As they were about to step outside,

Jessica quickly turned out of Mac's grasp and raced back to the stairs.

"Jess!" he shouted.

She hurried up the stairs. He followed her and saw her run into her room. As he reached the door, she was already coming back out carrying the doe-skin bundle.

"I can't let anything happen to this," she declared, hugging it to her chest.

He shook his head in disbelief but couldn't help smiling a little. Taking hold of her arm firmly enough to prevent any more delay in reaching safety, he led her back toward the stairs.

They reached the top of the stairway and hesitated. Acrid smoke hung in the air. The flames had spread to the walls around them. Red-orange waves seemed to boil along the ceiling; large chunks of plaster began falling. Exposed beams groaned against the consuming tongues of heat.

Jess drew back as the tapestry wall hangings along the stairway burst into wildly colored sheets of flame. Mac removed his coat and used it as a shield over them as they descended the steps together.

Just as they reached the main floor, part of the ceiling gave way, sending the large crystal chandelier crashing down, missing them by inches. Mac kicked the twisted framework out of their path, and they pressed forward through the suffocating smoke. The heat and smoke oppressed them; they struggled to breathe. The outer door seemed very far away. Suddenly, they heard a loud crash from the library. Turning, they could see a single form staggering toward the doorway. Mac quickly turned Jess back toward the front door and with only a few more steps they were standing out on the portico. Coughing and gasping for breath, they gratefully gulped in the cooler, fresh air as he led her down the steps.

Charles ran frantically toward the stables, screaming for water. He then turned and came running back as quickly as his aged legs could carry him. "Water, we must have water."

Mac led Jess away from the house and ordered her to stay put. He turned and ran back toward the blaze.

"Mac! No!" she screamed and started after him.

Young Molly, her eyes wide with terror, ran to Jess and grabbed her arm. "Miss McClaren, no," she screamed. "You can't."

Mac reached the house as a lone figure appeared, silhouetted against the blazing interior. He staggered forward, and Mac caught him as he fell. Hoisting the limp body across his shoulder, Mac carried him back down the steps to where Molly clung desperately to Jessica. Mac sank to his knees and laid his burden on the grass along the edge of the drive.

"Gregory!" Jess gasped at the sight of his terrible injuries. She knelt next to him.

His coat was smoldering and his face and hands were badly blistered. A large ragged gash stretched across his forehead. He reached for her, and she gingerly took his burned hand in hers.

"Jessica, my dear. Can you ever forgive me? It all went so wrong."

"Don't try to talk, Gregory," she said softly. "Someone will bring the doctor."

"I'm sorry I can't take you away from this wretched place, my dear. It's all Bradford's fault. He's been my ruination from the very beginning of my life. He threatened to lie and tell them all that I'm not Count Joseph Gregory Starkheim the Fourth at all."

"Gregory," she pleaded. "Please, just rest."

He smiled weakly. "You did forgive me for the letters, didn't you? It was wicked of me, but I didn't know you then." He groaned. "I loved you, Jessica, my dear. I would never have let Bradford hurt you. I just needed the money to take you back home in grand style. I'm glad they got the fire out, but it's so dark now . . ."

Jess did not have to look at the house to know it still blazed furiously. She gazed at Gregory through tearful eyes.

"You know I really wanted to make you happy, don't you?" he said.

"Yes, Gregory, I know that."

He smiled weakly and closed his eyes, breathing a last sigh.

Mac reached from behind her and placed his jacket over Gregory's face. He helped Jess to her feet. Tears streaked her face. Mac folded her in his arms, and they watched helplessly as flames engulfed the entire house.

The glow from the blaze had been seen from town, bringing out concerned folk ready to help. They busied themselves with dousing the stable roof with buckets of water passed from hand to hand. The stables were saved, but the house was a total loss.

The townspeople took Jess, Mac, Robbie, and the house staff back with them to temporary lodging at the inn in Ellensgate.

Jessica and Molly shared a room. Although they were both exhausted by the events of the evening, they sat for a long time, talking about everything. Neither slept until the sun crested the hills to the east of town.

30

Jessica, Mac, and Robbie stayed at Ellensgate two more days, making arrangements for the two funerals. It was never known whether Bradford had perished as a result of the fire, or if Gregory had killed him.

Jessica pondered the irony of Gregory's life and death. Abigail's fears had apparently come true; "the truth" had somehow been discovered by Gregory himself, leading ultimately to his destruction—and Bradford's as well.

Whether Bradford had been Gregory's real father or not would remain a mystery buried with Abigail. Gregory's alliance with Bradford in the British war effort and his cryptic comment about Bradford being his "ruination from the beginning of his life" indicated what he believed about his parentage. Bradford probably found this out and used it as leverage over Gregory, threatening to reveal the secret that would prevent him from claiming his title and his Austrian inheritance.

It was all mere speculation, and would be of little benefit to anyone, except to help Jessica understand the tragic events a little better. The entire matter would be left where it belonged—in the smoldering ruins of the Keene mansion at Ellensgate.

Lodgings were arranged for the staff members until they had received their portion of the inheritance and could find other work. Charles had suffered a stroke in all the excitement and was in serious condition at the doctor's home.

Bradford's two accomplices were returned to the prison stockade. Molly was invited to return with Robbie and Jessica to Cheltenham Farms. Jessica felt almost as if she had adopted a little sister; Robbie had other reasons for being glad she was returning to Cheltenham with them.

The trip home was not the frantic journey it had been coming to Ellensgate. Jessica could hardly believe only five days had passed since they had come this way. They traveled in the chaise, with David driving. Ettinsmoor and the two horses Jess and Robbie had ridden were tethered behind the carriage.

As they reached the crest of the hill where the road dropped down to the rolling fields of Cheltenham Farms, David pulled the carriage over to a small clearing on the side of the road and stopped.

"Time to stretch your legs," the young driver said, opening the door for them. "We'll give the horses a rest after that long haul up the mountain."

Stepping down from the coach, they walked to the side of the road overlooking the valley below. It was still cool, but the trees were forming buds early this year, and the promise of spring was in the air. Jess breathed deeply, drinking in the beauty of the surroundings and the lovely familiarity of home in the distance.

She and Mac looked at each other for a long moment, wondering what the next weeks and months would bring.

They felt that after what they had been through, with God's help and guidance, they could weather nearly anything—together.

"Jess," Mac said. "Look over there." She looked in the direction Mac indicated and saw the wide wing span of a bald eagle soaring majestically on the strong wind currents along the mountain ridge.

The eagle was flying high.